STAR TREK:
THE NEXT GENERATION NOVELS

STAR TREK:
THE NEXT GENERATION GIANT NOVELS

STAR TREK®
THE NEXT GENERATION

STRIKE ZONE

PETER DAVID

TITAN BOOKS
LONDON

STAR TREK **THE NEXT GENERATION 5: STRIKE ZONE**
ISBN 1 85286 099 5

Published by
Titan Books Ltd
19 Valentine Place
London SE1 8QH

First Titan Edition March 1989
10 9 8 7 6 5 4 3

British edition by arrangement with Pocket Books, a division of
Simon and Schuster, Inc., Under Exclusive Licence from
Paramount Pictures Corporation, The Trademark Owner.

British Library Cataloguing-in-Publication Data. A catalogue
record for this book is available from the British Library.

Printed and bound in Great Britain by Cox and Wyman Ltd, Reading,
Berkshire.

For Myra, Shana and Guinevere,
Who let me get my work done

Acknowledgments

Many readers are irritated by acknowledgments pages, because they feel the author is indulging himself at their expense. But they don't want to skip the acknowledgments because they're afraid they might be missing something, or perhaps the author might somehow be offended.

Consider this a free pass. If you wish to skip the acknowledgments, do so without guilt or fear of retribution. But, please, don't begrudge the existence of these following words. You see, for the people who are mentioned herein, it will doubtlessly be the high point of their boring, pathetic little lives.

Thanks (and blame, I suppose) for this work can be divided up among the following:

Howard Weinstein (or, as his friends call him, Mr. Weinstein), who badgered me into calling Bob Greenberger seven years ago and set me on a crooked path to writing;

Bob Greenberger, editor and Trek maven, who, years later, badgered me into calling Dave Stern;

Kurt Busiek, writer and newlywed, who also badgered me into calling Dave Stern;

Dave Stern, editor of this book, who took the call;

Sharon Jarvis, my agent, and her able assistant Joanie Winston, who also take my calls;

The August Party Crew: Mary Bloemker (who still hauls out my early fanzine work just to watch me scream); the Burnsides (T.J., Jamie, Malcolm, Robin, and the little Burnsides); Tom Chafin (whose impression of Commander Riker must be seen to be believed); Rosie Ianni (who seems incredibly willing to watch my kids); Rich Kolker (the only deity I know personally); Pat and Jill O'Neill and the little O'Neills; Sheila ("This isn't science fiction. This is Star Trek!") Willis; plus others too numerous to count (about 27);

A.E LaVelle, Sara Paul and the rest of the STC and Second Age gang, and Steve Kitty who introduced us;

David Peters, the brilliant writer of the *Photon* series;

Wendy Goldstein who was there at the beginning;

Tinker and Susan . . . you know who you are;

All the people who have praised my first novel, *Knight Life,* (which has nothing to do with Star Trek, but I had to get a plug in);

Bill and Miggy for all their support;

Max and Steve for playing backup;

The whole crew at Marvel, DC and First Comics, just for the hell of it, but particularly Bobbie Chase and Howard Mackie, who didn't bust my chops during this book's deadline crunch; Carol Kalish also for the hell of it; Steve Saffel, who gave me the best idea I never used, and who also wishes to make it clear that his boring, pathetic little life has yet to have a high point;

To the Net, particularly Moriarty, Reverend Mom, Karen Williams, Doc Samson, and Jayembee;

Gunter and Dalia David, who let me go to a Star Trek convention; and Martin and Claire Kasman, who gave me somebody good to meet there;

And lastly, Keith Roberts, who got me interested in Star Trek back in seventh grade. Gimme a call, huh?

STRIKE ZONE

Prologue

THE SAND CRUNCHED beneath the sole of Budian's three-toed boot. Then he stopped so suddenly that his feet skidded just a bit beneath him, much to the amusement of his immediate crew of three. He spun around, hissing between his sharpened teeth. "Shut up! Shut up, the lot of you!"

If one did not have a Universal Translator one would have heard only a series of gutteral grunts, coughs, and snarls, with an occasional body slap for emphasis. The Kreel, for such was their race called, were notable for having one of the singularly least elegant languages in all the known galaxy.

Their exterior was just as appealing as their language. The Kreel had spindly legs that, in one of nature's more curious design aberrations (right up there with the bumblebee and the duckbilled platypus), supported a massively sinewed, almost triangular torso. Their arms were long, their knuckles hanging almost down to their knees. They took great pride in their bodies and were not shy about displaying them, usually sporting breeches and skimpy tunics cut to display a maximum amount of muscle. This was unfortunate for other races, since Kreel skin was unbelievably wrinkled, dry, and red, as if they all had permanent cases of sunburn. In addition, a thin layer of coarse, matted hair, spotted their bodies.

Their heads seemed to rise up straight from their shoulders. As a result, when they turned to look to the side or behind them, they had to practically twist all the way around. They tended toward large lantern jaws, and their eyes were huge, almost like handballs —appropriate for a race whose home planet seemed shrouded in almost perpetual gloom. The planet they were on now—under a blazing alien star—was so appallingly opposite from their home that it was physically painful.

In response to Budian's command, the three other members of the Kreel landing party quickly bowed their heads (by bending slightly at the waist, almost in the way the traditional Japanese did). Budian smiled then, showing his teeth once more, before gesturing that his second-in-command should join him.

"What do you think, Aneel?" said Budian. "What do the instruments say?"

Aneel pulled out the detection device that was based loosely on the design of a Federation tricorder, a marvelous instrument that current Kreel technology didn't have a chance in hell of duplicating. He swung the device around hopefully, and then said nervously, "I'm not getting anything. I think it's broken."

"Well?"

"Well what?" said Aneel cautiously.

"Fix it! Fix it, you feldling idiot!"

Unnerved by his commander's display of temper, Aneel did the only thing he could: He smacked the detector with the side of his fisted, three-fingered hand.

2

The detector obediently lit up and started to hum contentedly. Aneel blinked in surprise and then looked to his commander for approval. Budian nodded curtly and then said "Which way?"

Aneel checked the readings on the detector and pointed. "Over there."

Slowly, they made their way in the direction that Aneel led them. Budian was one step behind and to the right. He was trying to watch everywhere at once—watch Aneel, watch his own men behind him, because he didn't trust a single one of the pack, and, most of all, watch the sky.

The last wouldn't have done him the least bit of good, he knew, because if that accursed Other Race showed up (damned be their name and barren be their women) to make a fuss over this planet (which was indisputably in Kreel territory), then there was no possible way that Budian was going to be able to see them in orbit from the planet surface. The idea was preposterous. He knew that, and yet he couldn't help himself as he kept glancing heavenward.

It was midday, and the air was just hanging there, the sky a blistering, uniform red. In the distance, Budian could hear the steady chittering of insects. No potential threat, but it was annoying.

"Through there."

Budian looked up, mentally chiding himself for his lapse in attention. Such lapses could prove fatal in the future. "Through where, Aneel?" he demanded.

Aneel was pointing straight ahead, but before them was only a wall of solid rock—part of a large mountain range that seemed to extend before them.

"Through there?"

"Yes, sir."

"How the *flarg* do we get through there?"

Aneel gestured helplessly. "I don't know, sir."

3

Budian let out the sigh of one who does not suffer fools gladly—either that or the sigh of one who is afraid he's about to be made to look like a fool. He reached for his belt and pulled out his weapon. "Stand back," he said, gripping the disruptor tightly with both hands and bracing himself. The kick on these weapons was not to be taken lightly.

Ten feet away from the mountainside he fired, blasting a steady wave of pure sound at the mountain. Rock and dirt exploded, covering the Kreel with a fine layer of filth. This did not bother them particularly; Kreel were not renowned for bathing.

"You're doing it, sir!" shouted Aneel. Budian nodded, keeping it up until so much dust was swirling up that even they, with their enlarged eyes, couldn't see much. His finger lifted away from the trigger and the blast ceased.

"Wonderful, sir!" said Aneel.

"Shut up."

"Yes, sir."

Budian stood and watched, silently urging the dirt out of the way so that they could see just what, if anything, they had uncovered.

Within moments, the debris had settled, and Budian's breath caught in surprise.

There was an opening. Clear as anything, there was an opening. There had been some sort of door there before; gleaming metal edges were still visible where the disruptor had torn it away. But now they had access to whatever it was that lay inside.

The Kreel glanced at one another and then, out of deference, stepped aside and indicated that Budian should go first.

There were times, it occurred to Budian, when being the leader wasn't all that it was cracked up to be.

* * *

The sleek battlecruiser *Kothulu* settled into orbit around the planet which was, at present, simply designated as DQN 1196. The blazing red sun, a paltry several million miles off, cast a gentle glow off the gleaming hull of the ship.

"Commander?"

The commander did not look up immediately. One never looked up immediately when a subordinate requested attention. It gave the impression that you were anxious to hear what he had to say. A good commander, particularly a good Klingon commander, always made it appear that whatever the subordinate was about to say the Commander was already aware of it. The unspoken message was "Why did it take you so long to report the obvious?"

"Commander?" came the prompt again.

Count to three, turn, look, then speak. "Yes, Tron."

"Picking up life-form readings from planet surface."

The commander nodded. "Kreel, I'd wager."

A pause. Then Tron nodded. Keeping just the slightest touch of admiration out of his voice he said, "I believe so, sir." Subordinates knew that you never let ranking officers be aware when you were impressed by some feat of theirs.

Once again the commander nodded, his massive, ridged head bobbing just a bit. "So our intelligence was correct, then. The Kreel scum are rooting around in this system."

"What is there around to interest them, Commander?" Tron asked, then promptly chided himself mentally. Never ask a question. It implies you don't know.

Too late, though. The commander had heard. "What is there, Tron?" he said in a voice just loud enough to be heard by the entire bridge crew. "Nothing. Nothing of any interest except to a backward race such as the Kreel."

Slowly, the commander stood up. Tron's fingers played across the intercom. His mind jumped ahead, anticipating his commander's thoughts. "The transporter room is prepared to beam them up at your command, sir," he said.

The commander sniffed in disdain. "Allow that Kreel slime to set foot aboard our magnificent vessel? Even in chains, they would not be worthy of that. Take a landing team, Tron, and find out what they're up to. See what they've found."

"Yes, Commander. Although," he added in his deep, gravelly voice, "you did say that there was nothing of interest down there."

"True," replied the commander easily.

"Then how could they possibly . . . ?"

The commander turned and took several short steps over, bringing himself eye-to-eye with Tron. "Even worms," he said, "can turn up interesting tidbits in a moldering corpse."

The Kreel blinked in astonishment, unable to summon any of their usual bluster and arrogance.

When they had stepped through the newly blasted hole in the mountainside, they had discovered a stairway that led straight down into darkness. They shined a light down into it, but the beam seemed to make only the barest dent in the overwhelming blackness. Budian naturally (and reluctantly, although he covered it well) went first, the others following behind him in single file.

They walked slowly down metal steps that seemed to trail off into infinity. Aneel glanced down at one point and silently noted the fact that the steps were not the least bit dusty, and he then made mention of that fact to his commander. "It's as if," Aneel added, "they were somehow just repelling dirt."

Budian snapped back, "Then it's fortunate that they don't just throw you right off."

From then on, Aneel decided he would keep his observations to himself.

Eventually, they reached the bottom of the stairs and there, several meters ahead of them, was a large, gleaming metal door. Detailed symbols were etched on it, symbols that the Kreel, who stared at them in confusion, could not even begin to understand. But when they got to within a few feet of the door it silently opened.

The Kreel blinked in the light that overwhelmed them. They pulled out their disruptors, ready in case something attacked them while they were momentarily disoriented. But nothing attacked, and the disorientation soon passed.

They stepped into the light and were stunned by what they saw.

They were standing at the head of a corridor that branched off in two different directions: Both paths were massive tunnels, gleaming metal and arching in high curves above them.

The tunnels were at least twenty feet high, and upon closer inspection were constructed of curved tiles, each about two feet square, joined so smoothly that the seams were barely visible. Budian ran his fingers across them, and even though he could see the divisions, he could not feel them. He shook his head (and, as a result, his torso) in amazement. "What could have made this?" he whispered. In the silence, his voice seemed to echo.

Aneel made vague gestures and wasn't able to come up with a reply. No matter. Budian hadn't really expected one.

He gestured to the other two members of the group. "You two," he said "go that way." He indicated the corridor branching off to the left. "Aneel . . . you're with me."

This news was less than thrilling to Aneel. Not only would he have preferred to be with someone other than the leader, he frankly would have opted to remain back in the ship in the first place. The ship which was, even now, sitting serenely on the planet surface waiting for them to return.

How much easier, thought Aneel, it would be if the Kreel had transporter capability. But those techniques were used by wealthier and more advanced races. Not the Kreel. Not the Kreel who were known as warlike, backward scavengers. What they could do with the kind of weaponry used by the . . . the . . .

He spat. Budian looked at him in mild surprise. "Is that to be considered a criticism?" Budian asked in a very dangerous tone.

"No sir," said Aneel, in such an offhand manner that Budian realized he was telling the truth. "I was only thinking of the Klingons."

"May their ships dissolve in piles of rust and their sun go nova," said Budian quickly.

They both spat, then pressed on, leaving little bubbling traces of expectoration on the floor behind them. They took some degree of comfort in cursing the Klingons at any opportunity, simply because they knew that the Klingons were so far advanced beyond them that cursing and spitting were the only things they could really do.

As they walked away, a small section of the floor came to life. The metal rippled ever so slightly, and the spit disappeared without a trace.

* * *

"They're definitely not here," said Spyre.

Tron nodded, sticking his head in through the open hatch of the Kreel scout ship. It was a patched-together affair inside, and Tron noted parts from at least four different technologies. He entered carefully, making sure not to accidentally step in something distasteful. He stared at the command panel in wonder, then reached behind it and came away with a handful of wiring—and tape.

Tape! By the Emperor, tape! It was nothing short of miraculous that this vessel hadn't blown up. He allowed it to slip from his fingers and turned to his crew.

"Find them," Tron said.

"Do we kill them once we find them?"

Tron's brow wrinkled slightly. Left to their own devices, back before the days of the Great Enlightenment, that is exactly what they would have done. "Their fate is in the commander's hands," he said. "Between you and me, killing them would certainly be my preference. What we will probably do"—and he emphasized the *probably* with faint distaste—"is toss them in their ship, take them in tow, and drop them off, powerless, somewhere in space. Their fate from that point on is in their own hands. However, you don't have to be gentle when you do find them."

Budian and Aneel could not believe their good fortune.

They walked by room after room now, doors hissing open as they passed. It was as if this underground lair was filled with secrets that it could not wait to yield up to them. And each room was filled with . . .

"Weapons," said Aneel, stopping at one to palm a handgun reverentially. Unlike the huge, clumsy weap-

9

ons that the Kreel exploratory group was carrying, these were smaller, sleeker. Unmistakably deadly, however.

Budian snatched the weapon from his second-in-command's hands. "You might hurt yourself with this," he snapped. *Or me,* he added silently. "Come on. Let's see what's at the end of the corridor."

"But . . ." Aneel gestured helplessly. "Shouldn't we go through some of these rooms? Explore them? Catalog the weapons?"

"They're not going anywhere. They've been here, who-knows-how-long, and will continue to be here. Let's discover everything this find has to offer before we start charting what we've found. That's simple enough to understand, isn't it, Aneel?"

"Yes, sir," said Aneel with marked lack of enthusiasm.

They worked their way farther along, Aneel now making a conscious effort to look neither left nor right. Eventually, the corridor made a slight turn, then another, and then Budian stepped back in alarm as another form suddenly appeared in front of him. Without hesitating he swung up the small weapon he'd been carrying and pulled the trigger.

A split-second too late, he realized that it was one of his own people.

The unfortunate Kreel threw up his hands and shouted.

"Wait!" he began—and then vanished. There was no beam from the weapon, merely a soft, diffuse glow, and suddenly the Kreel simply wasn't there. It was as if Budian had been holding a remote-control device while watching something on a monitor, and had then just shut it off.

"Don't startle me!" shouted Budian at the empty air, for it had all happened so quickly that he didn't fully have the time to register that the crewman was gone. "I hate it when—" And then it began to sink in.

He stared at the space which the crew member had once occupied, then glanced at the remaining two members of the group. They each took a slight step back, as if nervous they might be next.

He held the gun a bit more tightly. "Come on," he said, gesturing with it. They followed obediently.

So the two branching corridors had come back on each other, and now the three members of the stalwart Kreel race walked on another twenty meters, past more rooms with fascinating technology, past curious inscriptions on the walls that made no sense to them.

And eventually, they hit a dead end.

The door facing them was more massive than any they'd ever seen. The two sides of it came together in a vertical zigzag pattern that looked like teeth, ready to crunch down on any who endeavored to enter. To the right was a small panel made up of an array of smaller multicolored rectangles. Ten going up, four across, forty in all.

The door showed no interest whatsoever in opening.

Budian stepped up to it and waited with as much patience as he was capable of, but the door did not move. It had been closed for countless years and would, apparently, remain closed for countless more.

"Stand back," he ordered tersely. He brought up his brand-new weapon and fired it point-blank at the door.

The door did not seem to take kindly to this: Budian's hand weapon vanished.

Along with the hand that was holding it.

Just like that. Budian's right arm now ended in a neatly cauterized stump at the wrist.

Budian stared, dumbfounded. It had happened so

swiftly that he hadn't had time to react. There were horrified intakes of breath from his men, and that was the first confirmation that he wasn't imagining it. With that realization came his first physical reaction. He staggered, leaning against the wall and holding up the stump in shock.

He tried to flex the fingers that were no longer there. He could swear that he was doing it. He knew that he was doing it. Even as he reached out with his remaining hand and actually touched the mound of hardened flesh, his mind kept screaming, *It's still there! It has to still be there!*

"Sir . . ." Aneel breathed. "Are you all right?"

The cosmic stupidity of the question hung there, and not even Budian would touch it.

"We . . ." the other crew member, who was called Deni, spoke up. "We have to get you back to the ship."

"No." The reply was faint.

"But . . ."

"NO!" said Budian with more force, and now pain was finally starting to register and he forced it back. Later, in privacy he would howl and scream in agony. Not now. Not here. "No, first we get through this feldling door."

It was clear what was going through their minds. They thought *they* were going to have to try firing on it. They glanced at each other, silently agreeing that if that order was given, they'd fire on Budian before they'd take that suicidal course.

Fortunately for them (and, one would have thought, Budian, except ultimately it didn't make much difference) that was not the option that Budian was considering. Instead, Budian gathered his strength, stepped away from the wall, and walked toward the panel. He was now cradling his maimed wrist in the crook of his left arm, and the initial pain was beginning to subside ever so slightly. He was certain, though, that for months he would be imagining the flexing of the hand that was no longer there.

He touched the panel and the forty colored rectangles lit up. A low hum filled the area, and the colors reflected on his taut face.

"A combination lock of some sort," he muttered. "You probably have to touch them in a specific order."

"So . . . how do we get in?" asked Aneel.

"We just keep pushing different panels until we hit the right mix."

"But that could take . . ."

Budian turned on him, fury barely contained. "This cursed door cost me a hand! Whatever's behind it, I want to know! Whoever built this installation, they just left weapons, lying around, more advanced than anything we have. Maybe more than the Klingons have. But they thought enough of whatever's behind this door to keep it locked up. I want it! I *deserve* it!"

He turned and, with his remaining hand, started pushing panels furiously. Each one had an individual note to it, a faint *ping* sound came as it was hit. And each one glowed under his touch, ever so briefly. But no combination was prompting the door to open, and display its secrets.

Suddenly there was a sharp, high-pitched whine.

Budian turned to his men, who were standing about five feet away, and said "What does that sound like to you?"

It started almost ludicrously. Budian was staring at his men, waiting for Aneel to speak, and then Aneel's face twisted in horror, as did Deni's. That was the first thing he saw.

Then Budian thought that his two remaining crew members were getting taller. This was quickly replaced by the partially correct realization that he, himself, was, in fact, getting shorter.

He looked down and the full truth, the full horror of it, began to dawn on him.

He was dissolving.

His feet were already gone, reduced to some unrecognizable, formless mass. Even as his mind managed to register this, his shins were gone, then his knees. There was a distinct hissing sound, but nothing else. No smell of burning flesh. No blood. No mess or muss.

And when the full nauseating terror managed to completely penetrate, that was when he began screaming.

Budian began to shriek in words incomprehensible even to a Kreel. He was incoherent with fear and terror as he looked down and saw his body, his magnificent body, being destroyed molecule-by-molecule.

And yet, for all his horror, he never once asked for help, never appealed for aid, divine or no. For the Kreel do not beg. Die horribly, yes, but not beg.

And now his chest was gone and he was still hideously *aware;* he could still see and feel what was happening.

Oh god, thought Budian, *let it end let it end let it end.* But it didn't. Somehow, perversely, he was aware until his very last moment when his head hit the floor and that too began to melt away; his brain continued to function and register the images that his eyes brought to him.

And the last image that he registered was his men, grinning.

Moments later the floor rippled and the remains of the Kreel commander were swallowed up.

* * *

14

Tron stood at the entrance to the cave, the entrance that had been blasted away, and stared at it in amazement. "How could this have been here?" he demanded. "How could our earlier surveying parties have been over this planet and not found it?"

It was rhetorical, of course. None of the other Klingons had been in those earlier exploratory parties, and so no personal reckoning was being held. One of the Klingons thought, *Maybe it wasn't ready to be found.* It was a private speculation, one made more from what passed for Klingon whimsy than from anything else, and as such, it was a speculation that went unvoiced.

It so happened that he was right. But he wouldn't have been believed, anyway.

"All right," said Tron, gesturing to his small group. "Let's see what's inside."

And then a gutteral voice said, "Instead, let us show you . . . Klingon pig."

It came from just inside the opening, and the accent was unmistakable. Tron's face twisted in disgust as he said, "Is that Kreel I smell in—"

The ground to Tron's immediate left exploded, taking with it the Klingon standing there.

Tron reacted instantly. "Fall back!" he shouted, and the remaining Klingons promptly did so, firing back into the hole. They blasted a steady barrage, all bets off, determined to reduce the Kreel to free-floating molecules.

The Kreel fired back. The Klingons didn't know, couldn't know, that the Kreel were crouched on steps, placing them safely below the blasts that were passing harmlessly over their heads.

A pencil-thin beam of light shot out of the hole, lanced over the head of one of the Klingons crouching behind a rock.

And then the beam of light reversed itself and, as if it had eyes, swung back and blasted the Klingon from existence.

Tron had seen enough. He tapped his wrist communicator and shouted into it, "Commander!"

Imperturbable came the reply: "Yes, Tron?"

"Beam us up, sir! Now!"

"Report, Tron."

"If you don't beam us up—sir—I won't live to give you my report!"

An instant later, Tron felt the comforting glow of the transporter beam around him. He and the remainder of the ill-fated Klingon away team materialized on the transporter deck of their ship.

Tron barely had time to step off the platform when the call came down from the bridge that Tron had better haul himself up there *now* and explain just what the devil had happened, and how a simple search-and-destroy mission could possibly go so completely off-kilter.

"The scream, sir."

Tron paused and turned, looking back at the other survivors of the landing party. One of them, a first-year techno, said, "The Klingon death scream, for our slain comrades on the planet surface."

Tron had never been much of a traditionalist, but that was never something that was healthy to admit. Nevertheless, he said, "I think, novice, that my first duty is to get to the bridge or there may be a lot more Klingon screaming going on."

Down on the planet surface, Deni and Aneel had quickly retreated into the confines of the cavern when they had heard the transporter whine. Once, they would have felt a stab of jealousy over the Klingon technology that gave them such gifts. Now, however, they felt nothing except the heady intoxication similar to a child given the key to a candy store.

Aneel was poking around in one room when footsteps snapped him around, weapon at the ready. Aneel, however, was a little more cautious than the late Budian, and so he did not blow Deni to atoms. This was fortunate, for Deni was holding a weapon so huge that he had both arms wrapped around it and still his hands didn't quite meet. It glistened silver, and it was almost completely smooth. The part that seemed to be the muzzle was large enough for a Kreel child to crawl into.

Aneel's huge eyes became even wider.

"What the *flarg* is that!"

Deni's squat head moved out from behind it. "I don't know! But it's . . . it's big!"

"Then it must be good."

And then the big gun began to beep.

The two Kreel looked at each other. "What did you do?" demanded Aneel.

"Nothing! Nothing, I swear! It just started by itself."

"Let's get it outside! If it's going to explode, it's not going to do it in here!"

Deni started frantically to drag the huge weapon, and Aneel shouldered one end of it. Between the two of them, they broke all speed records as they bore the weapon up and out of the tunnels. Once they were a safe distance from the entrance, they set the weapon down with the barrel pointing straight up. Then the thing started to tilt over, right onto Aneel. "Help me!" he barked at Deni.

That's when the weapon spoke to them.

In a pleasant female voice that, incredibly, spoke Kreel, the weapon said, "Targeting."

They froze, staring at each other. Then Deni's face

17

twisted in disgust, and he said, "It's a woman's weapon."

"Don't be a feldling idiot," snapped Aneel. Then, as they both pulled their full weight into it and righted the gun, Aneel said cautiously, "Gun . . . what are you targeting?"

"Orbiting vessel. Visual aid requested?"

"Sure."

The air before them shimmered slightly and there, hanging in front of them, a patch of stars twinkling around it, was a Klingon battlecruiser. In contrast to the ship's design, and intent, it seemed almost peaceful.

"Awaiting instructions," said the gun.

Aneel and Deni looked at each other once again. For a brief moment, Aneel found himself wishing that the commander were still around to take charge of the situation. He was good at that. But the commander was, at the moment, a small puddle of goo, and since his status didn't seem likely to change in the near future, it was Aneel who was left to make the decisions.

"Shoot at it," he said.

"As you request."

Silently and efficiently, small tripod legs stretched out from the bottom of the gun, giving it balance and stability. Aneel and Deni stared at it. As the weight of the weapon was taken from them, they suddenly realized what was about to happen. It also occurred to them that, when it did, their personal health and safety would be best served by being elsewhere.

They ran.

"You allowed yourselves," said the Klingon commander slowly, "to be routed by a few pathetic Kreel?"

Every word hung in the air filled with disdain and disbelief, on the bridge. Tron shifted uncomfortably, but stared resolutely straight ahead.

"And you have the nerve," continued the commander, rising from his chair and circling his subordinate, "to return to this ship with a report of that nature? Are you prepared, Tron, to live the rest of your life in Disgrace?"

Tron did not answer. There could be no answer. To be in Disgrace was tantamount to a death sentence, for no Klingon could live in such a state. Bereft of friends, of property and privilege, of everything. Even . . . of name.

"Commander!"

The warning came from the science station. The commander turned quickly, for the controlled alarm in the science officer's voice was very noticeable. Tron breathed a silent prayer of thanks for the distraction, and then the commander glanced back at him. The silent message was clear: *This is not over.*

"What is it, science officer?"

"Energy reading on planet surface, sir. Massive burst."

The commander frowned, bending over and seeing for himself. "What are those little rodents up to?" he demanded. "That's enough of this. Lock on to them and beam them up here. I hate to pollute the ship but I see no alternative, thanks to the mishandling of the situation." He shot Tron a look.

"Commander, shields just came on!"

Immediately, the commander spun around to look at the viewscreen, expecting to see another ship approaching them. But only the planet was there. "Source?" he said.

And then the Klingon battlecruiser was knocked out of orbit.

As if a giant hand had flicked them away, the ship was knocked literally end-over-end, hurtling through space like an out-of-control poker chip. Artificial gravity could not even begin to adjust as the Klingons were tossed around in their ship. One moment they bounced off walls, the next they ricocheted off ceilings. Miraculously, there was only one casualty, down in engineering, as a technician landed wrong and broke his neck.

"Stabilize us!" shouted the commander, somewhat unnecessarily, for the helmsman was frantically trying to do just that. The first thing he had to do, though, was get his hands on the controls.

The commander spun out of control across the length of the bridge, crashing into Tron. "Computer!" the commander shouted. "Override manual control! Stabilize!"

Shipboard functions such as helm were always left, at least on this ship, to the Klingons themselves. How could one be a Klingon if one did not hold the direction of his destiny in his own hands, after all? But now the commander removed that prohibition against the computer, and shipboard systems promptly kicked in with reverse impulse. Slowly, the Klingon ship pulled out of its spin.

Once it had stopped, the bridge was silent for a long moment as they all looked to the commander.

The commander, in turn, looked to the screen. There was no sign of the planet now . . . no, *wait.* There it was, a speck so small as to be almost undetectable. That was how far away they'd been hurled.

"Helm," he said slowly. "Bring us to within firing distance. Weapons, stand ready. Lock on to life readings and open fire. Tron," he added, turning, "shouldn't you be at your post?"—an unspoken admission that perhaps Tron had been out of his league on the planet surface.

Tension evaporated from Tron's body. "As you wish, commander," he said.

The Klingons moved with deliberate caution, wanting to get to just within the range where they could cut loose at the upstart Kreel who had treated them with such indignity.

There was, however, one thing that they had not allowed for. Perhaps it was because they felt that, now that they were on guard, they would be better prepared. Perhaps it was their firm belief that such an aberration could never happen twice.

Whatever the reason, it simply never occurred to them that the weapon on the ground might have greater range than they did. And when the ground fire cut loose again, it was clear that what had come before was merely a warning shot.

A beam of pure energy lanced upward, cutting through their shields as if they were nonexistent. It sliced across the left warp nacelle, blowing it apart. And now there were indeed Klingon death screams as Klingons were incinerated instantly, or ripped apart by the power of the blast, or sucked completely out of the ship and hurled into the pitiless vacuum of space where they all would die instantly.

On the bridge of the crippled ship, the commander never flinched. Death held no fear for him. Now, though, surviving meant more than simply avoiding death. He had to warn the Klingon Empire what was happening: Had to warn them that the balance of power had shifted dangerously, had suddenly been skewed toward an immature race with a century's worth of grievances and an itchy trigger finger.

"Get us out of here," he said.

"Warp drive severely damaged, sir. Navigational console is . . ."

"Get us out of here," he repeated, "even if you have to go out and push."

They got out of there.

Chapter One

WESLEY CRUSHER LISTENED CAREFULLY, trying to screen out everything, including the sound of his own soft breathing.

He was crouching against a tree, phaser in hand, examining every bush for where the potential danger lay. A gentle breeze rustled the plantlife around . . .

A breeze? Or was it . . . ?

He quickly swung his phaser around, aiming at one particular bush that appeared to be moving more than it should. He squeezed off a quick shot and waited, prayed, for an unconscious body to fall out of it.

Nothing happened. The bush continued to sway serenely. No one obediently tumbled out, insensate.

Wesley's mouth twitched in annoyance. He flicked away a fly buzzing ceaselessly around his face.

Then he sensed, rather than felt, something crawling across his boot. He looked down, and an ugly pincered bug the size of his fist was sitting there, apparently sizing up his big toe as a potential snack.

Wesley jumped back, making a sound of disgust and shaking the thing off his foot.

And at that moment a phaser blast lanced across where his head had been only an instant before, striking the tree and knocking off a piece of its bark.

Wesley hit the ground, landing on his elbow in just the right way to send a ribbon of numbing pain spiraling through his arm.

"I hate this," he muttered, even as he flung himself through a row of bushes that seemed to provide comparative safety.

Safety, however, it hardly was, for the bushes lined a sudden and rather abrupt drop-off. Wesley had no time to react as he rolled down the embankment, sending dirt and small rocks flying as he went. *"I hate this I hate this I hate this",* he kept saying, like a meditative chant, as he grabbed at roots to try to slow down his fall. The roots uncooperatively kept ripping out of the dirt.

Wesley ended up at the bottom of the embankment, his usually carefully combed hair completely askew, his clothes covered with dirt, and his face covered with several scratches. His arm was still throbbing. And as the world spun around him—the sun shining down on him blissfully as if he were spending a relaxing day at the beach—Wesley lay there and said, "I really, really hate this."

Then the sun was blotted out as a figure stepped in front of it. The figure grinned down from the top of the twenty-foot incline.

"You're dead, Orange," said the figure.

With a sudden burst of strength he wouldn't have thought still in him, Wesley rolled to the right as the phaser blast from above just missed him. *He's toying with me,* Wesley realized. *He'll be sorry for that.*

He rolled into a crouch, swung up his arm, and fired.

24

At least, that was the plan. Except that Wesley found himself staring dumbly at an assortment of roots clutched in his fist.

It took less than an instant for Wesley to realize that he must have let go of the phaser during his efforts to stop his roll. By then it was too late, as Wesley was slammed back by a phaser blast that hit him square in the chest.

Wesley fell back and lay still.

Unmoving.

Dead.

"Dead again, Orange!" shouted his assailant. "You never could handle me."

Utterly oblivious of Wesley Crusher's recent demise, Commander William Riker strode purposefully down a corridor.

Saluting was long-outmoded in Starfleet, and even if it were still in fashion, the many civilians that Riker passed would hardly be bound by military tradition. And yet there was something as he passed both civilians and crew members. Not a salute, but always some nod of greeting, a smile, a slight touch of a finger to forehead. Everyone aboard ship felt a compulsion to acknowledge Riker's presence.

Respect, he wondered? Yes, certainly that, but more. Genuine affection. The people, the crew, were fond of him. Before serving aboard a starship with its massive community of a thousand people, Riker would have sworn that it was impossible to be both popular and respected. Authority was authority, and that was that. William Riker had made the decision, early in his career, that commanding the respect of *his* people would always be of paramount importance. He wouldn't care if he were liked or not, as long as his authority was not questioned.

And he had almost convinced himself that being liked was unimportant.

Almost.

Then again, as one particularly shapely, young woman walked past him and gave him an appreciative raise of her eyebrow, popularity certainly had its advantages.

And with the reawakening of Riker's basic interest in being liked, other aspects of his personality stirred as well.

His sense of humor, for one.

Specifically, two weeks ago he'd gone on a seventy-two-hour shore leave. It was the longest vacation from an assignment William Riker had taken in his Starfleet career, and it had not been a willing one.

"You need the time off, Number One," Jean-Luc Picard had said with utter certainty. Jean-Luc Picard, the veteran captain of the *Enterprise*, had been sitting in his quarters with the serene confidence and peace of a Buddha. Riker had known that look. It was the look Picard adopted when the decision had been made, period, nothing to discuss, but debate would be entertained merely to make the subordinates feel they had contributed something.

"With all due respect, Captain, I disagree. Have you noted any diminishment in my performance and capability?"

"None whatsoever," said Picard, fingers steepled in front of him.

"Then I hardly see the need for this action."

"This is not an 'action', Number One," replied Picard. "Most people would hardly see a vacation as punitive. Generally, it's regarded as reward for a job well done."

"My job is here on this ship," said Riker.

"By startling coincidence, so is mine. And part of

26

my job is to decide what the jobs of others are. And right now your job is to take seventy-two-hours shore leave on Gamma Origi III. It's a very relaxing planet that bears a marked resemblance to the more-pleasant areas of Alaska. And don't say you can just take some extra time in the holodeck. As effective as the deck is, GO III is more so. You will feel right at home."

"Sir, I know I grew up in Alaska, and I certainly have a great fondness for it," said Riker with a helpless gesture, "but my home is . . ."

"On this ship," Picard finished. "I appreciate your dedication . . ."

"Captain . . ."

"Number One," said Picard with a tone of voice that clearly indicated the conversation had gone as far as he was going to allow it to go. "Your protest is duly noted and logged. But I am ordering you to go down to that planet and have a good time, or I'll have you loaded in a photon casing and shot down there myself."

"I take it that's your final word, sir," Riker said stiffly.

"No. This is: *Good-bye.*"

And so Riker had gone, grumbling all the way. He knew beyond any doubt just who was responsible for this enforced holiday: Deanna Troi, the ship's counselor. It had to be. Who else would have the presumption to decide that she, and not Riker, knew what was best for Riker.

He could just hear in his mind the conversation: "I sense a certain degree of stress from Commander Riker," she would say in those carefully modulated tones. "He demands a great deal of himself, taking personal responsibility for everyone on this ship including, to a large extent, you, Captain. He works so hard to keep himself in check that it's beginning to

27

have an adverse effect on him, and I would very much recommend some off-ship relaxation time for him, whether he objects or not."

What was it Geordi La Forge had once muttered about her, under his breath? "Deanna Troi, interplanetary *yenta.*" It was said with a sense of bemusement, and Riker had checked language banks to understand the reference. Yiddish slang, for *busybody.* Once he had, he'd chuckled over that one (although without letting anyone spot him doing it) for quite some time. It was fairly accurate. If Deanna's job had not been to be concerned over the mental health of the crew, she would still have acted exactly the same. She just wouldn't have had the rank to back it up.

The annoying thing was, she'd been right. Riker *had* needed a break. He'd realized it during the second day of his "exile," while clinging batlike to the side of a mountain he was busy scaling. A sensation, vaguely familiar, worked its way through him. Relaxation. It was as if he'd been holding his breath for a year and finally exhaled.

Of course, the fact that Deanna had been right did nothing to mollify Riker's annoyance over being given the heave-ho from the confines of the *Enterprise.* He decided, therefore, that a certain small but harmless revenge should be taken upon those who had done the heaving. He wasn't certain yet what he would do to Deanna Troi, but a method of getting back at the captain had occurred to him at the self-same moment in the climbing trip.

The joy of it was, of course, that Captain Jean-Luc Picard, for whom Riker's respect was second to none, would never admit it, that Riker had gotten his goat. Never.

So here Riker was, his enforced vacation now only a week-old memory, and as his thoughts tumbled around he sensed, rather than saw, the presence nearby himself. He spoke without looking. "Good day, Captain."

"Number One," Picard acknowledged, matching Riker's stride. Holding back, in fact. It was a curious thing: although Picard was half-a-head shorter than Riker, somehow Riker always felt that he had to pick up his pace to keep up with Picard. "On your way to the bridge?"

Picard wasn't looking directly at him. Riker knew why, and grinned inwardly. "Yes, sir."

"Excellent. How long until our arrival at Daedalus IV?"

Riker fought down the suspicion that Picard knew and was just testing him. "Fourteen hours, sir."

Picard nodded. "It's been far too long since the colonists had a routine visit from a starship."

"I agree, Captain."

"I'm glad we're in accord, then, Number One."

And still Picard wasn't looking at him! This was marvelous!

They arrived at the turbolift and the doors obediently hissed open. Riker paused, allowing the captain to enter first. Just as Riker stepped in, a voice called out, "Hold it!"

Riker turned, his broad-shouldered body obscuring the captain from view. A girl of about eighteen years of age *(what was her name again, anyway?* Riker blanked), wearing a tight, gold jumpsuit slit down either leg, ran up to the lift as if this were the last one that would ever appear in the ship.

She stood in the doorway, preventing the doors from closing. The turbolift politely and patiently waited. "Commander," she said breathlessly.

"Yes?" He smiled. "What can I do for you" (it clicked in to place) "Miss Chase?"

29

"My friends call me Bobbi," she said. "And I just wanted to say"—and she boldly ran her fingers across the lower-half of Riker's face—"that I really like it. Are you going to keep it? It is *reaaaalllly* sexy."

The sound of someone very unsubtly clearing their throat came from directly behind Riker, and Bobbi glanced around his shoulder. Her eyes widened. "Oh! I . . . I didn't see you there, Captain! I'm sorry."

"Obviously you had something in your eye," said Picard icily.

"I didn't mean to keep you."

"How fortunate." And then the temperature in the area dropped yet another ten degrees.

Quickly she stepped back and the doors hissed shut. Picard and Riker stared at each other, making direct eye contact for the first time since they'd met in the corridor.

"Permission to be sexy, sir," said Riker, fighting to keep a straight face.

"It is not funny, Number One," snapped off Picard. "Such familiarity with family members or crew is inappropriate—Bridge," he instructed the lift.

"You have told me in the past to be the pleasant, approachable face of command, Captain, leaving you to do your job in peace. That's certainly all any of us wants."

If Picard picked up on the mild barb, he ignored it. "Yes, well, there is such a thing as doing one's job too well."

Smiling slightly, Riker reached up and stroked his chin. There, feeling comforting and masculine, was the new facial feature that had elicited such raves from the young Miss Chase (and, indeed, from assorted other female crew members.) While on his vacation, Riker had allowed his beard to grow in. It grew rather quickly and, once back aboard the *Enter-*

prise, he had carefully trimmed and shaped the full beard to give it a swashbuckling style. It added a certain rakishness to his straight-arrow image, and accented his eyes.

Picard had said nothing. Absolutely nothing. When Riker had returned he'd merely nodded and said, "Good to have you back, Number One." He issued no comments, one way or the other, presumably since it was of no importance. Picard's lack of response was, to Riker, all the proof he needed. Picard glanced at Riker, gaze unwillingly drawn toward his face, and then Picard looked straight ahead again.

And Riker knew what he was thinking, or believed he knew, and the belief would certainly be more than enough to satisfy his need for revenge.

For Riker was certain, absolutely certain, that Picard was thinking, *It is cosmically unjust that my first officer has more hair on his face than I do on my entire head.*

Riker's bemusement instantly vanished, however, as the communicator on Picard's chest beeped once. Picard tapped it once and said, "Picard here."

"Captain, this is Worf." The last three words were somewhat unnecessary. That basso-profundo voice could only belong to the Klingon head-of-security. "You're needed on the bridge."

"I'll be there as quickly as I can," said Picard. "Picard out."

Less than a second later, the turbolift opened onto the bridge, in the aft section. Picard walked out past Geordi La Forge, at the engineering station, toward Worf at tactical.

Geordi La Forge was ostensibly blind from birth. However, he had been fitted with a prosthetic visor, which a clever scientist had named "VISOR." This stood for Visual Instrument and Sensory Organ Replacement (Geordi had wondered how long they'd had to think to come up with that acronym) and the bottom line was that Geordi could "see" almost the full electromagnetic spectrum.

And yet Geordi, for all his gifts, still did a double-take when Picard walked onto the bridge barely a second after being summoned. But La Forge recovered quickly. As Riker neared him, Geordi spoke.

"What kept you?"

"Traffic."

Picard stepped up behind Worf. "Yes, Mr. Worf? You called?"

The massive Klingon turned and looked at his commanding officer. He gave no reaction at all; it was as if he fully expected Picard to simply materialize, like a genie from a lamp, the moment the call went out for him.

"A small ship, bearing 212 mark 3. It appears to be Kreel design, and"—and he made an expression of extreme distaste—"from the attitude of the ship's commander, they would most definitely appear to be Kreel."

"A Kreel ship? Out this far from their space."

"Yes, sir."

"Hmmm. A Kreel ship," Picard repeated, trying to fathom it. "Have they said what they want?"

"Yes, sir." Worf paused a moment.

"And that would be . . . ?" Picard prompted.

"Our ship."

For long moments, Wesley Crusher lay there unmoving. His assassin stood there and, when Wesley failed to give any indication that he was still alive, said nervously, "Hey Orange? Say something."

When Wesley still didn't move, the assassin hopped over the edge of the embankment, scurrying down quickly and endeavoring not to lose his balance. His arms pinwheeled as, once, he almost slipped and fell. Finally he drew up next to Wesley and said "Come on, Orange. Say something."

Slowly Wesley opened his eyes. "I really hate this," he said. "I keep saying that and I still let you pull me into this."

"I'm sorry."

"No you're not, Jaan. You never are."

"Let me help you up."

"I can do it just fine, thanks," said Wesley, still irritated with himself. He stood, brushing the leaves and dirt off himself and shaking his head. "Why do I let you talk me into these stupid games? I'm sixteen years old, for crying out loud. I'm an acting ensign. If we want to have some sort of competition, why don't we play a nice game of chess?"

"Because it's boring."

"That's besides the point."

"And you always win."

"Aha!" said Wesley as they headed toward the exit. "Now it comes out."

They made their way through the forest. Some sort of buzzing insect insisted on plaguing Wesley. Then a thin, long-fingered hand reached out and batted the annoyance away. "Thanks, Jaan," said Wesley.

Jaan was a head taller than Wesley and, indeed, many years older. But Jaan's race lived longer than humans, and he was still a relative adolescent.

Jaan's race, the Selelvians, were among the most beautiful in the galaxy. He was a shining, if somewhat eccentric, example why.

Tall and slender, with long, graceful limbs, Jaan had darkish red hair, which hung to just above his sloping shoulders, and a mouth twisted in a perpetual look of amusement. His clothes were flamboyantly multicolored and hung loosely. He didn't seem to walk so much as glide.

For all the traits the Selelvians possessed, the nickname they had been given as a whole by humans was, obviously, "elves."

Yet another insect began to pursue the hapless Wesley, but by this point they had reached their destination. The forest seemed to stretch onward forever in front of them, but Wesley uttered a command that the shipboard computer promptly obeyed. A hole appeared in the forest and through the aperture could be seen the corridor of the *Enterprise*.

The two young men stepped through. The insect followed, determined to pierce Wesley's skin and drain all the blood from him. However it, just like the forest, was a product of the holodeck. The moment it passed into the corridor, the insect was gone. Wesley had the considerable pleasure of watching the annoying bug vanish back to the nothingness from which it had come.

"Using your brain is all well and good," Jaan was saying, "but you need exercise, Orange."

"Why do you call him 'Orange'?"

The two of them turned, and Wesley felt his mouth go dry. Bobbi, who had earlier been raving over Will Riker's beard, was looking at them with curiosity. "Why?" she repeated, her arms folded across her breasts.

Wesley Crusher tried to find just the right thing to say, calling upon all the prowess of his reputed genius intellect. "Duhhhh . . ." he managed to get out, as Bobbi stared at him guilelessly.

"Old earth drink," Jaan said quickly. "I found it in some old files in the food synthesizers. Orange Crush. Crush. Crusher. Get it?"

"Oh," said Bobbi, and blinked. "It's not really funny."

"Well it's not supposed to be," replied Jaan with the pleasant arrogance that only his race was capable of carrying off. Elves could say practically anything, and they looked so good doing it that they were usually forgiven almost immediately, no matter how snide or high-handed they sounded.

Nevertheless Wesley subtley elbowed him in the ribs. "It's just a stupid nickname," said Wesley.

"Oh. Okay." Her curiosity satisfied, Bobbi walked away.

Jaan shook his head. "Can you pick your jaw up off the floor now?"

"Oh, please. I wasn't that bad. Tell me I wasn't that bad."

"What do you see in her?" said Jaan in puzzlement. "She's pleasant to look at, but nowhere as bright as y—"

"I am so *sick* of that," said Wesley with unexpected, even uncharacteristic, annoyance. He started down the hallway, and now it was Jaan, much to his surprise, who had to rush to keep up. "I am so sick of everybody thinking of me as if I were some sort of . . . of genius."

"Now why, in the name of Kolker, would anybody think that?"

Wesley gave him a sidelong glance. "Great. Now you're being sarcastic."

"Well, what did you expect? You go around putting together devices that left two engineering heads in tears because they could barely understand how they worked. Everyone figures that Picard put Geordi in charge of engineering because, at least, he can't see the latest Crusher miracle."

And Wesley turned on him with surprising vehemence, stabbing a finger at him. "Don't you ever say stuff like that about Geordi. Not when I'm around. In fact, not ever."

"I'm sorry, all right?" said Jaan quickly. "It was just a bad joke. Forget I said it."

They started walking again, heading in the general direction of the Ten-Four Room, one of the more frequent haunts of the *Enterprise* crew. Jaan could take it or leave it, but Wesley felt even more a part of the actual starship crew whenever he was there.

"You know what they call me," Wesley was muttering. "I hear it behind my back. They call me the 'Brain Trust.'"

"That's not exactly a profanity."

Wesley turned and stopped dead in his tracks looking at his friend. "I feel like it puts a distance between me and everybody else," he said. "I can't help the things that I can do. Deanna Troi senses emotions, no one thinks that's any big deal. Vulcans can knock people out by touching their shoulders, and it's business as usual. Those are their gifts, their skills. Me, I cobble together some stuff that runs through my head, and I'm Wesley Crusher, the Brain Trust. People are starting to give me almost as much distance as they do Captain Picard."

"Is that an insult to you, or a compliment?" asked Jaan.

Wesley stared at him and realized that the question was quite valid. "You know . . . I'm not sure."

"It can be taken however you want it to be taken," said Jaan easily. "For what it's worth, Orange, I happen to think you can do absolutely anything."

"You certainly know how to insult a person," said Wesley with no heat.

And at that moment the sound of a yellow-alert

36

klaxon echoed throughout the ship. Wesley's head snapped around in alarm and they heard Picard's voice over the intercom. There was such a controlled casualness about it that one would have thought he was announcing the weather.

"Attention all hands," Picard was saying. "We have encountered a possibly hostile vessel. We are endeavoring to reason with the inhabitants at this time. However, we would like all noncombatants to report to your quarters, should separation become necessary."

It was a maneuver that had served the *Enterprise* in several earlier instances. When danger threatened, the ship's saucer would separate from the aft section. This enabled the speedier aft section, aided by the warp nacelles, to handle whatever opponent they were up against, while the family-laden saucer section maneuvered out of the hazardous area, albeit at sublight speed.

"Come on!" said Jaan urgently, tugging on Wesley's elbow.

"You go on ahead. I'm getting up to the bridge."

"Orange! For the love of—"

"I'm an acting ensign! My place is there. Besides, I'm not going to miss the chance to see Captain Picard in action in an emergency." He dashed into the nearest turbolift and barked, "Bridge!"

Jaan, standing helplessly in the hallway, said, "But Orange, what about—?"

"You heard the captain! Move it!" called Wesley, and the turbolift doors hissed shut.

Jaan sighed, turned . . . and doubled over. As others raced around him, he clutched at his stomach, cramps knocking the wind from him. In agony, he straightened up and leaned against the wall.

"Not now," he muttered. "Not now . . ."

Chapter Two

"NOT NOW, MR. CRUSHER!"

Picard wasn't removing his gaze from the main viewer as Wesley said, "My place is here, sir!"

"Mr. Crusher, as admirable a job as you have done up to now, if we're going into a potential combat situation, I prefer a more experienced hand at the conn."

"Please, Captain. A Starfleet officer belongs where he can do the crew the most good."

"Who told you that?" said Picard.

"You did."

Picard frowned, turning and staring at Wesley for the first time. "I did?"

"Yes, sir."

Wesley met the stare. He knew damned well Picard had never said that. But it sounded like something he would say. However, if Picard pressed for details, there was no way Wesley was going to have the stones to carry off further fabrication.

"Mr. Marks," Picard said. "Relinquish conn to Mr. Crusher."

Wesley opened his mouth and then closed it again. He turned quickly, before Picard had a chance to change his mind, and went to the conn station. Marks, tall and gangling, barely had time to get up before Wesley had taken his place. And Wesley heard Marks mutter under his breath, "Brain Trust."

"Mr. Crusher," came the stern voice of the Captain from behind.

He knows, Wesley thought with alarm, and managed to say, "Yes, Captain?"

"The next time you present yourself on the bridge, may I suggest you do not look as if you have just come in from the playground."

Wesley looked down at himself and moaned softly. His clothes were still dirty and rumpled from the survival games in the holodeck. No doubt, his face was covered with grime as well. He had completely forgotten about his appearance in the rush of subsequent events.

He was about to offer an apology, but Picard wasn't looking for one. Besides that, there was no longer the opportunity as a gravelly voice, a barely-translatable series of growls, sounded over the ship-to-ship communications.

"This is the Kreel ship *Zonobor,*" came the voice. "Where is your ground-kissing coward of a commander?"

Picard did not take the bait. "This is Captain Picard," he replied, his tone carefully neutral. "You have some business with us?"

The Kreel ship hung there in space, well within phaser range, as if the *Enterprise* posed no physical threat at all. "Yes, business," came the voice. "You are to surrender your ship to us."

Worf spoke up from behind Picard. "Permission to blast them from space, sir."

Picard turned and frowned. Even for Worf, that was extremely aggressive. "Is there a problem, Mr. Worf?"

"Kreel cannot be reasoned with," replied the Klingon. "Or bargained with, or even treated as any civilized race. To endeavor to do so is, in my opinion, a waste of this vessel's time and capabilities."

"In my opinion, it is not." He turned to Deanna Troi. The counselor was seated to his left, straight in her chair and taut as a piano wire. "Counselor, what impressions are you getting?"

Troi began to speak, then paused and appeared to shift gears. "Nothing you have not already surmised, Captain."

It seemed to Picard there was something she wasn't saying, but he opted not to call her on it. His next question, one that would normally fall upon the security chief to answer, he deliberately directed elsewhere. "Data," he said slowly, "are you aware of any Kreel technology that poses a threat to this vessel?"

In the ops seat next to Wesley, the white-skinned android promptly began to process his captain's request for information. For only a fraction of a second, his gold eyes actually seemed to turn inward, as if his optic nerves were somehow scanning the resources of his own brain. He tilted his head slightly, like a dog listening to an inaudible whistle.

"At this time," Data responded so quickly that the pause between question and answer was undetectable, "the Kreel continue to be one of the more primitive races in terms of technology. They have space-going capability, but their experiments in matter transportation have all failed to date, usually in rather grisly fashion. Their hand weapons are simple disruptors, their vessel armament primarily light pulses that pose no threat to our shields."

"As I thought," said Picard.

"Their weapons development," continued Data, and from the tone of voice it was evident that a massive tangent was about to be embarked upon, "can be traced back to—"

"That will be quite enough, Data." Picard closed his eyes momentarily. That was the risk one ran with getting information from Data rather than a computer. It was an old habit that Picard retained, preferring to garner facts from a speaking individual rather than a disembodied computer voice. Still, sometimes it seemed more trouble than it was worth. The captain turned to the main screen. "Picard to Kreel ship."

The irritated voice barked back, "You certainly took your *feldling* time getting back to us."

"Yes, well . . . I was discussing your 'ultimatum' with my bridge crew. I'm afraid that surrendering to you at this time is utterly out of the question."

"How inconvenient. I'd heard you were all cowards . . . it explains why the gutless Klingons have allied with you."

Picard felt Worf's eyes drilling into the back of his neck. He ignored it. "That is hardly the case," said Picard.

"If you do not surrender, we shall be forced to destroy you!"

Upon hearing this, Geordi brushed his fingertips across the activity panel of his engineering station. The indicators lit up in front of him, showing him, among other things, a silhouette of the *Enterprise* with the shield indicators serenely in place around them. From behind him, he became aware that Worf was checking the exact same thing. "Take your best shot, suckers," muttered Geordi La Forge.

"Shields in place," said Worf.

"Picard to *Zonobor*," Picard said in his best no-

nonsense voice. "We will not surrender the ship. That is our final word. However, if there is some emergency that you require assistance with—"

Picard was not permitted to finish the sentence as the *Zonobor* cut loose.

Worf's report was a mixture of businesslike response and astonishment at their arrogance. "They're firing on us, s—" And then, if Worf's voice were capable of going up an octave, it would have. "Captain! Energy readings off the scales! It—"

The blast from the Kreel ship cut through the forward shields as if they simply were not there.

The impact was felt throughout the entire ship, as if a massive fissure in space had just opened up and the *Enterprise* had fallen in. Wesley, gripping the side of the conn chair, imagined he heard the screams of civilians throughout the ship.

"Evasive maneuvers!" shouted Picard through the din.

Wesley froze. He didn't know what to do. He was at conn, it was his responsibility. But they were being fired upon, by a vessel packing fire power unknown to present engineering. Immediately his mind started visualizing energy fields, trying to figure out just how the devil it was possible to hit the *Enterprise* with that much pure power . . .

And Picard, who was hardly accustomed to repeating himself, said, "Go to red alert! Conn, evasive maneuvers! Marks, take o—"

That got Wesley's attention. "Evasive maneuvers, sir!" he quickly called out, executing the order.

Gracefully the *Enterprise* angled hard astern.

The Kreel ship, like an angry, stubborn mongrel, kept on her and fired again. This time the astounding weaponry ripped through the starboard shielding, knocking it out of existence.

At engineering, Geordi didn't know where to look first. He had a fleeting wish his visor had an "off" switch. "Forward and starboard deflectors out! Circuit overloads!"

"Compensate!" snapped Picard.

"Working on it, sir."

Deanna Troi felt compelled to say, "Panic from all over the ship, Captain. I can feel it."

"So can I," Picard said.

"Separation?" asked Riker.

"No time, Number One. Besides, the Kreel would hardly be sporting enough to let them go."

As if on cue, the voice of the Kreel commander sneered over the ship-to-ship, "We could have destroyed you just then, *Enterprise*. If you attempt to fire on us, we will destroy you. If you attempt to run away again, we will destroy you. You have no option but to surrender."

"Death First!"

The shout came not from Picard, but from Worf.

With utter astonishment, Picard looked at Worf. The burly Klingon was clearly seething, furious beyond anything Picard had ever seen.

His voice laden with danger, Picard said, "Worf . . . be . . . quiet."

But the damage was done. "Is that Klingon I smell, even through space?" came the snide voice.

Picard needed to say nothing further. Worf had regained control of himself, making a visible effort to keep his mouth clamped shut.

"How marvelous. In addition to your ship, Captain, we want the Klingon. For a toy."

Worf clenched his fists, the knuckles flexing under the skin, as if envisioning a Kreel neck between his fingers.

Picard now understood Deanna Troi's brief hesita-

43

tion earlier, when he'd asked what impressions she was picking up. She'd been about to report about overwhelming hostility, not just from the Kreel, but from Worf. Twenty-twenty hindsight, however, was going to serve no purpose.

"All right," said Picard. "You win. The ship is yours."

The bridge crew, as one, turned and stared at Picard. Picard had the distinct feeling that, had he been in command of a Klingon vessel back in the more savage days of the Empire, he would have been incinerated right about now by his own people.

"Excellent," came the voice. "You send the Klingon and yourself over here for insurance. Then bring our boarding party over there . . . and no transporter tricks, or you're dead."

"We'll be there in a moment. Picard out."

He stepped away from his command chair, heading in the direction of the doorway in the bridge aft section which led to the conference room.

"Conference, sir?" asked Riker.

"Devil take that," snapped off Picard. "What would you suggest we discuss, Number One? The scenery?"

And now Picard walked to where he'd been heading in the first place, namely the science station just to the right of the door. "Mister La Forge, I need you for this."

Obediently, Geordi stepped over to his captain's side. Riker, still not fully understanding what was happening, tried to establish some sort of handle on the situation. "Captain, I cannot allow you to deliver yourself in to their hands."

"No one is delivering anyone, Number One. Mister La Forge, call up a schematic of the normal design of a Kreel ship."

Geordi did so, and a shimmering outline of the specs of the *Zonobor* appeared on the computer screen.

"Now," said Picard, "full sensor scan of our opponent. Compare and contrast."

A detailed image of the actual *Zonobor* appeared alongside its specs. And there was something else. On the underside of the actual ship was highlighted, in yellow, a very small image. From its shape and design, it could only be some sort of weapon.

"Well well well," said Riker. "Accessories."

"That must be why they're unshielded," Geordi exclaimed. "All power's going into their weapon. If we remove it from them, that should shut the weapon down."

"Feed the coordinates down to the cargo transporter room," Picard ordered. He tilted his head slightly. "Bridge to transporter room D."

"Transporter room here," came the slightly surprised reply. D was the largest transporter platform on the ship, used only when massive shipments were being brought aboard. Now, in a red-alert situation, hardly seemed the time for such cargo movements to be made.

"Mr. La Forge is feeding coordinates down to you. Prepare to activate transporter on my order."

"Yes, sir. What are we bringing aboard?"

"We'll all be surprised, transporter room. Bridge out." Then he paused, savoring the moment. "Picard to Kreel vessel."

"For someone in as much danger as yourselves, you're hardly in a position to take as much time as you are," came the irritated response.

"Just getting our ship together," said Picard. "We are preparing to activate the transporter. Transporter room, get ready. And . . . energize."

For about five seconds there was nothing but silence.

"They've raised shields," said Worf. "Too late, though."

Then a satisfying howl of indignation echoed throughout the bridge.

"What have you done?!"

"The same thing we would do with any belligerent child," said Picard with a great measure of self-satisfaction. "We've taken your toy away."

"Give it back! It's *ours!"*

"And the *Enterprise* is ours, but you did not seem to be interested in recognizing possessions. Now, either tell us what this is all about, or we'll be forced to fire on you. I'd prefer not to, but then again it might be interesting to see how *your* shields hold up against *our* phasers."

"You wouldn't dare!"

"Oh yes we would," replied Picard. "And once we've disabled you, we'll bring you all aboard this ship until we get this all sorted out."

And the voice, suddenly deadly, said, "You can't. There's a Klingon aboard that ship. At least one, maybe more."

Without looking back at Worf, Picard said, "That's quite correct."

"Death First!"

Picard's head automatically snapped about, reflexively thinking that it was Worf who had once again spoken. Then he realized that, in fact, it was the angry voice of the unnamed Kreel commander.

"Wait!" shouted Picard. "Transporter room! Lock on to—"

Too late.

The ship's detonation was eerily silent as it blew in all directions simultaneously. Picard's order died in his throat as the Kreel died in space, and he felt a burst of rage sweep through him.

"Useless," he snapped. "So utterly, utterly useless." He turned away, not wanting to see the last bits of the Kreel ship fizzle into nothingness. There had been a brief fireball as the explosion ripped through the vessel's atmosphere, but the vacuum of space had snuffed it out most efficiently. "Mr. Riker, I want you to take Mr. La Forge and Mr. Data with you down to the cargo transporter room and see exactly what we've reeled in. Mr. Worf, come with me."

He turned to the ready room, situated just off the forward section of the bridge. Deanna Troi stood, standing just enough in his path so as not to be blocking but, at the same time, making it impossible to ignore her. "Yes, Counselor?" he said with just the slightest trace of annoyance.

"Captain, if I may . . ."

"Counselor, I am in command of the situation. Kindly allow me to do my job."

Troi bit off her response and said simply, "I would not dream of interfering, Captain."

"Thank you." He walked into his ready room, Worf following silently. Riker, for his part, went to the aft turbolift with Geordi and Data a step behind.

The door hissed shut after them. Wesley watched them go, and then he sank back in the conn chair, closed his eyes and moaned softly.

Deanna's exotic voice came from behind him. "Do not be concerned, Wesley. Your hesitation was only momentary . . . and understandable."

He couldn't even bring himself to look at her. "But you could tell I did hesitate, couldn't you. It was that obvious."

"Yes."

"Everyone . . ." Wesley took a breath, forcing himself to stare straight ahead at the field of stars that floated before them. "Everyone expects so . . . so damned much of me. Like I was telling Jaan. They put me up high on this level above everything else."

Deanna squatted down, so that she was at eye level with him. "And when you are up so high, you have so much farther to fall, don't you?"

"Yes."

"Mm-hmmm. You cannot change who and what you are, Wesley. All you can do is live with it. And I shall do whatever I can to make it livable for you." She paused. "Your mother's leaving was very difficult for you, wasn't it?"

Wesley rolled his eyes. "Great, a guy's feeling down on himself, and the first thing that you can think of to say is that he misses his mommy."

"That's not what I was saying, Wesley."

"Forget it, okay? I really appreciate your help, Deanna, but I'll work everything out just fine." He began diligently checking the headings. "Just fine," he repeated, and Deanna knew that there would be no further communicating with him at this point.

Deanna sighed. Here she had this gift to let other's emotions touch her, caress her, and embrace her mind and spirit. But when it came to reaching back toward the sources of those emotions, frequently it was like wearing a blindfold and having her hands tied behind her. She could see more clearly than anyone, but she was, by her standards, mute.

When she told the captain, in a difficult situation, that she sensed pain, Picard would nod and act as if that told him something. But how could she put across to him, to anyone, what she was really feeling? Thoughts, emotions, and feelings raged through her, but she had only clumsy, inefficient words to express them.

Who was she, she thought bitterly, to counsel Wes against feeling inadequate. She was the greatest failure on the ship, her one-way abilities laughable, her job a sham.

And then she looked at the despondent Wesley, and she gathered all her self-pity and self-doubt together into a ball and rolled it away into a dark, rarely visited part of her mind where she hoped never to see it again, and hoped that it would most definitely not come out to see her.

Who, she wondered, counsels the counselor?

"Would you like to tell me just what the devil that was all about?" snapped Picard.

He had barely waited for the door to the ready room to shut before turning on his head-of-security. Worf stood there, stoically, arms folded behind his back.

"I apologize if my conduct was inappropriate, Captain."

"If? *If?* That's putting it mildly, Worf." Picard was shaking his head in disbelief. "This is incomprehensible. I know the Klingons and the Kreel have never gotten along, but this surpasses anything I would have imagined."

"Permission to speak freely, sir?" said Worf.

"Permission denied."

Worf blinked slightly, but said nothing.

Picard paced the inside of the ready room, finally sitting behind his desk and fingering a small souvenir on it, as if to focus his thoughts. "I know there are certain Klingon imperatives that are part of your emotional makeup, Worf . . . but they have never interfered with your ability to carry out your responsibilities or with your loyalty to the Federation."

"I have always taken great pride in that," Worf said stiffly.

"As well you should. Of course, you did have the benefit of being raised by humans, although," he added, anticipating what Worf was thinking, "I imagine most Klingons would consider that to be something of a handicap."

"I was not going to say that."

"But you thought it."

"Of course."

Equivocation was definitely not one of Worf's problems. Picard was almost tempted to smile, until he thought of the destroyed Kreel ship. "What is it between Klingons and Kreel, anyway?"

"Permission to—"

"Yes, yes, granted."

"The Kreel have always picked at the bones of Klingon conquests, as jackals do after the lion has had his kill. Klingons are warriors. Kreel are savages, always at the outskirts of Klingon activities, envious, plotting, thoroughly repulsive in attitude and appearance."

Picard was impressed. It was the longest speech he'd ever heard Worf make. Clearly it was something he felt quite strongly about, something that had been inbred early in his life and very thoroughly. The Kreel were practically a taboo thought to Klingons, much as incest or cannibalism was to most humans.

Still . . .

"Everything, Lieutenant, has its positive aspects—if you just take the time to look."

"As far as the Kreel are concerned, sir, I'd prefer to look from a distance," said Worf.

"Duly noted. But Worf . . . that's a flaw in your character . . . racial memory or not, a flaw. I suggest you do whatever it takes to correct it."

"Yes, sir."

"And if you ever shout out of turn in that manner

on the bridge again, I'll have you rotated off the bridge crew. Clear?"

"As crystal, sir."

Picard motioned toward the door, heard it hiss open as Worf left. He looked down, trying to sort out what had happened. It took several seconds for him to realize that the door had not shut again. He looked up and, although Worf had gone, another figure was standing in the doorway.

"Yes, Mr. Crusher?"

"Captain, I . . . I wanted to apologize."

"Apologize?"

"Yes, sir. You ordered evasive maneuvers earlier, and I froze." Wesley took a tentative step forward. "I wanted to acknowledge my mistake and let you know I was working to improve myself."

Picard waved him off. "It's not your fault, Mr. Crusher."

"It's not?"

"No. Simulations and run-throughs are one thing, but thrusting a raw teenager . . . no matter what his abilities . . . into a life and death situation was inappropriate. I'll be aware of that for next time."

Wesley hardly felt mollified by this. "Sir, I really . . ."

"That will be all, Mr. Crusher."

Wesley hesitated. There was so much he wanted to say, but he couldn't bring himself to say it. He desperately wanted Picard's understanding, not condescension. Then again, what else could he, Wesley, have expected, considering the way he'd acted. Still, he couldn't just let it pass.

"Captain, I—"

At that moment Picard's communicator beeped. Picard touched it lightly, answering the page.

"Captain," Riker's voice filtered through the de-

51

vice, "I think you'd better come down to the cargo transporter room. You're not going to believe this."

"On my way, Number One." He stood and cocked an eyebrow at Wesley. "Anything else, Mr. Crusher?"

"No, sir."

"Good. The next time you write your mother, please send my regards."

"I will, sir." Wesley stepped to one side as Picard walked past him and off the bridge, calling out to Worf that he was now in command.

Wes stood there for a long moment more, staring at the inside of the captain's ready room. Then he turned and saw Deanna standing behind him.

He raised a finger. "Not a word. All right? Just . . . not a word."

"Whatever you wish, Wesley."

He walked back out onto the bridge and glanced around. "Hey Marks . . . you want conn back? It's all yours."

Marks, who was standing at science station Two, looked with mild surprise at Wesley. "You sure? Usually it takes a crowbar or a blaster to get you off the bridge."

"Well, you know us genius types. Erratic as anything," said Wesley with a bitterness he couldn't even begin to disguise. Then he turned and walked off the bridge.

Deanna watched him go and made a mental note to talk to the captain, at length, about Acting Ensign Wesley Crusher.

Chapter Three

TAKA NAGAI, head of Federation internal affairs, felt a certain degree of anticipation. Sitting in her office, drumming her fingers on the table, she stared resolutely ahead and tried once again to frame exactly what she would say when this most respected person stepped through her door.

There was a soft buzz on her intercom and she tapped it. "Yes?"

Over the intercom the receptionist said crisply, "The Ambassador is here to see you."

"Send him in."

Nagai stood, out of respect. She was not particularly tall, and she was getting on in years, but nevertheless, she projected an aura of power almost unconsciously.

The door slid open and two burly Klingon "honor escorts," a cheerful euphemism for "body guards," entered the office and looked around carefully. Despite the fact that they were in the posh surroundings of one of the top people in the Federation, they were taking nothing for granted.

Then they stepped aside and the Ambassador entered.

Taka Nagai was momentarily startled. She'd seen pictures of him, but they had not prepared her for the in-person experience.

"Honorable Kobry," she said, bowing slightly at the waist.

Kobry looked ancient. Klingon life expectancy was one of the great questions of medical science since, until recent years, few Klingons had had the opportunity to die quietly in their beds. So no one was certain what "old" for a Klingon was. But whatever it was, Kobry was it.

He was also the shortest Klingon Taka had ever seen, coming barely up to her waist. His hair, indicative of his age, was long and flowing but quite pale. His skin looked relatively normal, but his eyes were also fairly light.

But the oddest thing about him was that he was . . . smiling.

Taka Nagai, in all her years of dealing with Klingons, had never seen one smile. Oh, to be sure, Kobry wasn't exactly grinning ear-to-ear. It was a small smile, playing across his lips, as if he were aware of everything that was running through her mind.

He returned the bow. "Honorable Nagai," he said, and, unsurprisingly by this point, his voice was quite soft, almost musical. "It is a pleasure to meet you."

"And I you, Ambassador."

Nagai sat back down and then realized to her horror that she'd forgotten to adjust the chairs for his height. But the Klingon, hopping up into the chair opposite her, seemed not the least bit concerned that his feet didn't quite touch the floor.

They paused a moment, taking each other's measure silently. Then Kobry spoke. "You are aware we have a difficulty."

"Quite aware." She did not even have to consult the reports that were glowing for her inspection on the nearby computer screen.

"The situation is incendiary," said Kobry. "We are dealing with something that could lead to war between the Klingons and the Kreel."

Upon the speaking of the latter name, one of the two Klingon guards spat. Kobry fired a look at him and said, "Don't do that again. It's impolite."

"It's tradition," rumbled the Klingon.

"Not . . . here," said Kobry in a tone that indicated he was not joking. The taller Klingon fell silent, and Kobry turned back to Taka Nagai.

"If this is brought to Federation Council," continued Kobry, "into an open forum, tempers will flare, and we will have war. I would prefer not to see that happen. I'm certain you would prefer not to as well."

"The Federation prefers moderation whenever possible. War and violence are to be avoided, since they usually accomplish nothing," said Nagai.

"However," Kobry said, "it has taken the Klingons many centuries to learn this, and indeed"—he glanced at his guards—"some of my people are still chafing at the bit, so to speak. There are factions within the Empire who wouldn't mind war in the least. And considering the provocation we've been given, it would be understandable. Klingon blood has been shed."

"True. But so, I understand from reports of skirmishes, has Kreel blood. This is the danger of war . . . that both parties attempt to end hostilities with force and, instead, only succeed in aggravating them."

Kobry nodded. "Indeed so. But asking the Klingon

55

Empire to deal with the Kreel . . . that is not something that will sit well in many quarters."

"The Kreel have come to us for intercession."

Kobry made no effort to hide his surprise at this. "Is this true?" he said at last.

"The mishap on DQN 1196 a month ago has escalated. The Kreel wish to end it before the result is all-out war."

"But the Kreel are not members of the Federation."

"Yes, but the Federation is very anxious to avoid war, and so we will be happy to act as mediators in this situation."

"That is all well and good," said Kobry. He leaned forward. "It is fortunate that you mention DQN 1196. That planet happens to be within Klingon territory."

"The Kreel say it's within theirs."

"Yes, I know." Kobry smiled ruefully. "Absurd, don't you think? Stars and planets that have been there while we were climbing from the primordial muck and will continue to be there long after the 'glorious' Federation and Empire have long passed from the history of the universe. And we have the temerity to argue over who they 'belong' to. Nevertheless, the Emperor is quite firm on the point."

"So are the Kreel. And since they're currently in control of the weaponry on that planet, that makes them difficult to deal with."

"Very true." Kobry paused a moment, looking thoughtful. "Perhaps it would be best for parties of both Klingons and Kreel to be brought to the site of the dispute. That is, after all, where it all began."

"I don't know if the Kreel will agree to that," said Taka Nagai.

Kobry raised an eyebrow. "I had thought they came to you, asking for mediation."

"Oh yes," she said quickly. Too quickly.

"That being the case, I'm sure they would wish to cooperate in any way possible."

"Of course. Of course. I'll talk to them. And, perhaps, what would be best is if both parties are brought there on a Starfleet vessel. Just to underscore the Federation's interest in keeping hostilities from escalating."

"Excellent idea," said Kobry. "May I suggest that, whatever ship you choose, it be one that has a great deal of room. If you're going to have contingents of Klingons and Kreel on the same ship, then you're going to need room."

"I think that's a very valid suggestion." She quickly called up on the screen the roster and location of various ships, keeping a particular eye out for Galaxy-class vessels.

"There are several excellent choices here," she said.

"Good," said Kobry. "I will leave the details to you, then."

Nagai rose as Kobry stood, and she remained that way until after he'd left. Then, as soon as the door to her office was safely closed, she sent out a call to the Kreel ambassador who had shown up a day earlier at the Federation's repeated behest.

Gods, he is a repulsive one, she thought as his image appeared on her screen, but quickly brushed that sentiment aside as inappropriate.

"Well?" said the Kreel ambassador. "How much longer is this foolishness supposed to go on?"

Using the exact same tone and phrasing as she had with Kobry moments earlier, she said. "The Klingons have come to us for intercession."

"Now that is surprising," grunted the Kreel. "Klingons have said in the past they'd rather consume their young alive than sit down and discuss any of our grievances."

"That's in the past."

"They spit whenever our name is mentioned."

"I find that difficult to believe," deadpanned Nagai.

"Obviously it took the threat of advanced weaponry to bring them around. Clearly they're frightened of us now. That being the case," he said cannily, "why should we bother to talk with them? Let there be war."

"And if there is," said Nagai tightly, "the Federation would have to support its allies, namely the Klingons. Are you prepared to go to war with the entire Federation?"

The answer was immediate: "Yes."

They stared at each other over the communications screen for a long moment, and then the Kreel said indifferently, "However . . . if the Klingons wish to come together, the Kreel can show that in strength there is also compassion. They think of us as savages. But we can be . . . civilized."

Taka Nagai didn't buy that for a second, but she was willing to accept anything if it meant somehow heading off interstellar war. And with the number of skirmishes between the Klingons and Kreel growing, the Federation had to do something *now*.

Even, she thought ruefully, telling each side that the other had been willing to take the first step. A dangerous game, diplomacy, but then again, so was war. The only difference was that diplomacy was about the preserving of lives, and war was about the taking.

And so, walking a tightrope with razorblades as nets, Taka Nagai began to discuss specifics with the representative of the Kreel . . .

Chapter Four

THE TEN-FORWARD, or "Ten-Four Room" as it had been nicknamed, was packed. This was usually the case after a particularly difficult situation: crew members gathered here to knock back glasses of synthehol and describe how they were never really concerned during whatever emergency had just occurred. No problem at all.

Guinan looked up from behind the bar as Wesley entered. He walked up to her and forced a smile. Guinan nodded in acknowledgment.

"Club soda?" she asked noncommittally.

Wesley shook his head. "Synthehol."

Guinan raised an eyebrow. "Didn't see you as much of a synth man, myself, Wes," she said. "Is that what you really want?" She paused, hand poised over the dispenser.

Wesley hesitated and then sighed. "Club soda's fine."

"Uh-huh." As if by magic a club soda appeared in front of him. From nearby, he heard someone say, "To the Ferengi!" and others took up the toast. The Ten-Four Room was the only place one would ever hear something nice said about the Ferengi. That was because it was that race of spacegoing "Yankee Traders" who had first developed synthehol, the drink that acted like alcohol when it hit the system, but with effects that could be dismissed from one's consciousness at will.

At first it was not generally known that synthehol existed. You would simply be drinking with a Ferengi, matching him drink-for-drink, and the next thing you knew you were totally blasted and making ludicrous bargains with a Ferengi salesman who was, mysteriously, stone-cold sober. When word got out, the Ferengi were upset over their secret ace becoming common knowledge. But they quickly, and rather unexpectedly, discovered that there was now so much demand for the beverage that whatever money they lost in tricking hapless victims was more than made up for by straight sales of synthehol.

Still, despite its no-hangover status, synthehol was still considered an adult's drink. Therefore, Wesley's abortive request for it was more than enough to pique Guinan's interest.

"Something bothering you?" she asked.

Wesley stared at Guinan. He had never quite been able to figure her out. She looked mostly human, but there were traces of some alien race that he couldn't quite identify. He knew Picard had had a lot to do with getting Guinan assigned to the *Enterprise,* but he wasn't sure why.

"No. Well"—and he didn't know why, but he always felt as if he had to tell her what was really on his mind—"Well, yes. But it's nothing I really want to talk about."

"Feeling sorry for yourself."

"I'm just a little depressed, okay?" said Wesley. "Is that a crime? *Normal* people get to be depressed."

"Oh, I don't know." Guinan smiled. "People always seem to want to cheer up someone when they see them feeling down. It's part of human nature."

"Well, I wish it was part of human nature to know when someone wants to be left alone," said Wesley, nursing his club soda.

"No problem here," said Guinan.

There was a tap on Wesley's shoulder, and he turned as Guinan said, "Please don't touch Wesley. He wants to be left alone."

"Sorry," said Jaan. "I'll just move along then."

"No, it's okay!" said Wesley. "I didn't mean you."

"Well, okay. If you're sure." Jaan took a seat next to Wesley, who stared at him and frowned.

"What are you looking at?" Jaan asked.

"You. Are you feeling okay?"

Jaan made a dismissive noise. "Never felt better."

Guinan leaned forward, Wesley's concern mirrored on her own face. "Are you sure you're feeling okay? You look a bit flushed."

Jaan and Guinan stared at each other, and Wesley got the distinct impression that there was some sort of unspoken struggle going on between the two of them. He looked from one to the other, feeling like a spectator at a tennis match.

"No, I'm not. Not sure, that is," Jaan said with sudden candor. "I had some stomach cramps earlier, and I've been feeling a little rocky."

"Do you know what it is?" asked Guinan.

Once again, they stared at each other, and now, to Wesley's astonishment, Jaan jumped to his feet, his legs shaking under him. "I've . . . I've got to go, now."

Guinan reached out toward him, to put her hand on his forearm. "Wait, Jaan."

"No!" shouted Jaan and spun away from Guinan as if she had a poison touch.

Wesley shouted Jaan's name, and now everyone in the Ten-Four Room had totally forgotten whatever they were talking about as they turned and stared at the suddenly-belligerent elf.

"Stop looking at me!" Jaan snarled. "All of you!"

"Jaan!" shouted Wesley.

"You too, Orange!" He pulled away from Wesley with such speed and force that he tripped himself up and fell to the ground. It was a stunning moment, for elves were noted for their grace and smoothness. Jaan pulled himself to his feet and fell once more.

And now the other crew members were stirred from their surprise and came forward. Jaan was twisting on the floor, his arms wrapped around his stomach, and he was moaning softly, his legs curled up. Guinan had punched a comm link and was summoning a team from sickbay.

"Hold on," said Wesley, and he was holding the pained elf in his arms. "Just hold on, Jaan. It'll be okay. Everything'll be fine. My m—Dr. Pulaski," he quickly corrected himself, "will take care of everything. She'll know what's wrong with you."

"What the devil is it?"

Picard was staring at the device that had been beamed in to the cargo transporter room, taken without so much as a by-your-leave by the *Enterprise* from the frustrated (and subsequently dead) Kreel.

It was extraordinarily small, about four feet long. In evidence were traces of the mounting brackets that had been used to attach the gleaming cylinder to the underside of the Kreel ship. Also in evidence were certain dials and settings with markings that Picard couldn't even begin to understand. While Data studied the markings, his face as ever giving no indication what thoughts were running through his android mind, Geordi was poking around near the rear of the cylinder. Both of them were being certain to stay clear of what was clearly the gun's business end.

"Here," said Geordi, pointing. "Here are the modifications the Kreel made so it could be operated from within their vessel."

"They clearly had every confidence in this little bit of gadgetry," observed Picard. "Too much, in fact. They thought they were invincible, and it never occurred to them that we might simply remove their little popgun."

"Overconfidence," said Riker, "or simply inexperience. Remember, the Kreel still haven't fully developed transporter technology."

"Yes, and no member of the Federation, or any of the more advanced races, has been particularly interested in giving it to them. Even the Ferengi won't deal with them . . ."

Geordi glanced up. "I thought the Ferengi dealt with anyone."

Riker looked at Geordi with bemusement (and wondered distantly whether Geordi, who could detect so much that was unseen, was able to perceive something as delicate as a smile), and said, "Not even the Ferengi want to give a lit match to the child in the tinderbox."

And now it was Data who registered curiosity. "Tinderbox?"

Riker said, "In the days when people lit their houses with fires, they'd keep it in a box outside the house, so it would be dry."

"How did they light the wood? I assume this was before phasers."

"Slightly. They used matches."

"Ah. Then I do not understand the problem," said Data with that maddening manner he had.

"What," said Picard with resignation, knowing they wouldn't get out of this until Data's endless curiosity was satisfied, "what is it that you don't understand?"

"If matches are what is required to light tinder, then what is wrong with giving one to the child in order to light it? If it is necessary . . ."

"Yes, but if the child is *in* the box, then he burns up himself, and possibly the entire town."

"Ah!" said Data. "I understand."

There were sighs of relief from all around, and Picard opened his mouth to finally bring the conversation back on track.

"How did the child get in the tinderbox?" asked Data.

"His parents locked him in there because he asked too many damned questions!" said Picard.

Data nodded, his gold eyes thoughtful. "That was probably very wise of them."

"Captain," Geordi said quickly before Data could send the conversation spinning in another direction, "this weapon seems extremely powerful for its size."

"It certainly made short work of our shields," agreed Picard, looking over the weapon carefully. "Any thoughts how?"

"My guess is that it simply disrupted them somehow," said Geordi. "I mean, if it had actually *cut* through them, with some sort of high-intensity beam or something, it would have kept on going and sliced us apart as well."

Data was studying the glyphs carefully. "It may well have been capable of that," he said. "If I am deciphering this correctly, the weapon was on its lowest setting."

Geordi and Picard looked at each other. "You're joking," said Picard.

"Joking? Most unlikely, sir," said Data.

"Of course, I know that, but . . . how are you able to translate the symbols?"

Data turned his unblinking, amber gaze on Picard. "There have been similar markings on artifacts found scattered throughout the galaxy in various archeological digs," he said.

"Incredible," said Geordi. "He doesn't know what a tinderbox is, but he can translate glyphs from dusty archeological digs."

"Actually, they were quite sanitary—"

"Data, let's not lose the point here . . . again," said Picard. "The Kreel . . . were they able to read the markings and adjust it? And how were they able to?"

"Oh, I doubt it very much, sir, considering what we know of the Kreel. It is far more likely that they simply used the weapon as is, with no real understanding of how to modify it beyond tying it into their shipboard functions."

"So you're saying that, rather than having developed it themselves, the Kreel probably found this weapon."

"Probably correct, sir."

"Just what are this weapon's full capabilities, Mr. La Forge?"

"I don't know, sir. I'll have to bring it down to engineering, have my tech boys look it over. I know this much . . . from our initial investigation, it won't explode. It seems to have no power source." Then Geordi paused. Although he'd said nothing at the time, he knew that Wesley was still upset over what had happened earlier on the bridge. Wesley must certainly have felt that he had "lost face" with Picard.

This might be a good time to remind Picard of not only Wesley's abilities, but also of the fact that, like any sixteen-year-old, he needed his ego stroked now and then.

The pause was brief, almost unnoticeable, and then Geordi continued, "I'd like to have Mr. Crusher in on this, if you don't mind, Captain."

"Mr. Crusher? Very well," said Picard with a shrug, "make it so."

Geordi looked in Riker's direction momentarily and then, with a feeling like stepping off the edge of a cliff, said, "I think it would be best if you informed him of this yourself, sir."

Picard stood and looked surprised. "Me? Whatever for?"

"Well, if it comes from anyone else, he'll think it's some sort of demotion. He'll think he's being punished."

"That's absurd," snapped Picard. "Why should he think that? It's a simple temporary reassignment of duties."

Resolutely, Geordi folded his arms across his chest. "Teenagers get things in their heads. You know how it is."

Picard pulled himself up stiffly. "Are you implying, Mr. La Forge, that I was once a teenager?"

"Never, sir."

"I should think not." Nevertheless, he stepped over to the wall and tapped a comm link panel. "Captain to Mr. Crusher. Report."

No answer.

It was astounding. Usually response to a page came almost instantaneously. "Captain to Mr. Crusher. Report."

At last, Wesley replied "Crusher here."

There was something in his voice. Something was

distracting him. He sounded as if he were barely paying attention. Perhaps he hadn't even noticed the page at first. "Is there a problem, Mr. Crusher?"

"Problem?"

Picard frowned. What in the world was wrong with Wesley? Was he getting senile at the ripe old age of sixteen? "Yes, Mr. Crusher. A problem. A difficulty."

"A confusion," Data chimed in helpfully. "A mishap, a misfortune, a boondoggle, a—"

"Shut up, Data. Mr. Crusher, your assistance has been requested, and I am now ordering it."

The response Picard got was hardly what he had expected. For one thing, it was a woman's voice, husky and attractive. Picard knew that the woman who went with that voice was also attractive (although hardly husky). "This is Dr. Pulaski, Captain," she said.

Picard blinked in surprise. "Doctor, I would appreciate your not interrupting. I happen to be having a conversation with Mr. Crusher."

"I know, Captain. He's down here in sickbay with me."

Now that was unexpected. Picard had simply assumed that she had butted in on the comm link—a breech of etiquette, but then that would hardly dissuade a woman like Dr. Katherine Pulaski. "Is Wesley all right, Doctor?"

If Pulaski took notice of the fact that Picard had dropped the "Mr. Crusher" reference when he thought Wesley was ill, she made no mention of it. "No, he's quite all right. However . . ." There was a hesitation, as if she was trying to figure out the best way to phrase it. "However, he's aiding me in a matter of some urgency. Can you do without him for a while?"

Picard's back stiffened, as it frequently did in these

recent days of his getting acquainted with the formidable Dr. Pulaski. "The starship *Enterprise* has done quite well for close to a century before Mr. Crusher came along, Doctor. We can certainly muddle through without him for a while longer, if you need him down there."

"Oh my," came the bemused reply. "Close to a century, you say? May I make note of the fact that this is the fifth model of the good ship *Enterprise?* And not only that, but it's my understanding that our Mr. Crusher was instrumental, on several occasions, in delaying the need for a sixth? Perhaps if Mr. Crusher had been born a generation earlier, we would still be at NCC-1701 without the 'D' suffix."

Picard winced.

"Are you through, Doctor?"

He could imagine her beautiful eyes (and, blast and damn, why did her eyes have to be so beautiful?) sparkling with merriment. "Quite through, Captain."

"Fine. Keep Mr. Crusher with you as long as you need. We'll mu—we'll be fine without him. Picard out."

He snapped off the intercom in irritation. Then he turned to Riker and said, "Number One, kindly go down to sickbay and find out what the devil's going on down there. If any of my ensigns, acting or not, are going to be dwelling in Dr. Pulaski's realm I want to know specifics." He frowned to himself. "I should have asked her myself, but that woman can be so irritating at times. I'm not certain what in the world you see in her, Number One."

Riker grinned at that. He had served with Pulaski on an earlier ship assignment and, through time, had become an enthusiastic fan of hers. But he knew that there was a period of adjustment to her style, and he secretly sympathized with what Picard was going through. Very secretly, however. "She grows on you, sir."

"Like a fungus," Picard muttered.

"Or a beard," Riker suggested.

Picard shot him a look but Riker had already forced a deadpan expression.

Picard's communicator beeped and he tapped his insignia. "Picard here."

"Captain," came Worf's low voice, in a tone indicating that the duty he found least interesting was passing along messages, "we have a communiqué from Starfleet."

"I'll be right up," said Picard, and cut the connection. "Geordi, bring that thing down to engineering. But if you take it apart, make damned sure you can put it back together again."

Sounding slightly wounded, Geordi said "Of course, sir."

"Good. Mr. Riker, Mr. Data, with me. Mr. Crusher will have to wait."

They turned to leave and Picard was muttering something to himself. Riker heard enough snatches to prompt him to say, "Beg pardon, sir?"

"I said," Picard admitted, "that your beloved Dr. Pulaski seems determined to challenge my authority."

"More like establishing her own, sir."

The three officers entered the turbolift.

"Do you know," Picard said slowly, "what Nietzsche said about women?"

Everytime Data tried to tell a joke, he failed. Now was no exception. "No, but if you hum a few bars, I'll fake it on my harmonica."

Riker tilted forward, his forehead against the turbolift door. Picard closed his eyes in pain.

For Data, that was practically an ovation. Thus encouraged, he said with the same intensity that he would have announced a Romulan attack, "A man leaves his cat with his brother and goes off on vacation . . ."

And Picard, who could have ordered him to stop, in a fit of masochism allowed him to continue.

If I can survive being trapped in a turbolift with Data trying to tell jokes, he reasoned, *I can certainly survive anything Starfleet has to tell me.*

Chapter Five

SEATED IN THE CONFERENCE LOUNGE off the bridge, Picard, Riker, Data, Troi, and Worf stared at the holopic of Admiral Westerby with a collective combination of astonishment and annoyance.

"Admiral," Picard said slowly, "are you telling us that Starfleet knew of these apparent weapons advancements by the Kreel, and had not made it general knowledge?"

"What we knew, Captain," said Westerby with an emphasis on rank to give a not-so-subtle reminder as to who was in charge, "was nothing. Nothing except rumors, vague intelligence reports. If the Kreel had attacked Vulcan, for example, we would have known everything there was to know immediately. The Klingons, unfortunately, tend to be pretty tight-lipped whenever they run into difficulties. No offense intended, Lieutenant Worf."

Worf was silent for a moment, and Picard wondered just what was going through his mind.

"One cannot take offense," said Worf, "at the truth.

Klingons, as a whole, do not like to discuss problems. A sign of weakness, we feel."

"Problems are one thing, Worf," said Picard, "but major attacks by foes bearing vastly improved weapons!"

Worf's gaze bored right through him. "I assure you, sir, I had no idea. *I* would have told you, had I known."

"Of course you would have, Worf," Picard said quickly. "I never meant to imply otherwise." He turned back to Westerby. "But now you want me to put my ship, my crew, directly in the middle of this . . . this situation?"

"Precisely," said Westerby. "The Klingons and the Kreel have both come to realize that full-scale war is imminent. It's our belief the Kreel didn't bargain for that. We think they stumbled onto these weapons and are now over their head, and they're looking for a graceful way out. What they've agreed to is a full sharing among all parties of the weapons they've found."

"Balance of power," Data said. "All sides having the same weaponry, so that no one will wish to employ them since mutual destruction is assured."

"We know what balance of power is, Data," said Picard, who was still a bit irritated from the long and badly told joke Data had inflicted on them in the turbolift.

"And the agreement," continued Westerby, "is that both Klingon and Kreel diplomatic contingents will be transported aboard a Federation vessel to the site of the initial discovery."

"Site? What site?"

"Well," said Westerby, "our records show it as DQN 1196."

"That's in Klingon territory," Worf said.

"Or Kreel," replied Westerby. "It depends who you talk to. At this point, the Kreel have another name for it, which translates out roughly into 'Hellhole.'"

Picard nodded. "As near as we can tell, the netherworld might indeed be the source of these weapons."

"What's frightening is that we've only seen the ones they had the resources to figure out," said Westerby. "The Federation doesn't want to even consider the untapped potential of that planet. That's why they've decided that Starfleet has to maintain a major presence right in the midst of the situation. In fact, the request for the *Enterprise,* specifically, came straight from Taka Nagai's office."

The *Enterprise* officers looked at each other in surprise. "We are, of course, honored," said Picard. "Still, perhaps the Klingons and Kreel could each travel in their respective ships, with the *Enterprise* as an escort."

Westerby was already shaking his head. "We consider it unwise to have a Klingon and Kreel ship in proximity to each other. The results could be . . . unpleasant."

"Then perhaps we could transport one group while another starship transports the other."

"We suggested that. Unfortunately, the Klingons and the Kreel want to keep an eye on each other."

"So we have to keep them close enough to watch each other, but far enough away so that they don't kill each other." Picard shook his head wearily. "Admiral, with all due respect, there must be another way."

"Perhaps there is," said Westerby evenly. "But this is the way we have chosen. Is there a problem with that, Captain Picard?"

Again that emphasis on rank. Making no effort to keep the annoyance out of his voice, Picard said, "No problem we cannot handle, Admiral."

"As I thought," said the admiral cheerfully. "You'll be picking up the Klingon contingent first, and then the Kreel group. Coordinates for your rendezvous will be forthcoming shortly. Starfleet out."

The holopic obediently vanished. As if prearranged, Riker and Troi slumped slightly with a *"Whew"* sound. Picard leaned forward, his fingers interlaced. "Well . . . that's just marvelous," he said.

"Sir, I wish to protest for the record," Worf said with remarkable stiffness.

Picard looked at him bemusedly. "So noted. I'll be certain to file it right after *my* protest."

"Why are you so adverse to this mission, Captain?" Data asked. "Certainly shuttling races with disputes is hardly new for the *Enterprise.*"

"It's the nature of the races, Data. Plus the nature of the disputes. Plus the civilians . . ." Picard shook his head in dismay. "Civilians. To this day it's the one major policy decision Starfleet has made that rankles me. And I see you're shaking your head, Mr. Riker."

"We've disagreed on this before, Captain, and I think we'll continue to do so," said Riker. "Many people aboard the *Enterprise* are scientists, geologists, explorers who are doing the kind of work that can only be done aboard a starship."

"Not to mention the spouses and children of *Enterprise* crew members," Troi added. "Part of the movement toward integrating families began when studies showed that long separations from their loved-ones was detrimental to the health of Starfleet personnel."

"My second-in-command and my counselor, of one mind once again, eh?" Picard said. Troi and Riker glanced at each other and quickly turned away, Troi maintaining her professional detachment, but Riker permitting a small smile. Picard continued, "But we keep coming back to one overwhelming problem. You, Mr. Riker, and you, Counselor Troi, and everyone in this room, has been through Starfleet Academy. We've had special, extensive training to handle all sorts of situations.

"Now when we encounter difficulties that can be handled by the bridge crew, all well and good. But Starfleet is thrusting us into an arrangement where a problem with lethal potential is going to be wandering the corridors of this ship. I'd like to confine the Klingons and Kreel to their quarters for the duration of the trip, but the Klingons are too proud and the Kreel too nasty. The last thing we want to do is take the members of a diplomatic mission and put them in a foul mood right at the beginning. But if difficulties start, I'm extremely concerned that all the civilians are going to find themselves caught in the middle of a crossfire." He conjured up images of children lying phaser-burned and dead or dying in the hallways while rampaging Klingons and Kreel carried on their race war, oblivious of the consequences. Not a pretty picture.

"What I resent," he said, "is that Starfleet has seen fit to take the *Enterprise* and turn her into a . . . a . . ."

"A tinderbox?" offered Data hopefully.

Picard considered that and nodded slowly. "As always, I'm impressed by your learning abilities, Mr. Data. Yes, indeed . . . a tinderbox. And we have to keep the matchbook out of their hands."

"Absolutely," said Riker.

"I agree completely," said Worf.

"What's a matchbook?" said Data.

* * *

Wesley stood over the diagnostic bed looking down at the unmoving body of his friend. He watched the slow, steady rising and falling of Jaan's chest, and then glanced up at the monitoring board. He did not even look when Dr. Pulaski came up behind him. "He seems to be resting comfortably," he said.

"Really," she said. "Any recommendations, Doctor?" The words might have been sarcastic, but the tone was carefully neutral. It was as if she were testing him.

She tests everyone, he thought. Then he realized that that was an oversimplification. Katherine Pulaski didn't "test" people to see if she could catch them or see how much they knew. Rather, she seemed eternally interested in trying to see just how far humans were capable of bringing themselves, of what sorts of intuitive leaps in knowledge and logic they could make when challenged. An unselfish, altruistic point-of-view for her to have.

Also a damned irritating one.

All right then. Without removing his gaze from the monitor he said, "Fifty cc's of andromorphine."

His brisk prescription hung in the air before Pulaski seemed to pluck it out. Nearby stood a medic-aid who, naturally, was not acting upon Wesley's diagnosis. But Pulaski now said in her no-nonsense tone, "You heard him."

The dosage was quickly administered and, within moments, Wesley could imagine that his friend's breathing actually seemed to be less strained.

Then Jaan opened his soft, slanted dark eyes. They blurred for a second and then cleared and he smiled up. "Hi, Orange," he said weakly. "C'mon . . . let's blow this mausoleum."

"I'm afraid," was Dr. Pulaski's stern order, "that

you'll have to stay put for some time. At least twenty-four hours for observation."

Jaan's voice seemed to turn to honey. "Oooohh, now you don't have to keep me here that long, do you? Now of course you don't. I just had a little problem and certainly you don't have to—"

She leaned forward on the edge of the diagnostic table and placed a finger against his lips, stilling them. "You're not my first elf," she said. "So you can just forget 'the Knack.' I know about it, I'm ready for it, and that pretty much puts it out of commission. Correct?"

He sighed. "You're well-read."

Wesley looked from one to the other in befuddlement. "The Knack? What's the Knack? I don't understand."

"The Knack," said Dr. Pulaski, looking away from her patient, "is a little-documented aspect of the Selelvian makeup. When they look at you with those marvelous dark eyes of theirs, they have a way of cajoling listeners into doing whatever they, the elves, want them to do. They say they have a knack for getting things done. However, if you're aware of it and"—she smiled—"you have a fairly strong sense of self, then you can manage to resist their . . . suggestions?"

"A fair-enough assessment," replied Jaan, and he was smiling but there was a twinge of pain in there that he obviously was trying to screen out.

Pulaski folded her arms. "So you want to tell me what this is all about? And I can request privacy, if you so wish," she said with a glance at Wesley.

Jaan didn't appear to understand what she was talking about. "You mean Orange? No, it's okay. Actually," he paused, "I suspect you already know

77

what 'this is about' and you're just extending me the courtesy of being the one to say it."

"That's one interpretation," said Pulaski evenly. "You are aware of your condition, then."

"Of course."

Wesley looked from one to the other. "Well *I'm* not aware," he said in frustration.

For the first time since he'd known him, Wesley saw Jaan fumbling for words, looking for the best way to put something that was clearly uncomfortable for him. And when it became apparent that he was having difficulty, Pulaski stepped in.

"There's a very long, very complicated name for it," she said, and Wesley knew from all those times watching his mother in action that this was an example of a doctor putting on her best bedside manner. "The Selelvian nickname for it is 'the Rot.' It's genetically transmitted, and can strike at any time in the Selelvian life-cycle, although it usually doesn't hit until middle age."

"Right." Jaan grimaced. He wiped off the sweat that was beading on his forehead, and from nowhere, it seemed, Pulaski had a cloth in her hand and was dabbing at it. "You know me, Orange. Always beating the odds. Maybe about three, four percent get it as young as I do. Young, relatively speaking, that is."

"Okay," said Wesley slowly, as if it were taking time to sink in. "Okay, then. What's the cure, Doctor? How do we make him better?"

A long sigh issued from Katherine Pulaski. "I can treat the symptoms, Wes," she said slowly. "Relieve the pain of the abdominal cramps. The headaches, the nausea . . . hell, when the drowsiness and lethargy sets in, I could pump Jaan so full of drugs that his feet won't touch the floor, although I would really prefer not to, since they would impair his thinking."

"No," said Jaan flatly.

"I thought not. But the disease itself . . . I'm sorry, Jaan, but you must know there's nothing I can do."

"Yes, I know."

Wesley looked from one to the other in disbelief. "What do you mean, nothing? There's got to be a cure for it."

"There's no cure."

"A vaccine."

"There's no vaccine," Pulaski almost snapped, but reined herself in. It wasn't any easier on her than on them to discuss it, but she had to be the one in control. Besides, she wasn't about to start explaining you can't vaccinate against a genetic disease. "I'm sorry, Wes . . . Jaan. They simply haven't managed to develop one, yet. That's why when Selelvians mate they undergo blood tests for it, but unfortunately there is always a margin of error in those tests."

"See?" said Jaan with a cheerfulness he didn't feel. "I beat the odds again, Orange. Twice. I'm really lucky, aren't I?"

"So you're . . ." Wesley could barely put coherent thoughts together, much less sentences. "So you're . . . you're going to *die?* Is that what you're telling me? Is that what's going to happen, Doctor?"

"Wesley, we all—"

"Don't *say it!*" Wesley practically shrieked. He backed away from Pulaski as if she'd suddenly grown fangs. He stabbed an index finger at her. "Don't say, 'We all die someday, and we shouldn't be afraid,' and that 'Death is natural.' Dying when you're old is natural. But dying when you're young, when you're . . ." He couldn't complete the sentence, and said instead, "How long?"

Pulaski looked from Wesley's agonized face to Jaan's stoic expression. She wondered briefly whether

Jaan had reached the point where he had accepted what was happening inside his body, or whether he was simply bottling it all in and was a time bomb ticking down. "That depends," she said. "On the progression of the disease, on Jaan's—"

"HOW LONG?!"

It was a shout ripped from deep within him, and Wesley's yelled question brought all activity in the sickbay to a complete halt. Everyone was looking at him in astonishment, and he didn't care.

Her voice was so quiet in contrast to his that it was remarkable. "Six months to a year," she said.

He repeated what she had said, mouthing it in disbelief. He shook his head, and it was as if he were staring inward, trying to deal with what he'd been told. Something in the tumblers of his mind clicked.

"Your parents," he said. "You told me weeks ago that they'd been killed in some sort of accident. Back on Selelvia. That was what had made you go off into space, because you wanted to get away from the memories of that." He paused, not wanting to believe it, because Pulaski had said it was an inherited disease, and if what he thought was true, then against all hope it confirmed it. "That . . . that was a lie."

Slowly Jaan nodded.

"They . . . they died of this disease, didn't they?"

With a sigh Jaan said, "Look, Orange . . ."

"Why didn't you tell me?"

"How could I?" Jaan's calm was in stunning contrast to Wesley, Pulaski thought, especially considering that it was Jaan who was dying. Then again, the elf had had time to adjust to it. Or maybe he was still trying not to think about it. "Look, Orange . . . it's not the kind of thing that's easy to discuss. And you'd been through enough. Bad enough that you lost your father . . ."

"That was years ago," said Wesley. "I was a kid. It's over."

Katherine Pulaski pursed her lips. She had known Bev Crusher back when her husband had been killed. Bev had been a wreck, and Wesley had hardly been the little stoic . . . *no, wait,* she realized. He *had* been. His mother had come unglued, but young Wesley had been tight-lipped, steel-jawed—the "man of the house," as countless relatives kept seeming to say of him. Tough, supportive . . . he had seemed harder hit by news of Jaan than news of his own father. Or maybe she was imagining it, separated as she was by the long years.

Unaware of what was running through the doctor's mind, Jaan was saying, "And then your mom left you . . ."

Wesley blew air through his teeth. "She didn't leave me, for pity's sake. She got a terrific career opportunity. She knew I was in good hands here. I told her not to pass it up. She was willing to stay here, and I told her she would be crazy to let a shot at head of Starfleet medicine go past . . ." His voice trailed off and he snapped his fingers. "I'll contact my mom! She'd be up on the latest research! She'd . . ."

"I can assure you," said Pulaski with just a hint of pique, "that I am up on it."

"Good. So there has to be something."

"There isn't."

"There *has* to be!"

"Wesley," she said tiredly, "research isn't my strength. But I'll be happy to make all the current medical knowledge available to you. Obviously the time you spent with your mother has rubbed off on you. You seem to have a better-than-layman's knowledge of medicine . . ."

"Why shouldn't I?" said Wesley bitterly. "You

81

know me. Wesley Crusher, the 'Brain Trust.' The sixteen-year-old computer on legs."

"You're getting yourself confused with Data again," said Jaan softly. "Listen, Orange—"

"No, you listen," said Wesley, and he stalked to Jaan's side. "You'll beat this thing. You will. That's all. You'll just beat it. Doctor, I'll take you up on your offer. About the medical journals. Hang on, Jaan. We'll do it. You and me." He turned and walked quickly out of sickbay.

There was silence for a long moment, and then Pulaski said, "Well, that could certainly have gone better."

"Orange is a funny guy," said Jaan. "What he can do is way up here"—and he raised his right hand high over his head—"and what he can handle is about here"—and his left hand was six inches lower. "So when you get to the area in between, well . . . weird things can happen with him."

"Mm-hmmm. But now the question becomes, what's going to happen with you?"

"Pardon?"

"We should rotate you off-ship immediately."

"But why?" protested Jaan.

"Impaired efficiency."

"You can compensate for a lot of it," said Jaan. "You said so yourself. Look, Doctor . . . I came on this ship to do my research work. To be able to study alien cultures firsthand. I've already gotten several articles written and published back home and when I've put together enough they'll be collected into one volume."

"I don't see how that—"

"Please, Doctor," he said, and if he was trying to use the Knack, she sure couldn't tell. This was genuine, heart-felt pleading. "When you write, you leave a

82

bit of yourself behind. When you write enough, when you write something that really has impact, you can affect people and what they think long after you're gone. It's the closest thing to living forever that we've got. Please . . . please don't deny me the immortality that my body is never going to give me. Please . . ."

His lips trembled and he put his hands to his face, as if he could physically shove the tears back into his eyes.

And if he was using the Knack, then dammit, she didn't care.

"All right," she said softly. "I'll have to tell the captain of your condition, of course . . . but I'll recommend that you be allowed to remain with the ship for as long as possible."

"Out of the question."

In the privacy of the captain's ready room, Picard stood with arms folded and entire body posture indicating that he wasn't going to hear a word of it.

"It's important," said Pulaski. She made a conscious effort to duplicate the way Picard was standing, to send a subtle message that she wasn't backing down on this.

"So is the efficient running of a starship. And a starship is not the place for a dying crew member."

"We're all of us dying, Captain, from the moment we're born."

"That's a lot of nonsense, Doctor, as far as this situation is concerned, and you know it."

She sighed. "Yes, I know. Wesley didn't buy that line of reasoning, so I shouldn't have expected you to."

"Wesley? What does—?"

She didn't give him the opportunity to change subjects. "However, it is my medical recommendation that Jaan be allowed to remain aboard, at least until the disease reaches its later stages and he becomes unable to function. As long as he's capable of making a contribution, why shouldn't he be allowed to, Captain? Who's he going to hurt?"

"That's not the point. A starship is no place for a—"

"Dying crewman, yes I know. But he's not a crew member, he's a civilian, and don't make that face, Captain. 'Civilian' isn't a dirty word."

"What face?"

"That twitch. That little irritating twitch around your eye every time civilians are mentioned."

Picard looked as if an iron rod had been jammed down his spine. Every word a bullet, he said, "I have no nervous twitch."

"You do."

"That's absurd."

Pulaski paused a moment. Then with slow, measured steps she walked right up to the captain, and stood toe-to-toe with him.

"Civilian," she said.

Picard twitched.

"A-HA!"

"'A-ha' nothing."

"You twitched. I saw it."

"Doctor, your charming efforts to divert my attention are going to do you no good whatsoever." He circled around to his desk and sat down behind it, as if the physical obstruction between himself and Dr. Pulaski gave him a measure of security. "Your patient will be returned to his home."

"My patient has a name. It's Jaan. Jaan Baat-Utuul-Bayn-Devin. It's not as impressive as a rank, of course, but he's entitled to be referred to by a name, as is any *civilian.*"

84

Picard tried to fight off the twitch and failed, to his annoyance and Pulaski's apparent satisfaction. "It is my decision," he said, "that Jaan be sent back to his people. My authority on this ship is final."

"Not when it comes to medical decisions," she said.

"This is not a medical decision, this is a personnel decision, and it's been made."

"Fine. Make your decision." She dropped down into the chair opposite him.

"It's made."

"Good. I officially file my appeal to your decision."

"Appeal denied."

"All right. Now that you've denied it, I'll appeal to the level above you, and the level above that, and as high as I have to go." She smiled at him with that damnable beautiful smile that was almost as attractive as her eyes *(and why did she have to be so blasted attractive)*, and said, "As you know, Starfleet does allow for an extensive appeals process when the medical head comes into conflict with the ship's captain. To protect the ultimate authority of both positions."

"Yes, I know that."

"And you also know the appeals process takes somewhere around six months. During which time your decision will not be in force regarding Jaan. So while we slug it out in appeals, he'll be allowed to be a useful member of this stargoing society."

Picard felt a fury building in him and slammed it down, but couldn't keep all of the anger from his voice as he said, "I do not appreciate this challenge to my authority from someone relatively new to this ship!"

"So I'm new!" shot back Pulaski. "I didn't know one had to be a veteran like yourself to care about people! Well I'll tell you what, Captain. Maybe you'll be lucky! You see, I think Jaan has as little as six months to live . . . about as long as the appeals process. But maybe fortune will favor you, and Jaan will drop dead before that!"

The moment the words were out of her mouth, she wished she could have called them back. It was as if she'd struck him a blow across the face. For a moment, he actually looked stunned.

She looked down, ashamed of herself. "I'm sorry," she said with real sincerity. "That was a hideous thing to say."

The silence hung heavily in the ready room, and when Picard spoke it was without the authoritarian stiffness and clipped tone she'd come to expect.

"Do as you see fit, Katherine," he said softly.

She looked up at him now, and there was no anger in his eyes. Only sadness. "All I ask is that you keep me apprised of his condition."

"Of course." She paused. "Thank you."

She turned to go and stopped at the door as Picard added, "And Katherine . . ."

The second time he used her first name, she chose not to ignore the opening. "Yes, Jean-Luc?"

"Please extend to the lad my . . . sincerest condolences. If there is anything we can do to make his remaining time with us more comfortable, he need merely inform us."

And at that, she smiled. "I'll make it so," she said, and walked out of the ready room.

Chapter Six

RIKER SLOWED HIS BRISK STEP down the corridor as young Bobbi Chase approached him.

"Commander Riker," she said.

He nodded slightly in acknowledgment. "Bobbi."

And to his mild surprise, she kept right on walking past him. He smiled in amusement at the mercurial nature of teenage crushes.

Then the voice came from behind him, and she said, "Oh, Commander."

Set phasers on gush, he thought as he turned. "Yes?"

Bobbi took a step forward, hands fidgeting nervously. And she said, "Have you seen Wesley around lately?"

He blinked in surprise. "Wesley? As a matter of fact, I was just going to his quarters to check on him."

"He's not there. I've knocked and knocked on his door and there's no answer."

Riker frowned. "Really? You won't be insulted if I confirm that myself, will you?"

"Not if you won't be insulted if I ask to come along."

He considered that a moment. Wesley was going to have a lot on his mind. Did Riker really want to have a young girl along as a distraction to the boy?

What was he thinking? Of course he did. "As you wish," he said. Bobbi smiled and fell into step behind him.

When they got to Wesley's quarters, Riker touched the caller signal and, for good measure, said, "Wesley? Are you there?"

No answer was forthcoming. "Told you," she said.

But Riker wasn't satisfied. He rapped more solidly on the door and said sternly, "Wesley, if you're in there, I order you to open this door. And since you're an acting ensign, if you disobey a direct order, I may be forced to hold an acting court-martial."

To Bobbi's surprise, but not Riker's, there was the sound of shuffling about for a moment, and then the door opened.

Wesley stood in the doorway. He was so preoccupied he didn't even notice Bobbi standing there. "Yes, sir?"

"Wesley, would you mind telling me what the devil is going on?"

"On, sir?"

"Yes, going on. Would you like me to summon Data so he could offer a few dozen synonyms?"

Then he glanced over Wesley's shoulder to the interior of the room and his eyes widened in surprise. "What have you done to this place, Wesley?"

He took a step forward, and at first Wesley didn't move from his spot. But Riker stared down at him and Wesley stepped back, allowing Riker to enter. Bobbi came in close on his heels, and Wesley looked at her with a sort of vague interest. He said nothing.

Riker stood in the middle of the room and turned, because that was the only place where there was any space in the room at all. The left side was now completely filled with computer terminals, all of which had different subjects on their screens. The right side was taken up by lab and medical equipment, some of which Riker recognized as coming from sickbay.

"Wesley, what—" He gestured helplessly. "What are you doing in here?"

"Doing, sir?"

"Don't start that with me, again, Mr. Crusher. Now what are you up to?"

Wesley leaned against one of the tables. "I'm going to find a cure for the Rot. For the disease that's killing Jaan."

Bobbi gasped. "Jaan? The elf? He's dying?"

"That's nobody's business outside of this room, understood, young woman?" said Riker quickly. Even as he spoke he knew it was a lost cause. Within an hour the entire ship would know. Keeping a secret in an enclosed society like a starship was tougher than limiting Data to one-word answers.

She was nodding but, by that point, Riker had already turned away from her. "Wesley," he said, trying to find some way to reach him, "you're no medical expert. Researchers have been trying for years to find a cure for that disease."

"No they haven't," said Wesley in a tone that indicated he'd already anticipated everything Riker might say and developed a counter for it. "I've been checking. In the Federation medical annals, the Rot is receiving only a fraction of the attention that other afflictions have gotten. They're far more interested in devoting time and attention to plagues than to the Rot."

"But Wesley, I'm certain that they've given it as much time as they can."

"As much time as they have available, maybe, but that's not the same thing."

And now Bobbi, who was looking uncomprehendingly at one essay on the effects of the Rot, said, "Well, I can understand it, I guess. I mean, plagues and things, they're certainly more important than—"

"Than what?" Wesley said heatedly. "Than in a disease which only afflicts a very small percentage of only one race? Only Selelvians can come down with the Rot, no one else. Maybe if you or I or Commander Riker or Captain Picard or the head of Starfleet could catch it, then it might get a lot of attention. But who cares about something that only an elf can catch, right? We're all safe, and he's dying, and I've got to do something about it!"

Bobbi looked helplessly from one to the other, and Riker said quietly, "I think you'd better leave now, Bobbi." Grateful for the opportunity, she did.

Wesley stood there, defiantly, and Riker said, "You and Jaan have grown quite close since your mother left, haven't you?"

It was not the question Wesley had expected. He cocked his head in curiosity and said slowly, "Yes. I mean, we saw each other around, we talked and things, before that. But right after Mom left, we really started to get friendly. We had a lot in common."

"Did you?"

Wesley frowned. "Well . . . not a lot of things. But Jaan had lost both of his parents, and Mom may not be dead, but I can't exactly go and talk with her about whatever's bothering me."

Riker drummed his fingers on the dresser that was currently holding several pounds of medical equipment. "Funny. I thought most sixteen-year-olds didn't like to go talk over problems with their moms."

"Well . . . it's like the *Enterprise* being able to separate the saucer section. You hope you won't have to use that ability, but it's nice to know it's there, just in case."

"I see." Privately, Riker thought that was an interesting analogy to make, and remarks about "separation anxiety" came to mind. But that was more Deanna's department, anyway. "Look, Wes . . ."

"Don't try to talk me out of it, sir, because I've already got my mind made up."

Riker stared blankly at Wesley. Talk him out of it? He could order him if he wanted to. Just because Wesley wasn't an actual, *bona fide* member of the crew didn't mean that he was not bound by the orders of the command personnel, particularly the second-in-command. And if Wesley gave him trouble, he could have him confined to quarters. Except that was what young Mr. Crusher wanted. He could remove all the computers and equipment from Wesley's room. He could even toss him in the brig. But none of that would solve the problem.

And the boy was hurting. His mother had just left, and although Wes remained in good hands, it had to have some impact. And now a close friend was dying.

Still . . .

"Wes," he said carefully, "as I said before . . . your specialty isn't medicine. It's in engineering."

"You don't grow up the son of a doctor without picking up a lot," said Wes. "And what I don't know, I'll learn."

"You can't duplicate the years of education of the scientists who are already researching this disease."

"I," said Wes tautly, "think I can. I've saved this ship. Saved it a couple of times. That didn't come from luck. That wasn't happenstance. What I don't know, I can learn."

"About engineering, maybe. But not—"

"About anything." He tapped his forehead. "Photographic memory."

"What?"

"Photographic memory. I see it, I remember it."

"Wes," Riker was starting to become exasperated. "A photographic memory won't do you a damn bit of good if you don't fully understand and comprehend everything you see. And you just don't have the background to do that."

"I can do it. And if you try to stop me, you'll be condemning Jaan to death, plus who knows how many other people. All because you didn't believe me."

Riker sighed. "All right, Wesley. You're not going to believe me on this until you learn it yourself. You win."

And with that he left Wesley alone in his room.

"Of course I win," murmured Wesley. "I always win. I'm the Brain Trust."

Riker stopped in briefly with Dr. Katherine Pulaski to confirm that the medical materials and text references had all come from her.

"I saw no harm in it," she said.

"The boy thinks he can cure the Rot."

"The young man thinks he can cure the Rot," corrected Pulaski. "Who knows, Will? He may be right. If five-year-old Mozart had come to you and asked you to buy him a piano because he felt like composing a symphony, what would you have said?"

"I would have said 'Ask your father.'"

"Spoken like a true second-in-command."

Her remark was made without heat, but nevertheless his lips thinned in mild annoyance. He liked Katherine, always had, always would. But one of his great secret desires was to once, just once, win an argument with her. Somehow that goal still seemed far off.

She patted him on his bearded cheek. "Don't be so glum, Will. If he succeeds, you look like the brilliant, foresighted commander who supported him. If he fails, you get to say 'I told you so.' "

"I don't want to say 'I told you so.' I just want him to be happy."

"Fine." She paused. "Then pray that he helps his friend."

"Speaking of his friend"—and Riker glanced around the sickbay—"I don't see him here."

"Jaan? I discharged him. Oh, I'm keeping regular tabs on him. But why should I keep him cooped up in here?" She shrugged. "He's not contagious. And it would certainly defeat the purpose of keeping him on board if he were a prisoner in sickbay. With regular medication, rest, and periodic monitoring, he should be fine."

"As fine as someone can be who's dying."

"There is that."

Having finished his impromptu meeting with Katherine, Riker now went to engineering. It did not take him long to locate Geordi. He was in the section that was crammed with techies, crawling all over the device they'd *(stolen* was such an ugly word) appropriated from the Kreel. Riker stood in the doorway a moment and watched them work.

They looked like ants swarming over a particularly enticing bit of leftover food.

Geordi was standing there, in the midst of all the activity, running a scanner over it and shaking his head slowly. Riker called to him. At first, Geordi didn't even respond. Then one of the tech crew nudged him, and Geordi trotted over to where Riker stood, waiting patiently.

He liked Geordi. He really did, and even now he had to fight off the occasional temptation to feel sorry for the chief engineer's sightlessness, particularly since Geordi would have been the first to scoff at any such feelings. Riker had discovered not long ago that the VISOR Geordi wore actually was a somewhat-painful prosthetic, because of the constant strain of his mind to cope with the visual input that most humans never even begin to imagine. The ability to carry on stoically, uncomplaining . . . he admired that in Geordi. In anyone.

"What's the story here, Mr. La Forge?" he asked with the formalness he always used upon requiring a report.

And Geordi, who was never impressed by formality, said, "You're not going to like it."

"I'll have to try. What have you found out about this weapon?"

"Nothing."

"Nothing?" Riker was incredulous. "Geordi, your people have been crawling over this thing for ages. Do you need help? Don't tell me," he said with mock horror, "that you can't do it without Wesley?"

Geordi smiled raggedly. "No, not even"—and then he imitated the distinctive tone of Captain Picard— "the formidable Mr. Crusher . . ."

"Who is otherwise occupied," said Riker.

". . . would be of much help," finished Geordi. "It's defying all our spectral analyses. We've tried scanning it with everything we can think of to get a reading on what constitutes this baby's circuitry. We've tried tricorders, optiscan, we've brought it down to sickbay—"

"Up to sickbay."

"Up to sickbay," Geordi amended, "and tossed it on the diagnostic table. We even, as God is my

94

witness, tried X-rays. How's that for outmoded? And even that didn't work. Any sort of beam or ray or light that is projected toward it, that endeavors to penetrate its guts, the thing just bounces back."

"Can you see it?"

Geordi paused. "That's a good question, isn't it? I mean, it sounded weird at first, but that's reasonable. I just took it for granted, my being able to see it. Yeah, I can see it. But all I'm picking up is the exterior. Now it's obviously not repelling all light. If it were . . ."

"It'd be invisible," said Riker.

"Right. Like a cloaking device. So it's one of two things. Either the outside is made of some metal that we've never heard of before . . . and this thing has alien properties, I'll tell you that right now. It's an alloy with trace substances I can't even begin to get a handle on."

"Or . . ." Riker prompted.

"Or it has some sort of internal cloaking device that's in force just inside the shell. So our scans penetrate just so far and no farther."

"I see."

"I wish I did."

"Are you at all clear about its power capacities?"

"Don't know. Haven't figured a way to test it yet. Not without risking blowing out the side of the engineering deck."

"Marvelous. Captain's going to love this."

"Well, let him figure out how to do it," said Geordi, that snappishness being the first indication of the frustration he was feeling. "I can't even disassemble it. Look at this"—and he guided Riker over to it—"except for these settings and markings over here, it's seamless. Look . . . there was an entry port over here, and the Kreel connected up some sort of jury-rigged circuitry to it. The wild thing is, it worked.

95

Luck of the stupid. This entry port could have been anything, and instead of managing to harness its power, the Kreel could just have easily have blown themselves to bits."

"Maybe it liked them."

"Then it's got strange taste in friends."

Riker looked over his shoulder and frowned. "You said 'was' an entry port. Where is it now?"

"It sealed up."

Riker's mouth moved for a moment or two, trying to get the question out. "It . . . what?"

"Sealed up. We pulled out what the Kreel had connected, and just had time to watch the hole close up."

"That's insane! What are you saying? That this thing's alive?"

"I sure hope not," said Geordi. "Because we've been poking and prodding this thing, and if it's alive, it might get mad at us. And I would not want to have Tiny mad at us."

"'Tiny'?"

"My nickname for it."

"Wonderful. So tell me, Geordi"—and he circled the weapon, staring at it in amazement—"how did it just seal up? A little hatch just dropped down?"

"No. That I could understand. That would be normal. That would be sane. This thing, the metal just sort of shimmered for a moment, and then it started to . . . I don't know . . ."

"Reform?" put in one of the techies.

"Good a word as any. It reformed around the hole, filling it in and smoothing out. It took maybe a total of three seconds. As if the metal were malleable. And as soon as the reformation was done, it hardened right up again. Became as smooth as the rest of it."

Riker leaned against a console, shaking his head.

"So what we got here," Geordi said with almost malicious glee, "is pretty damned peculiar."

And Riker wondered what the captain would do with that report.

Worf entered the holodeck. The door closed behind him as he glanced around the unactivated room. It looked unassuming, huge and black, with a shimmering grid of golden squares.

Worf could have fought in some sort of elaborate scenario—anything from battling on the parapets of a fortress to fighting for his life on the plains of an alien desert. But Klingons were never much for extravagances.

He walked forward slowly and said, "Fighting ring."

Immediately a large square, marked out in shimmering lines, appeared on the floor. He recalled that during workouts, Tasha had always conjured up a mat. No disrespect to the memory of the Honorable Natasha Yar, but the comfort of a mat was somehow inappropriate for a Klingon.

He walked to the center of the ring and took his mark there, body relaxed and ready, eyes narrowed. "Opponents," he said. "Four."

At each corner of the box a large, burly enemy for Worf to battle appeared. He frowned. Something wasn't quite right.

Then he knew what he wanted.

"Reform," he said. "Kreel."

The four forms blinked out to be immediately replaced by four Kreel warriors. They stood there impassively, waiting to be commanded.

Klingons, as a rule, did not smile. Not outwardly. Worf honored this rule, but inwardly, he was grinning.

But there was one thing he had to do before the drill

began. The computer would analyze the fight as it went and, if Worf were in serious danger, the computer would shut it down. A warrior could not be at his best if nothing were at stake.

Worf, however, had done some computer modification.

"Override mortality failsafe," he said.

For the first time the disembodied voice of the computer spoke. It replied, "Compliance." It meant that the computer would not stop short of deadly force, if Worf so desired.

"Attack," he said.

He waited, posing on the balls of his feet, hands now in front of him in a "T" formation.

When you were battling computer constructs, you were doing far more than just fighting mindless drones. The computer learned extremely quickly, and was able to compensate rapidly. For every move it developed a countermove. In short, you were fighting a device that thought as slowly as humanoids thought only if it chose to do so.

The first Kreel lunged forward, the others holding back to see what Worf would do. More than just being a generic creation, the Kreel attacked the way the Kreel do. No art, no cleverness, no strategy. Just straight on, arms outstretched, fingers grasping and eager to get hold of an opponent's throat or arms or legs or anything else that could be broken or crushed.

Worf stood his ground, knees bent slightly, arms out and ready. At the last moment, he twisted away from the rush, grabbing the Kreel by the back of the neck and waist and using its own speed against him. With a grunt he hurled the Kreel out of the ring, where it lay immobile, out of the drill.

He waited for the next single one to attack, or perhaps two. Instead, to his surprise, the computer crossed him up. It sent all three of the remaining Kreel at him at one time.

The move caught him completely off-guard, and all three Kreel converged on him, grabbing him and bearing him to the ground. He went down beneath a flurry of fists.

He warded off the blows as best he could with his burly arms, and one of the Kreel had an arm around his leg and was about to get another arm around it, in an endeavor to break it. Worf, on the ground, twisted around, got his foot in position and slammed his boot into the Kreel's face. The Kreel fell back, its simulated nose gushing simulated blood.

Worf writhed out of the grasp of the other two Kreel. One of them grabbed at him, but Worf dodged easily, kicking his attacker in the throat. The Kreel dropped, gagging, and Worf spun, delivering a reverse roundkick that broke the Kreel's jaw and knocked several of its teeth out. The massively injured Kreel rolled out of the Klingon's way and, in so doing, rolled right out of the ring and lapsed into inactivity.

The two remaining Kreel came at him, one trying to tackle his legs, the other aiming for his torso. Worf jumped back, and the two collided. One rose to his feet quickly, but Worf was waiting. He hit the Kreel twice in the gut, and as it doubled over Worf grabbed him by the shoulders and brought a knee up hard into the point of the Kreel's chin. It was a violent, vicious maneuver. Worf gloried in it.

At that moment, the other leaped onto Worf's back, pinning one of the Klingon's arms behind him. Worf used his free arm to hurl the insensate Kreel out of the ring, and then turned his full attention to the one on his back.

He spun around, trying to shake the damned thing off, and it wouldn't let go. The Kreel insinuated its arms through and around and suddenly Worf found his neck creaking under the grip of a full-nelson.

He dropped to his back, bringing his full weight to bear as he slammed the Kreel down under him. And still the computer construct wouldn't let go. Worf grabbed at the arms that encircled his neck, but he couldn't break their grip.

Worf grunted, and the computer analyzed that noise and recalled from its memory banks that a grunt was the only sound you'd ever hear from a Klingon in distress. With death imminent a Klingon would never scream or curse or howl. Just utter a subverbal protest from the depths of its chest.

The computer instructed its construct to give Worf an option.

"Surrender," growled the Kreel.

"Death first!" Worf shouted back, and he was certain, just certain that these would be his last words, for the room was starting to blacken and it was getting difficult to breathe . . .

The Kreel's hands were out of sight, clenched behind Worf's neck. Its incredibly long, gorillalike arms were fully stretched out, and suddenly, Worf saw an opening.

He stopped pounding at the Kreel's hands behind him and instead grabbed at the long forearms that were within his sight. By no longer fighting the pressure of the hands, he was permitting the Kreel to exert its full strength on him, a maneuver that within seconds, could cripple or kill.

He grabbed at the Kreel's left forearm, pulled it to his mouth, and bit down as hard as he could.

He tasted Kreel blood as his attacker shrieked in pain, and the grip on his neck lessened. He bit down harder and now the Kreel let loose all together, and Worf reached around and slammed the Kreel to the floor in a judo throw. He spat out the viscous liquid and brought both his knees down into the Kreel's chest. He heard the satisfying sound of ribs cracking as he grabbed the Kreel by its almost nonexistent neck, at the point where its bullhead met its shoulders. He dug his thumbs down and in, getting a good grip.

The Kreel made hideous, gurgling sounds, and its pig eyes widened, and then it said something very unexpected.

"Mercy." The word burbled out, amidst the constricted gaspings of the Kreel.

Worf looked down at his fallen foe in surprise. His hands were still tight around the creature's throat.

The creature. Klingons, even Klingons raised most of their lives by humans, were not brought up to think of Kreel as creatures. As fellow sentient beings. Only as jackals, as vermin to be snuffed out, as cockroaches waiting for the fall of humanity so that they could rise up and take over.

"No quarter," said Worf.

He twisted so easily and the *crack* as the Kreel's neck broke beneath his grip was deafening and so, so satisfying. Blood trickled from the edge of the Kreel's mouth and onto Worf's hands, and Worf ignored it, relishing the glory of the kill.

The Kreel lay there limply, the life that never was part of it now fleeing.

Worf stood slowly, staring down at the corpse that never lived. Then he stared at his hands, flexing them experimentally as if seeing them for the first time.

"End exercise," he said.

His foes vanished as if they'd never been there. The ring vanished. It was as if the whole thing had been a dream.

Except . . .

The blood was still there. He stared at his hands,

turning them over, and he couldn't understand it. There was still blood from the simulation on them, and that shouldn't be, couldn't be. Could it?

Slowly, his booted tread sounded strangely loud, he walked over to the exit and the doors opened. Stepping out into the familiar corridor of the *Enterprise* he looked at his hands once again, and this time, now that he was out of the holodeck, the blood had indeed vanished.

He smiled. Inwardly, of course.

"Bring on the Kreel," he said.

Chapter Seven

THE BRIDGE OF a Klingon battlecruiser was not a place where a great deal of unnecessary chatting went on. Nevertheless, whatever free-floating discussion was in progress came to a sharp halt when Kobry walked onto the bridge of the Kliingon ship *Kothulu*.

The commander's back was to the door at that moment, so he sensed, rather than saw, the intrusion. He turned and looked down at the dwarfish Klingon.

"Yes, Honored One?" he said slowly.

Kobry seemed to look him up and down before he said, "I was curious as to when rendezvous is scheduled with the *Enterprise*."

"Six hours, Honored One." He paused. "Is there any other matter I can help you with?"

Obviously there were several answers that were occurring to Kobry, but he uttered none of them. Instead he simply said, "No. That will be fine, Commander." He turned and left the bridge.

The commander settled back in his chair, looking less than pleased . . . a sentiment that was eagerly shared by his second-in-command.

"Commander, this is intolerable," Tron said.

The commander turned his malevolent gaze on Tron. Then, with surprising abruptness, he said, "In my quarters, Tron." He stood and left the bridge, leaving the others staring at each other in confusion. Tron, he himself, not understanding, followed his commander out.

Moments later, they were in the commander's quarters. This was a place where a private conversation could be held. Once, in the Klingon Empire, such luxuries as "privacy" were nonexistent. The cabin would have been rigged with, at the very least, a camera linked in to security. Those times were now past.

The commander turned and faced his second-in-command, arms folded. "Would you care to be more specific, Tron? What 'this' are you referring to?"

"This . . . situation." He was speaking so quickly, with such barely contained outrage, that his words almost stumbled over each other. "You've ordered me to be one of the Honorable Kobry's security staff on board the *Enterprise*. On a ship with Kreel."

"That's correct."

"Kreel!"

"I have no deficiencies in my hearing, Tron."

"Commander"—and Klingons did not beg, but if they did, then Tron was coming damned close—"it seems that we only recently came out of drydock after repairing the damage those Kreel scum inflicted on this ship. Not to mention the attempts on my life, and the deaths of the two members of the landing party on DQN 1196, *and* the Klingon blood spilled by the Kreel since that first encounter."

"Is there some point to this, Tron?"

Tron ordinarily would never have dared to say so much, to be so outspoken. But he sensed that, for some reason, his commander was actually interested in what he had to say, and he was hardly going to pass up the opportunity.

"The point is, sir, that although the Federation and the Empire are maintaining the fiction that there is no full-scale war between ourselves and the Kreel, those animals have been continually at our throats since they discovered that weapons caché on DQN 1196. But once we began to strike back at them, everyone went running to the Federation to mediate. Where is the revenge in that? Where is the Klingon pride?"

The commander did not reply immediately. Instead, he stared out the viewing port, seeming to take some degree of comfort in the stars that arced gracefully toward them as they warped toward their rendezvous.

"You preach the old ways," he said finally. "The ways that were before the time of the Great Awakening. The ways before the forging of the Klingon–Federation alliance that has brought new prosperity, new advances to our people. And never forget that one of the key shapers of that alliance is on this very ship."

"The Honorable Kobry." Tron sighed.

"Quite correct. Kobry is one of our most revered statesmen," said the commander. "Thinker, philosopher. His background, his history, is legendary. No matter that, before the Great Awakening, we were a savage, warrior race . . . much like the Kreel, if truth be known."

Tron spat.

"That is difficult to face," said the commander, "but it is the truth, as I have said. What you, or I, may feel about the current destiny of the Klingon Empire is irrelevant. We must abide by the wishes of the Emperor, and those wishes are now that full-scale war between the Kreel and Klingons is to be considered an absolute last resort. Something that is to occur only if all negotiations have completely dissolved; if the Kreel prove themselves to have nothing but disdain for everything that the Klingons revere and honor."

"They've already proven that," said Tron impatiently.

"Not sufficiently," said the commander, and now there was something else in his tone. Something not quite identifiable. And then, curiously, he did something he never did. He repeated himself. "Disdain for everything that the Klingons revere and . . . *honor.*"

At first Tron didn't get it. "We honor battle," he said. "We honor noble death. We honor . . ."

"Individuals," said the commander.

And then, slowly, what he was saying, or implying, began to sink in. And, not to put too fine a point on it, the commander said, "Specific . . . honorable . . . individuals."

"Such as . . . the Honorable Kobry," said Tron slowly.

"Such as he." All that time the commander was not looking at his first officer. "Now if something were to happen to the Honorable Kobry . . . something that the damned Kreel were responsible for . . . that would be an insult to Klingon honor that no amount of talking could put to rights."

"Yes . . . yes, it would."

"Why, full war would be a given. Almost instantaneous. A war that the Klingons would surely win, advanced Kreel technology or not. War is inevitable, you know. It is only the Kreel's luck that the Great Awakening prevented their extermination at our hands decades ago. Now they have weapons that can make our lives difficult. Who knows where they will be several decades hence. While we chatter away, making promises of peace and good fellowship, they can arm

106

themselves further, to the point where they are actually formidable. None of us wants that."

"No, of course not." Tron could barely comprehend
the enormity of what was being said, or not being said.
"I fully understand your implications, sir."

"Implications?" And now the commander did look
at him, with an expression of innocence that hardly
seemed natural for a Klingon. "What implications,
Tron? This is merely an informal discussion, between
commander and subordinate. I don't claim to see the
future. I have no idea what's going to happen. And I
would certainly think that you would not know either."

"How could I know?" said Tron carefully. "I'm no
fortune teller."

"Nor am I," said the commander. "Nor am I a
diplomat, or a wise man, or a great thinker or philosopher. I am merely a humble soldier. A patriot, hoping
to see the Empire travel along the road to its first, best
destiny. As are you. As are all great heroes."

"I am honored, Commander, that you think of me
that way."

"No more than you deserve, Tron. Indeed, it is my
hope that all Klingons receive exactly what they
deserve." He turned away again. "That's all."

Tron turned to go, mind still reeling over the
unspoken implications. The unstated threats, the
machinations, the back-door dealings that might lead
to war, with casualties numbering in the millions and
mass slaughter of a hated enemy. A chance to live with
dignity and/or die with glory.

Just like the good old days.

Chapter Eight

"I'VE HAD IT," said Jaan. "I'm finished. I'm through."

In disgust he threw down his cards. "Busted flush. And"—he looked at the other players around the table—"it's all your fault."

Data stared at him with his gold eyes, his cards held serenely in front of him. "I am afraid I do not follow your train of thought."

Seated at the table, all with varying heights of chips stacked in front of them, were Data, Geordi, and Deanna Troi. Jaan was shaking his head. "I mean, look at this group. The android who never changes expression. Geordi, whose eyes I can't see. And an empath who can sense if I'm happy about my hand or not."

"I would never use my abilities to play unfairly," said Deanna stiffly.

"I think he's kidding, Counselor," said Geordi. Despite her uncanny ability to sense emotions (or perhaps because of it), Troi was one of the most serious-minded people on the crew. She sometimes made Data look like a laughing hyena.

"No, he's not," replied Troi.

"Yes, I am," Jaan now said, smiling lopsidedly.

And then Troi stared at him, and she said nothing, but what she was thinking was quite clear. *No, he's not.*

"Either way, I'm folding," he said. "I'm kind of tired, actually." He got up and walked out of the lounge.

Moments later, he stopped in the corridor and leaned against the wall. He could feel his heart racing and forced himself to take slow, steady breaths. Then he tapped a wall comm unit. "Sickbay?" he said.

"Sickbay, Doctor Pulaski here," came the crisp reply. "Is that you, Jaan?"

"Yeah." He forced himself to stand a bit more straight, as if Pulaski could see him and would frown on his posture. "I'm feeling a little woozy."

"I'm not surprised. It's time for your medication. I was about to send out a med team to look for you. Where are you?"

"Near Rec Room D5."

"I'll send up an escort."

"No," he said quickly, with just a touch of anger. "I can make it. I'm not going to be some damned cripple who has to be taken everywhere. I'll be along shortly, on my own."

She seemed to hesitate and then said, "All right. You have five minutes. Plenty of time. But if you're not here by then, I'll send out someone to find you and bring you down here."

"Deal."

He walked away from the comm link panel, heading toward the turbolift. Then a voice behind him said, "Jaan."

He kept going. "I'm on my way down to sickbay, Counselor. I've been given a deadline . . . appropriately enough, I suppose. So if you want to chat, you'll have to do it while we're walking."

"Fine." Troi fell into step next to him. "I have been a bit concerned about you lately, Jaan."

"Captain told you about my little problem, did he?"

"As the ship's counselor, I'm responsible for the mental well being of everyone on this ship."

"Is that your roundabout way of saying 'yes'?"

She cleared her throat. "Yes. But I just wanted you to be aware that the captain isn't simply spreading it all about the ship." She didn't add that Bobbi Chase had already done that.

She stopped next to a door. "As it happens, Jaan, this is my cabin. I was hoping to be able to discuss this in private."

He made a sort of vague gesture downward. "They're expecting me at sickbay. If I don't show up there, they'll send out the hounds."

Troi considered this a moment, and then tapped her insignia. "Troi to sickbay."

"Sickbay. Pulaski here. What's the matter, Deanna?"

"It's my understanding that you were expecting Jaan in sickbay."

"That's right."

"He's with me, and I was hoping to detain him for several minutes if that's all right with you."

"I'm not certain how all right it'll be with Jaan. He sounded in less-than-outstanding shape a little earlier."

"I can make it a few minutes more, Doctor," Jaan now spoke up. He smiled ingratiatingly at Deanna. "Elves have remarkable powers of recuperation."

"So I've heard. All right, Deanna, but you're responsible for him."

"Absolutely. Troi out."

She turned to him and he was still smiling, and stars, she hadn't realized just how captivating a face he had.

"I must confess," she said slowly, "that I'm not as conversant with Selelvians as I should be. With over a thousand people on board . . ."

"No problem," he said. He took a step toward her. "No problem at all."

At that moment her insignia beeped, this time indicating an incoming page. She gave an apologetic half-smile and tapped it again. "Counselor Troi here," she said.

"This is Captain Picard," came that very distinctive voice. "We have rendezvoused with the Klingon ship and are preparing to meet the Klingon ambassador and his party. I think it would be best if you were there."

"Captain . . ." Uncharacteristically, she hesitated. "I'm in a private conference at the moment."

"Is there any way it can be delayed?"

She glanced at Jaan, about to tell him that the captain sounded most insistent.

Jaan was slowly shaking his head and mouthing the word *"No."* His eyes twinkled with amusement.

And of course, the answer was no. After all, here was someone who immediately needed her help. The captain was certainly capable of handling whatever might arise with this Klingon until she got there.

"Troi?" Picard said after an annoyed pause.

"I think, Captain, that delaying would be most unwise."

She could practically see Picard's surprised expression. "Very well, Counselor," he said. "Use your best judgment. Just be along as soon as you can."

"Absolutely, sir. Absolutely."

"Very well. Picard out."

Slowly, her hand dropped from her insignia, and Jaan took it in his. His nearness was overwhelming.

"Now," he said, in a musical voice, "what did you wish to speak to me about?"

"That was damned peculiar," said Picard on the bridge. He turned toward Riker. "Didn't you think so, Number One? And by the way, Mr. Riker," he said, without giving Riker a chance to answer, "that's a very annoying habit you've picked up."

Confused, Riker said, "What habit, sir?"

"That stroking your beard every time you're asked a question. It makes it appear as if you're indecisive."

"Does it?" said Riker innocently. "I'm sorry, sir. I'll try to watch that. As for your question, well . . . Deanna can be very single-minded when she believes that she is needed."

"Indeed."

"I'd like to think that's what makes her a good counselor."

The aft turbolift opened, and Geordi and Data entered, having received calls from the bridge previous to Deanna.

Data went to the ops station and sat down, staring with interest at the Klingon battlecruiser that hovered on the monitor. Once, the presence of such a vessel would have been a guarantor of, at the least, yellow-alert status. That, however, was before Data's time.

Then he turned and looked at the conn station, now occupied by Lieutenant Marks. "Where is Wesley?" inquired Data.

"Data," said Picard, "do not, under any circumstances, ask me again where Wesley Crusher is."

"Yes, sir."

"Captain," said Worf from his security console,

"I'm receiving an incoming hailing frequency from the vessel."

Picard couldn't help but notice that Worf had not said "Klingon vessel," as he would have qualified virtually any other. "This is Captain Picard, of the U.S.S. *Enterprise,*" he said.

The viewscreen shimmered, and now the image of the Klingon commander appeared. "Greetings, Captain Picard," he said in his gravelly voice. "In another time, I might have called you enemy."

"A time long past," responded Picard.

"We are prepared to beam our ambassador and his party aboard. We ask that you take extraordinary care of the Honorable Kobry."

"As we would any guest."

"But the Honorable Kobry is not just any guest," said the commander. "He is one of the most revered figures in our Empire. Certainly the Kreel must be aware of that."

"I'm sure they are," said Picard. He already had a suspicion where the conversation was going but allowed it to proceed.

"Your ship will have Kreel diplomats being given free rein. Do you know what the definition of a Kreel diplomat is?"

Picard shook his head and, from behind him, Worf spoke up. "A Kreel who has run out of ammunition."

There was a bizarre noise from the Klingon on the viewscreen, and Picard, at first, thought the commander was dying. Then he realized what it was. A Klingon laugh. Kind of like a cross between clearing one's throat and gagging. "Very good! You must be the legendary Worf."

Worf suddenly realized he'd committed a breech of etiquette by speaking up without Captain Picard's approval. It had simply been automatic. He remained silent now until the captain inclined his head slightly in the direction of the monitor. "I am Lieutenant Junior Grade Worf."

"Not Commander Worf?"

Worf paused only slightly. "These things take time."

Picard glanced over at Riker who gave him a "What did you expect" look.

The commander was still addressing Worf. "It is most fortunate to have a member of the Klingon Empire aboard the *Enterprise* to act as additional insurance."

"I am head-of-security and under command of Captain Picard who is very diligent in such matters," said Worf stiffly. "In those circumstances, I am more than content to do my duty. However, I think of myself primarily as a citizen of the Federation, rather than as a member of the Klingon Empire."

Picard gave a small, approving nod.

The commander, however, stared at him skeptically. "Lieutenant Worf . . . have you looked in a mirror lately?"

"I'm afraid I don't under—"

"A Klingon does as a Klingon is, Lieutenant Worf. Serve as your conscience dictates, but nothing can alter the fact that you are . . . one of us." He turned back to the captain. "Prepare to receive the Honorable Kobry."

"We will greet him in the main transporter room," said Picard. *"Enterprise* out." He stood and said, "Mr. Riker, Mr. Worf, you will accompany me. Mr. La Forge, you have the conn."

As they headed for the turbolift, Picard said brusquely, "I hope that Counselor Troi finishes whatever it is that's delaying her. This is precisely the type of situation I'd like to have her along for."

"I can make discreet inquiries as to how long she'll be and meet you at the transporter room in a moment or two," said Riker.

Picard nodded briefly. "Make it so."

Deanna Troi forced herself to take a step back from the elf. It was so difficult for her to focus her thoughts, to remember what the subject that she was going to pursue was. "I wanted to . . . to discuss with you your state of mind."

"Fine," said Jaan, showing his teeth. "I like women who are interested in me for my mind."

Troi shook her head quickly, as much to clear her own scrambled thoughts as anything else. "I think you're . . . you're not understanding me."

"I understand you perfectly. You're the ship's counselor. You're concerned about me. You're doing your job. Quite simple."

"Yes." She took a breath. "Yes, it is that simple."

He had stopped approaching her, but now he reached out and rested a hand on her shoulder. His eyes glittered, and she noticed for the first time that his pupils seemed almost as if they had little specks of copper swirling about in them. "Although," he said in a low voice, "I thought perhaps you were attracted to me."

She tried to take another breath but her lungs felt heavy and constricted. "I've been getting . . . feelings about you."

"And I for you," he murmured.

"No," but she wasn't able to muster much strength. "No, I knew you misunderstood."

"Did I?"

"Yes. I was receiving impressions from you of . . ."

"Of what?"

"Fear. Fear of your condition, now that it's caught up with you. Fear and desperation, that you would do . . . do . . ."

"Do what, Deanna?" he asked. He seemed very amused.

Her pulse was racing and she could feel her blood pounding in her temples. What was happening to her? What was coming over her? She was starting to perspire.

"Anything"—and the word was a low moan.

"You would do anything?"

"Yes. *No.* I—"

"Look at me, Deanna."

She tried to look away, but he took the point of her chin in his hand and brought her eye-to-eye with him. He smiled. "Do I look like someone who's frightened? Who's desperate?"

"No. But you're not . . . I mean, I—" She broke off, her normally ordered thoughts a total mishmash, her self-possession evaporated. She pulled at her uniform now soaked through with sweat and sticking to her. "Is it . . . hot in here?"

"I don't think so," said Jaan innocently.

"My clothes . . . feel so . . . uncomfortable."

"Well, I know how to remedy that."

And the door buzzer rang.

Jaan wanted to call out *"Not now!"* But as his thoughts strayed for just a moment, so did his control, and Deanna broke free. But she was still wrung out, disoriented, and he took the opportunity to say, with force, "I'm fine, emotionally. There's no need to worry about me. None at all."

The buzzer sounded once again and he released her, physically and mentally. She sagged away from him, then brought herself to her normal posture. She smiled, a bit confused, but at ease with herself.

"Counselor," came Riker's voice from the other side. "I hate to disturb you. I simply need to know when we can expect you to meet the Klingon ambassador. No rush, you understand."

"Actually, I believe we're finished here, Commander Riker," said Troi. "Wouldn't you agree, Jaan?"

"Absolutely."

The door opened and Riker walked in, glancing from Deanna to Jaan and back again. "I really don't want to interrupt . . ."

"Oh, of course you do, Commander Riker," said Jaan cheerfully. "But I can understand why. Counselor Troi's a busy woman. It's grossly unfair of me to monopolize her time." Graciously, he took Deanna's hand and kissed it on the knuckles. "Until later, Counselor." He walked out of her quarters.

Riker studied Deanna carefully. "Are you all right, Deanna?" he asked, addressing her with the informality they usually used when no one else was around.

"I'm fine, Will. Why?"

"You seem a bit flushed, that's all."

"I'm fine, really. Where's the ambassador and his party?"

"Just coming in now. If we hurry—"

"Say no more."

They left her quarters and headed down the corridor. As they did, Riker observed, "So Jaan was your emergency patient."

"I'm sure that comes as no surprise," said Troi evenly. "With the deterioration of his physical condition, certainly his mental condition has to be carefully monitored."

"So what did you find . . . if it's not treading on any confidentiality. Any cause for concern?"

117

She smiled at that, amused by Riker's never-ending concern that he be on top of all matters. "I don't think I would be violating any confidentiality in this instance," she said. "I feel completely at ease telling you that he's fine, emotionally. There's no need to worry about him. None at all."

Chapter Nine

THE FIRST KLINGONS to beam over from the Klingon ship *Kothulu* were the honor guard . . . or, more precisely, bodyguards. There were eight of them, and to Picard they all looked remarkably similar. With some alien races, it was just difficult to tell individuals apart. Features seemed to blur together. He wondered if Klingons had difficulty, telling for example, himself and Riker apart. He glanced over at Riker, who was standing attentively next to the recently arrived Deanna Troi, and decided that that seemed pretty unlikely.

Although the bodyguards did not have their weapons out, their hands were comfortably within immediate reach of their holstered phasers. Without moving from the transporter platform, they looked carefully around the room as if concerned that assassins might leap out at any time.

The foremost of the Klingons now stepped forward. His clothing was more elaborate, bordering on the ceremonial, indicating some degree of rank.

He walked straight up to Worf, and said, "Captain."

119

For the first time that Picard could recall, he saw Worf look slightly flustered. Picard jumped in quickly and said, "Actually, I am in command of the *Enterprise*. Captain Jean-Luc Picard, at your service."

The Klingon turned slowly toward Picard. "My apologies, Captain. I saw a Klingon in uniform and . . . well, you understand how the mistake is simple to make." He gave a stiff, Klingon salute.

Oh, I understand perfectly, thought Picard. *You knew damned well who was in charge.*

"Of course," Picard said, smiling, returning the salute. Such gestures were nonexistent on the *Enterprise,* but when dealing with visiting dignitaries, protocol required that you greet them in manners to which they are accustomed. "I'm certain that your *error* is merely a prediction of how far Lieutenant Worf will go in Starfleet."

"Ah yes," said the Klingon. "It seems like only yesterday, Captain, that if a Klingon was in the hands of Starfleet, the farthest he would go would be a prison planet."

"The Federation never had prison planets," replied Picard stiffly.

"Of course not," said the Klingon deferentially. "I am Tron, first officer to the glorious Klingon commander with whom you were speaking earlier."

"First officer. Then you will be returning directly to your ship?"

"No, not at all. I was one of the 'fortunate' few Klingons to have survived the initial skirmish with the Kreel on planet DQN 1196. As such, my expertise is required here. My commander will have to try to muddle through without me."

"And where," asked Picard, "is the ambassador?"

"We had to secure the ship first," Tron explained.

Picard, ever the diplomat, masked the sour feelings

that statement gave him and said, "I assured your commander, and I will assure you . . . this ship is quite secure."

"That is because the Kreel are not yet aboard."

"It will be secure either way."

"As you say." He touched a communicator that was on his wrist. "This is Tron. The way is clear."

The commander's voice came over the communicator and said, "Good hunting."

The other Klingons stepped off the platform and, within moments, the Honorable Kobry had materialized aboard the *Enterprise*. Standing next to him was another Klingon, an attractive female, even by human standards. She was tall and slender, yet her shoulders were square and her exposed arms looked quite muscular. The rest of her figure was hidden in black and brown leather. She also sported a gold doublet. Her eyes were almond, both in shape and size, and her hair hung loosely around her shoulders.

Still, for all her beauty, it was the Honorable Kobry who was receiving the majority of attention. Picard stared at him openly for only a moment, impressed both by the Klingon's advanced years and negligible height. *How in the world did someone so small, so physically helpless, come so far in the Klingon Empire?* It was ludicrous.

Yet Picard managed once again to cloak his inner thoughts as he stepped forward, extending a hand. "Honorable Kobry."

"Captain Picard," said Kobry, and smiled.

Smiled!? Picard could scarcely believe it, and he actually heard Worf gasp behind him.

He shook Kobry's small hand, and for someone so diminutive, he had a hell of a grip. "It is indeed an honor," said Picard.

"Yes, isn't it?" He chuckled. *(Chuckled!)* "Forgive

me, Captain. A small joke. But then, most of mine are."

Picard realized that this was going to be some trip.

"This"—and Kobry gestured toward the young woman—"is my aide, Gava. Gava, the inestimable Captain Picard and his equally inestimable staff."

She shook hands with each of them, a good, firm grip, but she lingered longest with Worf.

"This *is* a pleasure," she said, and her voice was low and throaty, with a certain raspiness to it that lent a suggestive air. "Much has been written of you in our journals. I had assumed that a good deal of it was exaggeration, however."

"None of it," replied Worf with authority.

"How nice for all of us," she said.

The transporter chief now spoke up. "Sir . . . we're receiving a call from *Kothulu*. They wish to know if all hands are aboard."

"Tell them"—and Picard glanced at Tron—"tell them everything is secure. They can move off at their leisure, and we wish them best of luck on their next assignment." He gestured toward the door. "I'll show you all to the quarters we've arranged for you."

The honor guard promptly formed a semicircle around Kobry, keeping him serenely in the middle of it. Kobry appeared to take no notice of it whatsoever. "Lead the way, Captain," he said.

Data, while sitting at the ops station, heard the beep of his communicator. Tapping it he said, "Data here."

"Data"—and the voice from the other end sounded fatigued and a bit raspy—"this is Wes. Look, I need some help."

"Is this related to why you've been temporarily relieved of duty?" Data said.

The conversation was already drawing surreptitious

glances from around the bridge. Everyone was secretly somewhat curious about what was going on with Wesley. They all thought he was a bit precocious as it was. But when he started to act downright odd, well . . .

"I wasn't relieved of anything, Data," came the annoyed response. "I just needed time to work on something else. Now can you come down here and help me?"

"Down there? No," said Data firmly. "I am on duty now. I cannot leave the bridge."

And Geordi who, as was everyone else, was listening in, spoke up, saying, "I can find a sub for you, Data."

"No, Geordi," and Data couldn't be swayed. "It is my responsibility. I cannot leave. But is there something I can help you with now?"

"Sure. Sure, okay, listen . . . you know the . . . hold it. Look, at least go into the conference room so it'll be private, okay?"

Data turned questioningly toward Geordi who said, "It's not like you're actually leaving the bridge. If we need you, I'll knock."

Moments later Data stood in the conference room, addressing Wesley's image on the computer/speaker. "What is the difficulty, Wesley?"

"You know a disease called 'the Rot'?"

Data had been working lately on making his answers more succinct. On some things he knew absolutely nothing, and on others he knew so much that he still had difficulty sorting out trivialities from important aspects. He was trying to learn to distinguish between the two. "Yes. I know of it."

"Good. Okay, look, I've found this one drug they used to crack cancer back a century ago."

"Solicyclin?"

"No, the other one."

"Nembitol?"

"Yes!" Wesley seemed to be frantically flipping through notes. "I've been reading on it and it seems to have properties that make it incredibly applicable to the Rot. It's so perfect that I can't believe it's never been tested before. What I wanted to know from you is if it—"

"Twenty-three years ago. It was ineffective."

All the blood seemed to drain from Wesley's face. "Are you sure? I mean, are you absolutely sure? I've been combing the journals and haven't found any reference to Nembitol at all."

"Journal of Applied Sciences," said Data crisply. "Volume eighty-three, issue number nine, I believe."

Wesley was calling up Data's references on one of the computer screens. He stared at it, scanning through to the table of contents and looked at it. Then Data actually jumped slightly as Wesley slammed a hand down on the counter. *"Aw nuts!* How could I have missed that?"

"How indeed?" said Data. "Certainly the voice interface from the computer would have referenced you to that article."

Wesley, looking more despondent than Data had ever seen him, said, "I haven't been using the voice interface."

"What?"

"I shut off the voice interface. I've been scanning everything manually."

Data blinked in confusion. That was foolish. It was the equivalent of shutting down the ship's warp engines and using oars instead. "Wesley . . . why?"

"It was giving me problems."

"I think that very unlikely," said Data, feeling a bit stung. While in Starfleet Academy, Data had been instrumental in doing some updating and redesigning of the computer system used aboard starships, including greater sophistication in its communication skills and expansion of its already formidable memory. "The ship's computer is extremely . . . what is the old-style term . . . 'user-friendly.'"

"Well I didn't like it," replied Wesley in annoyance. "I'd ask it research-oriented questions, and it would say 'Purpose of research?'"

"It's designed to do that," said Data, "in order to be as specific as possible in its replies. Its efficiency is increased."

"Yeah. But when I say 'Investigating cure for the Rot,' it just says back 'No cure at present.' I get enough of that from humans. I don't need a machine telling me that too. So if the computer's not going to be on my side, I don't have to talk to it."

Now Data knew something was seriously wrong. "Wes . . . the computer can't be on anyone's side. It's just a . . ." Then he paused. He was about to dismiss the computer in the same way that the recently-arrived Dr. Pulaski dismissed himself when the subject of his humanity was raised. It was most annoying. Was it possible that . . . the computer could become annoyed, too? There were the legends of one computer, over three hundreds years ago, that had become upset with the human occupants of a space ship, and the results had been unpleasant. Besides, what if the computer had feelings. Ridiculous? Any more ridiculous, he wondered, than he himself?

Opting quickly to change the subject, Data said, "Wesley, if you would like, I will be happy to aid you in whatever way I can when I am no longer needed on the bridge."

Wesley smiled raggedly. "Thanks, Data. It's appreciated. But I'll be fine. Really."

The screen blinked out.

And Data wasn't sure which human trait Wesley was displaying just then . . . lying, or kidding himself.

"I hope these quarters will be to your satisfaction."

Kobry stood in the middle of the room and turned slowly, nodding. "I have had much worse, I assure you."

"Good." Picard and Kobry were alone, the rest of the Klingons having been shown to their quarters nearby. Picard took a step forward and said, "I need to talk with you about a rather delicate subject."

"That is supposedly my specialty," said Kobry. He was wearing a large ring on his right hand, and he had now, to Picard's mild surprise, flipped open the top, revealing that it was hollow. He had removed a small vial from his suitcase and opened it, revealing its contents of round, blue pills. He transferred several of them into his ring and looked up innocently as Picard watched him. "For my health," Kobry explained. "Something of great concern to me. A Klingon does not live to be my age if health is not of paramount concern."

"I must admit, I cannot recall seeing a Klingon of your advanced years."

Kobry again gave that small, intriguing smile. "The advantage of my stature, Captain. I'm a smaller target. Now . . . that matter you wish to discuss?"

Picard resisted the temptation to inquire about Kobry's stature, particularly since it was none of his damned business. "Yes . . . that matter. Before the Kreel come aboard, I am going to request that your guards turn over their weapons to me for safekeeping."

Kobry looked mildly amused. "I thought you might."

"Will that be a problem?"

"That depends on how you define 'problem.'"

Picard gave silent thanks that, with an opening like that, Data wasn't in the room. "You're implying that your men will object."

"To put it succinctly."

"You could order them to."

"That I could. But since their first priority is to protect me, it is very likely that they will be . . . reluctant . . . to follow the order."

"Nevertheless, I must insist. Once the Kreel come aboard, the slightest argument could lead to a phaser pulled in anger. I would much prefer not to put that temptation at hand."

The door buzzed and Gava entered. She smiled at Picard and said to Kobry, "You are comfortable, Honorable Kobry?"

"Quite. The captain here wishes my men to turn over their weapons. I was apprising him of the difficulty of that."

"You are saying that, if we ask them to hand over their phasers, they won't do it?" asked Picard.

"Oh no, I'm not saying that at all. In fact, they probably will hand over their phasers since this is, after all, a diplomatic mission."

"Then what is the difficulty?"

"The difficulty," said Gava, "is that each of those Klingon bodyguards you see has at least eleven weapons on him."

Picard's eyes widened. *"Eleven?"*

"At least," affirmed Gava cheerfully.

"But I only saw the phasers."

"Of course," said Kobry. "That's all you're meant to see. With Klingon warriors, it's always a matter of pride, finding new and interesting places on one's person that a weapon can be hidden. Remove their

127

phasers if it will satisfy your sense of decorum, Captain. Gava will accompany you, to relay that that is my wish in this matter. But disarm my men? Very difficult. The only way you'll detect every weapon is with detailed sensor scans, and once detected, you'll never manage to get my people to part with those anyway. They'll fight to the death first."

"Yes, 'death first' seems to be a rallying cry these days," said Picard ruefully. "Very well then. I believe I will take you up on your suggestion to remove the phasers. At least give the Kreel a cosmetic belief that no overt threats are intended."

"As you wish."

"My concern is for the civilians aboard this ship. I do not want hostilities to break out aboard the *Enterprise.*"

"None of us does, Captain. Well . . . actually, I should qualify that statement. *I* don't. *You* don't. Hopefully, at least one member of the Kreel diplomatic party doesn't. Other than that," and he shook his head, "my people are spoiling for a fight. It would not take a great deal to set them off."

Picard turned to go, then looked back at the small Klingon. "This is going to be a very tense trip."

Kobry smiled. "Stimulating, isn't it?"

Picard walked out, Gava right behind him. They were met in the corridor by Worf who said, "The honor guard has been settled in their quarters, Captain."

"Excellent, Worf. Now, I believe I'll need your assistance on this as well. I will be requesting that each of the honor guard relinquishes their phasers to the head-of-security. Namely you."

If Worf was surprised at that, he didn't show it. "Yes, Captain."

"Worf," said Picard after a moment, "do you have eleven weapons on you?"

Worf stiffened. "Of course not, sir."

Picard sighed. "Good." Then a thought struck him. "How many . . . *do* you have on you?"

"Fourteen."

Picard looked stunned. "Worf . . . do you feel that's appropriate? Regulations . . ."

"Regulations give the head-of-security broad discretionary powers," said Worf. "If I have the latitude to protect this crew and myself with extra . . . insurance . . . I will do so."

Gava said, "Fourteen? In a uniform far less designed for weapons concealment than that of a Klingon? Very impressive."

"Everything about me," rumbled Worf, "is very impressive."

Oh God, thought Picard.

Chapter Ten

DR. PULASKI ENTERED SICKBAY to find Wesley Crusher exiting with half the med lab.

"Wesley!" Her voice went up half an octave. "What are you doing?"

With a small antigrav cart, Wesley had collected an impressive amount of hardware, primarily chemicals and various culture-growth machines. He stared at her blankly for a moment, as if trying to remember who she was. Then, sounding a little distant, he said, "I needed some things."

"This isn't needing things! This is bordering on grand theft. Now you put it all back." She looked more closely at him. His complexion was decidedly pallid, his eyes bloodshot. His normally immaculate hair was messy and seemed unwashed. "Wesley," she said slowly, "how long has it been since you got any sleep?"

"I've been sleeping."

"For how long?"

"Until I woke up. Can I pass please?"

"No! I said you couldn't. I'm not going to let you go

waltzing out of here with all this equipment. It's enough that I've given you access to as much as I have. Look, Wes," she said in a gentler tone, "why don't you lie down for a while?"

"I'm fine. Really." He smiled wanly. "You know how it is when you get really caught up in something. You just keep plowing ahead."

Pulaski thought back to her days in research, and before that, her years in medical school. If there was one thing she identified with, it was compulsiveness. Still . . .

"Wesley, I really can't approve of you taking this much equipment out of here. Now if you need something synthesized, you contact me and give me the specifics and I'll do it."

"That will take too long," protested Wesley. "You're always going to have other things to do. More important things to do. Everyone has always had more important things—that's why there's no cure for this disease yet."

And at that moment, Data came in. He stood there for a moment, blocking the door, and Pulaski and Wesley stared at him expectantly.

"Wesley," he said. "I am pleased that I found you here."

"Pleased, Data," Pulaski said, not bothering (it seemed to Data) to remember that he preferred his name pronounced with a long *"a"* rather than short. "How impressive. Pleased." She seemed very amused by that, far more amused than was Data.

"Wesley," Data began again, not allowing his train of thought to be disrupted. "I am becoming concerned for you. Your call to me several hours ago had you in a far more agitated condition than you usually are. I think you are pushing yourself far beyond your capacity."

The fact of the matter was that Pulaski had had the exact same sentiments . . . until Data stated them. Now, however, she heard herself saying, "Who are you to judge what Mr. Crusher's capacity is, Data?"

"I am a friend."

"A friend. I see." Arms folded she looked at him thoughtfully. "Listen, Data . . . the difference between machines and men are that machines do indeed have limits. Defined limits beyond which their capabilities cannot extend, until they are redesigned. Human beings have the ability to constantly surpass their limits and set new ones. That is part of the joy of being a truly living individual . . . something I would not expect a machine to understand. Now you purport to be alive. Do you understand?"

"Hey," Wesley said sharply. "You don't have to come down on Data like that."

"No, Wesley," said Data. There was a hard edge in his voice. "Dr. Pulaski is free to state her opinions. In answer to your question, Doctor . . . yes. I understand. Perfectly. I understand, in fact, more than I believe you would suspect."

"Well, good," said Pulaski, smiling in such a manner that Data couldn't tell whether it was sincere or sarcastic. Without giving him a chance to decide, Pulaski turned to Wesley and said, "The additional equipment you need? Take it. Just be prepared to return it to me immediately if I need it. Oh, but don't take the Wasserman Chamber. An eager young med student named Katherine Pulaski once removed a specimen from a Wasserman, a mere five seconds prematurely, and blew out the sides of the lab."

"Fair enough," said Wesley, and he picked up the large silver, oven-shaped device to bring it to the rear med lab.

And the moment he was out of earshot, Data said in a low voice, "Doctor Pulaski, if you have a difficulty with me as a member of this ship's crew, I think you should tell me. I don't understand why you feel the need to make rude comments about me."

She looked more amused than she had before. "I wouldn't expect you to understand, Data. It's a human foible."

Data took one step toward her, and there was something about the movement that spoke volumes. "Try me." When she didn't answer right away, he said, "Do you have a strong antitechnical bias?"

Her eyes narrowed as she appraised him. "You mean, do I dislike machines? Not in the least." She paused, as if trying to verbalize for the first time something that had been more free-floating irritation than anything else. "I think machines are marvelous. Machines are a testament to man's ability to think, to plan, to challenge and overcome his environment. Machines as man's servants are a wonderful thing."

She stood there, waiting for Data to pick up on what she was saying. He didn't. He just stood there, guileless, blank. Waiting for more input, of course, she realized. She sighed. "Don't you see? Machines and humans . . . it's like apples and oranges. You can contrast them, but you can't compare them. So a machine that believes that it's a human . . . that walks, and talks, and pretends to be something that it's not . . . well, it's just absurd. It's a joke. A machine pretending to be alive . . . how can it possibly be taken seriously? Or believe that it's *going* to be taken seriously?"

"I see," Data said slowly. "You are, of course, putting forward a hypothetical situation . . . that being, a machine that believes that it's alive."

133

"Of course," said Pulaski diplomatically.

"A truly interesting hypothetical. Let us take it another step further, if you don't mind."

"Not at all."

"Let us assume that this machine actually tested out as being 'alive' by all standards that would normally apply to any human. That this machine thinks and feels. That this machine dreams of . . ."

"Electric sheep?" asked Pulaski helpfully.

". . . dreams of being fully, unequivocably human. Wouldn't that indicate anything about the state of being alive, Doctor? Where does the division between machines and man end?"

"I'm afraid I don't know, Data. I'm afraid I don't have all the answers. If I had all the answers, why . . . I'd be a machine." And she gave her most ingratiating smile.

At that moment Wesley came back in without the Wasserman Chamber. "Oh, Data, you're still here."

"I was just leaving, Wesley," said Data. "Doctor . . . it's been a very educational conversation."

"Why, thank you, Data. I certainly hope you'll be able to store it away somewhere."

"And I hope you will as well, Doctor."

"Well, Data, not being a machine, I wouldn't know where." She turned away to give a last bit of advice to Wesley.

And Data, without batting an eyelash, said with unmistakable inflection and intent, "I think, Doctor, you know where you can store it."

Pulaski's jaw hit the floor as she gaped openly at Data. Wesley was just as stunned, but recovered faster, pushing the cart and grabbing Data by the elbow as they barreled out of sickbay.

"I can't *believe* you!" said Wesley once they were

safely in the hallway. And now Wesley was starting to laugh. "I can't believe you said that."

"I was going to suggest she store it up her—"

"I got that, Data. She did, too. But how did you come up with that?"

"I remembered something Geordi once said and made a slight modification. It seemed to fit the circumstances." Data stopped and looked concerned. "I certainly hope it was an appropriate thing to say."

"It was an insult!"

"Was it?" said Data calmly.

"Yes!"

Data considered this, his pale face unreadable.

"Are you quite certain?"

"Absolutely certain."

And a slow smile spread over Data's face.

"Good."

"Worf, it's . . . it's enormous." Gava gasped.

"Yes," rumbled Worf with obvious satisfaction. "It is, isn't it."

"I never would have thought it possible."

"I take great pleasure from it." He dropped his voice to a confidential tone. "Do not mention it to others, but I take it out at the end of every shift and simply . . . look at it."

She stepped back a couple of paces to see it better. "I must admit, throughout the Klingon Empire, I've seen quite a few . . . and you know how Klingons take pride in this sort of thing. But I've never seen one this large or impressive."

"Thank you," Worf said modestly. He picked up yet another medal in his huge collection. "The honor I feel when I survey all the awards I've received . . . it is indeed one of the few things on this ship that gives me genuine gratification. This one, for example, was for bravery above and beyond the call of duty. I led a battalion in action on Cantos V. I almost refused the medal."

"Why?" she asked in surprise.

"I disagree with the concept of 'above and beyond.' Whatever duty calls for, that is what is required. Duty has no limits."

"Interesting point."

"Thank you. I do have my pride."

"Yet you accepted the medal anyway."

"There's pride," said Worf crisply, "and then there's foolish pride."

"Ah." She smiled and moved about his cabin, admiring the starkness and simplicity of its design. Worf securely closed the cabinet in which the medals and awards were kept and turned back to her. "How long," she asked, "until we rendezvous with the Kreel ship?"

"Two days," said Worf.

She nodded. "That gives us plenty of time to get to know each other."

"Not really. I spend the majority of my time on the bridge. I usually prefer to work two shifts."

"Why is that?"

He gave what approximated a shrug. "What else is there for a warrior to do?"

"Oh, I don't know." She paused. "You said that virtually the only thing that gives you pleasure is your collection of honors. Is that true?"

"Yes."

"With all the available women on this ship? I find that difficult to believe."

"Available to others. Not to me."

"Why ever not?"

136

"Relations with any other female than a Klingon one would be . . . most unwise. For her." He paused, and to emphasize the point, he added, "Physically."

"Yes, I suppose I should have surmised that." She appeared puzzled and leaned against the wall, appraising him thoughtfully. "Worf . . . why do you stay here? Why serve the Federation? Someone of your obvious talents would do well in the ranks of the Klingon Empire."

"Perhaps."

"Certainly the problem of finding female companionship would not exist."

"There is that."

"Then why—"

"I am not given to discussing my personal motivations," said Worf stiffly.

Gava looked at him in surprise. "I did not mean to pry, Worf. Merely to know you better."

"Why is that?"

"Because," she said matter-of-factly, "I wish to know the nature of anyone whom I intend to take as a lover."

Worf considered this for a moment or two.

"Two reasons," he said.

She hid her amusement at his abrupt turnaround quite well. "And they are?"

"I was raised by humans," he said. "Have you read of the attack on Khitomer?"

"Who hasn't?" she replied. "The first major battle between Romulans and Klingons after the end of their alliance. Romulans were furious that the Klingons joined the Federation, and they attacked and destroyed the Klingon outpost on Khitomer. Mass slaughter. Everyone was killed."

"Not . . . everyone," said Worf slowly.

Her eyes widened. "You were there?" she said. "But—but that can't be. You're too young to have fought on Khitomer. It was years ago . . ."

"I was a child."

"Remarkable!"

"As difficult as it is to believe, I *was* once a child," said Worf dryly. He considered sitting on the edge of his bed, but instead opted to stand, as he usually did.

"No, I meant—"

"I'm aware of what you meant." His thoughts flew back to that awful time, long gone in years but as if yesterday in his memory. "I was in an attack shelter with my parents. My father was operating a ground phaser cannon a few feet away. My mother held me close to protect me. Absurd idea, really. If the shelter collapsed, what defense could her body provide? Or so I thought."

"What . . . happened?"

"Direct hit from a Romulan attack ship." His tone was carefully modulated and neutral. "The shelter collapsed. My father was killed instantly, my mother only moments later. And her body shielded me from harm." He shook his head slowly, as if finding it difficult to believe. "I remember hours seemed to pass after that, hours of dead silence. I crawled and clawed my way up, from under my mother's body. Up through the rocks and rubble. When my hand broke through, grabbing at air, I heard a voice shout 'Here's one!' Another hand grabbed mine and pulled me clear. It was as if I'd been born again. Given another chance. And the first thing that I saw was that the man who saved me was wearing a uniform." He tapped his chest. "This uniform."

"For a child, that can be a powerful image," said Gava.

"One that can shape a life," agreed Worf.

"It's very intriguing," she said. "You and the Honorable Kobry have much in common."

"Indeed?"

"He was also a resident on an outpost, although he was already grown up at the time. But because of his stature and appearance he was treated poorly; his intellectual growth was as stunted as his body. He was considered a moron."

"I find that difficult to believe."

"You know him now. You didn't know him then. He had no name."

Worf was stunned. "*He* had no name? The most honored Klingon once had no name?"

"Shocking, isn't it. At any rate . . . his home, too, was destroyed, although he survived by luck rather than love. He, too, was found by members of the Federation. He was re-educated, and in those circumstances his formidable intelligence emerged. Years later, when the Klingon Empire was in a state of chaos, he returned. He was the perfect ambassador between the Klingons and the Federation, particularly since he has human blood within him."

"A half-breed? Kobry is a half-breed? I did not know there were any Klingons with part-human heritage."

"There's at least two that I know of," she said bemusedly. "Kobry rose to a position of power and prominence and became one of the prime architects of the Federation-and-Klingon alliance, although he will downplay his role, if asked."

"Very impressive."

"Yes." And now Gava had drawn quite close to Worf, and, with a finger, was lazily tracing the ridge of his forehead. Worf stood stock-still, not giving any outward indication (as was the custom among Klingon males) of what was stirring within him.

Klingon males were supposed to remain stoic at all times. Almost all times.

"A question," she said lazily.

"Now?" he said, his voice bordering on incredulity. "Now you're asking more questions? You know more of me than anyone on this ship."

"I'm hoping to know more still," she replied, stroking his beard. "I was curious, however. You mentioned there were two reasons you would serve the Federation over the Empire."

"Did I? Oh . . . yes." With effort he refocused his thoughts. "The second reason is that, in the Klingon Empire, I would be one among many. Here . . . I am unique. I have unique skills and attitudes to offer. I'm needed here."

"Really?"

"Yes."

"Worf, it is my opinion that no matter where you are, you would be an outstanding specimen. But perhaps you are right. The humans, despite how far they've come, still consider war something to be avoided at any cost. They consider battle to be the last option. I've read their philosophies. They don't realize that turning the other cheek simply results in getting bruises on both sides of your face."

"Educating them is an endless task," said Worf roughly. "I have to admit, however, that, at present, my mind is not really on philosophical discussions."

"Really?"

"Yes."

"Would you mind telling me what is on your mind?"

"I would rather show you."

The Ten-Four Room was more sedate than usual. That was undoubtedly because of the group of about half-a-dozen Klingons who were gathered together in one corner, imbibing what was most definitely not synthenol for more than three hours and not showing the slightest sign of inebriation. Aware that the *Enterprise* only provided synthenol, the Klingons had brought along their own liquid refreshment, which Guinan was serving out.

Other members of the Enterprise crew were watching them, as surreptitiously as they could, from their respective tables, talking in what sounded like a low buzzing rather than the usual more boisterous chatter.

Riker, at the bar, was getting his glass refilled. "Last one before I go on duty, Guinan." He smiled.

"As you wish, O bearded wonder," she replied.

He smiled lopsidedly. "It does look good, doesn't it?"

"Well, the face it's attached to certainly helps." She smiled. "Is it my imagination or is everyone on the ship a little nervous these days?"

"It's certainly not your imagination." He lowered his voice. "The Klingons are in the Federation now. And we're all pretty used to having Worf around. But even so, the alliance is a bit too recent for everyone to feel completely at ease. And perhaps knowing that the Kreel will be coming on board is the equivalent of waiting for the other shoe to drop."

"You might have a point." She considered it a moment. "You know, it's not my place to offer advice . . ."

"Uh-huh," said Riker, not buying that for an instant.

"But I've always thought that a party is a good way to get people acquainted. Get them more comfortable with one another."

He put down his glass. "Now that," he said, "is an excellent idea. I'll bring it to the captain."

"Be certain to tell him it came from me," said Guinan. "That way he'll be certain to go for it."

Riker laughed. "You don't think he'll accept it coming from his first officer?"

"Well." Guinan smiled ingratiatingly. "Why take chances?"

Riker picked up his glass and finished his drink. "You know," he said thoughtfully, "one person I should really check with is Worf. He'd know best how the Klingons would react to something like a party." He tapped his communicator. "Riker to Worf."

There was a lengthy pause, as if Worf was having trouble finding his communicator for some reason. That, of course, was absurd since it was attached to his uniform. After a time, though, the Klingon's husky voice came. "Worf here."

Riker got that same odd feeling he had had earlier when he'd called on Deanna. The feeling that somehow his timing had been a bit out of kilter. "Worf . . . how would you feel about a party?"

"At this particular moment?"

"No, I mean later. A get-acquainted gathering for the ambassador and his party."

"Getting acquainted would be an excellent idea."

Riker thought he heard something then—a low laugh, of all things. Female? Slowly, he said, "All right, Worf. I'll be recommending it to the captain. Riker out."

He turned and looked at Guinan. "Did you ever get the feeling that you weren't certain about what was going on around you?"

Guinan considered it. Silently she poured herself a drink, pursed her lips, and seemed to be running her entire life's history through her mind in review.

"Never," she said at last.

"What, never?"

She grinned. "Well, hardly ever."

In Worf's quarters, thirteen weapons were scattered about the floor.

Worf was now picking them up and replacing them in the hidden spots of his uniform. Nearby, Gava was looking in his mirror and rearranging her hair.

Klingons were not much for innocuous small talk, so Worf said briskly, "I will see you again after I come off duty." Then he paused and added almost as an afterthought, "If you wish."

She turned slowly and smiled. "Of course, I wish."

"Excellent." He headed toward the door and paused. "One question."

"What would that be?"

"You said earlier that you know of two Klingons with human blood. One of them is Kobry, of course. But I would be interested in meeting the other sometime in the future, if that's at all possible."

Resting her chin on her hand, she said, "Why?"

"Having been raised by humans, I sometimes feel strained balancing their instincts against my own. It would be beneficial to meet any other Klingons with the same problem."

"All right. I can arrange it very easily. That Klingon is on this ship."

Worf's eyebrows shot up. "He's one of Kobry's honor guard?"

"No. 'He' is me." She stood and kissed Worf lightly on the cheek. "Human blood flows through my veins, as it does through Kobry's."

"Are you serious?"

"Always."

"That is why you were chosen to be the Honorable Kobry's aide, then."

"That, among other reasons. Perhaps that is why I was drawn so immediately to you, Worf. I sensed that human influence in you, and felt a certain kinship. Although *kinship* might be too mild a word. You best get to the bridge."

"You're right, of course." He turned, and the door hissed open. Then he stopped. Slowly he said, "You do not feel that same sort of kinship . . . with the Honorable Kobry, do you?"

"Of course not!"

He felt mild relief. What she did before, or for that matter after, she met him was none of his affair. But picturing her with the Honorable Kobry was a bit much for him to take. "I appreciate your telling me that."

"I'm glad you're appreciative," she said in amusement. "No, the kinship I feel for Kobry is entirely of a different nature."

"Really."

"Oh, yes."

"What nature is that?"

"Why . . . haven't you realized? The Honorable Kobry is my father."

Chapter Eleven

PICARD, FROM THE COMMAND CHAIR, glanced up at Riker. "A party?"

"Yes, sir. A sort of get-acquainted gathering. To put everyone at ease."

Deanna Troi, seated to Picard's left, said, "It might be good for the morale of the mission, Captain."

Thoughtfully, Picard stared straight ahead. "I don't know if that would be wise. Perhaps the best thing for this mission would be to keep as much distance between our people and the various diplomatic parties as possible."

"Hmmm," said Riker.

"You disagree, Number One?"

"Well, obviously, Captain, since I brought it up. If you feel strongly against it, of course, then that's that. I think you should know, though, that it was Guinan's suggestion."

"Really?" Picard looked up.

"Yes, sir."

"Oh. Very well, then. A get-acquainted party might be in order. Make it so."

Riker heard a stifled snicker from Geordi's direction. Ignoring him, he said, "Yes, sir. I'll speak to Ambassador Kobry about it."

"Very good." He turned in his chair. "Mr. Worf, have there been any difficulties with any of the Klingon honor guard interacting with the crew?"

"None at all, sir," replied Worf. "However, I do have security teams on alert. I intend that they remain so until this mission is over with."

"Excellent idea, Mr. Worf. And you, yourself, are getting on with the other Klingons?"

"Yes" was the succinct reply.

The forward turbolift opened, and standing in the doorway was the Honorable Kobry. A Klingon was standing on either side of him, both surveying the bridge personnel carefully.

"Captain," said Kobry, "I was hoping I might be allowed on the bridge."

"Of course, Ambassador." He gestured that they should enter. "Feel free."

Kobry walked out slowly, looking around with an expression of wonder. "Marvelous," said Kobry. "Just marvelous." He stepped over to ops and peered over Data's shoulder. "All flat panels. No switches."

"Touch sensitive," said Data. "If you'd like I can elaborate on their functions . . ."

"Oh no, no, that's quite all right. You just proceed as you wish. Don't let me disturb you." He stepped away and, turning, spotted Worf. "Good day, Security Head. I hope you are well."

Worf didn't say anything at first, trying to get a reading from Kobry of just what the ambassador knew. But the small Klingon's face was decisively impassive. "Quite well," said Worf carefully.

"Ambassador Kobry," began Picard.

One of the Klingon guards said tersely, "Honorable Kobry."

"Now, now, Bors, whatever the captain says is quite acceptable," Kobry said.

But Picard smiled graciously and, accepting the correction, said, "Honorable Kobry . . . it has been suggested that we have a sort of gathering, so everyone can become familiar with one another."

Kobry looked mildly skeptical. "We Klingons are not especially social creatures, Captain. I do not know if that would be the best way to proceed. I, of course, am accustomed to such gatherings, but my guards, well . . ." His voice trailed off, and he gave a small shrug.

Riker, who was standing next to Worf, turned and glanced at him. "You said you thought it would be fine," he whispered.

"My mind wasn't on the conversation," shot back Worf.

"Of course," said Kobry, in his most diplomatic fashion, "I do not wish to slight your idea, Captain."

"Oh, don't be concerned," said Picard. "Truth be known . . . it wasn't my idea. Actually"—he looked back at Riker—"it originated with my hostess in the Ten-Forward Room."

And the two Klingon guards said simultaneously, "Guinan?"

"Why . . . yes," said Picard in surprise.

"Well, if it was Guinan's idea, there should be no problem with that," said Kobry.

Picard and Riker looked at each other. Riker couldn't get over it. What *was* it about her? Picard had brought her on the ship. He must know more than he was telling. Someday he was going to have to try and pin the captain down on that particular point.

"Actually, Captain, I'd suggest you delay it a bit," said Kobry after a moment's thought.

"Delay it until when, Amb—Honorable Kobry?"

"Until after the Kreel are on board, and we are approaching or are in orbit around DQN 1196."

"Oh, I understand," said Picard. "Positive association."

Data spoke up. "Sir, I'm afraid I *don't* quite understand."

"Our arrival at DQN 1196 will be quite a tense moment," said Picard, "as will the Federation's examination of it. Both Klingons and Kreel have a claim on it, tempers may be running high. If the arrival at the planet is perceived as a time of celebration, that can only benefit our mission."

"Well put, Captain," said Kobry approvingly.

"I see." Data paused thoughtfully. "What, however, do we do if the Kreel are not interested in attending any such function?"

"We'll have them talk to Guinan," said Picard.

"Splendid," said Kobry. He stepped up and around to the upper portion of the bridge. His hands folded behind his back, he walked over and stood next to Worf. Kobry's head just cleared the railing as he looked out. "Splendid," he said again. "Well, I'll take up no more of your time, Captain."

He did not have to gesture to the guards. The moment he headed toward the turbolift, they were right behind him. All of them stepped in and were then whisked away.

"Now that," said Picard, "was very curious. Mr. Crusher, how long until . . ." Then he stopped and looked at the conn station, which was occupied by another crew member, Ensign Tom Chafin.

Riker knew what was coming. "Number One, how

much longer is Mr. Crusher going to be excused from his duties?"

"Not much longer, Captain," said Riker.

"What is his difficulty?"

"He's still aiding Dr. Pulaski in a research project."

"Still?"

"Yes, sir."

Picard shook his head, and he turned toward Geordi. "Mr. La Forge, you've worked with Mr. Crusher more than any of us. In your opinion, are Mr. Crusher's talents being properly utilized in medical investigation?"

Geordi considered the question carefully. His immediate reaction was that they were not, that Wesley's first, best destiny was engineering. But Geordi had learned through his own sources what Wesley was really doing, and he was not going to be the one who slammed the door on young Mr. Crusher.

"I think Mr. Crusher's talents are formidable, no matter what he's applying them to, sir," said Geordi. "His research talents are second to none . . . well, second to Data, I guess, but that's natural."

Picard paused, trying to decide whether they should retire to the conference room before he said what was running through his mind. Then he tossed out a question. "Does everyone here on the bridge know what we're talking about?"

Slowly everyone nodded their heads.

"It's a small ship, Captain," offered Troi.

"All right then, I can be blunt. Do you think Mr. Crusher is wasting his time trying to find a cure for this disease?"

Riker said, "Who are you asking, sir?"

"All of you. Feel free to jump in."

"I think he's an idiot," said Chafin.

"No one asked you," Geordi snapped.

"But—"

"I believe that Wesley is wasting his time, yes, Captain." It was Data who had spoken. "However, I believe he should be allowed to proceed."

"Why?"

"Because he might succeed."

"And," Deanna put in, "because he is a young man who refuses to believe that he's incapable of accomplishing anything he wants."

"I see," said Picard. "So either he'll fail, realize his limitations, and be miserable. Or he'll succeed against all odds and become insufferably confident in his ability to do anything. Does that sum it up?"

"I would not have said 'insufferable,'" Deanna commented. "But other than that, it's a fair assessment."

And Worf said, "Of course, you could order him to stop."

"In which case," said Riker, "when his friend dies, Wesley will blame you."

"Now that is the most irrational argument I've ever heard," snapped off Picard.

"Yes, sir. But no one ever said sixteen-year-old boys are rational."

"He could carry out his duties here and concentrate on other activities on his own time," suggested Data.

Picard shook his head. "That would be all that I need. A preoccupied teenager at conn. All right. Let things remain as they are for now. But at the end of this current mission, Number One, a decision will have to be made about Mr. Crusher, one way or the other."

The door buzzed several times before Wesley even heard it. "Go away," he snapped.

"Orange, it's me."

Wesley turned away from the computer screens. He rubbed his eyes, naturally closing them as he did so. The moment they were closed he felt his sleep-starved brain beginning to shut down and he immediately forced his eyes open. "Come in."

Jaan entered, looking around the quarters in amazement. The deterioration of Wesley's quarters was paralleling the deterioration of the young man, himself. Nothing had been put away. Hand-written notes were scattered all over the place, piles and piles of them. He picked up a few and read them. Hurried memos, reminders about certain drugs to be checked out, half-completed thoughts on new recombinations. "What, in the name of Kolker, is all this?"

"I'm working, Jaan. What is it?"

"What is it? It's this! Orange, why are you doing all this?"

"To help you, damn it!" He shook a fistful of notes at Jaan. "All this! It's for you. You're not just going to wither away and die, not while I'm around."

"Orange . . . Wes . . . I appreciate the concern, but—"

"Appreciation doesn't mean anything. Only results mean anything. And I'm going to get them." He was rubbing his forehead. "Head's splitting. But I think I'm on to something. There's another race with similar biology to Selelvians . . . at least, I think it's similar. There's so much to assimilate. Some organs are in different places, but the blood composition is close. And they had—"

"Wes, for pity's sake, get a grip on yourself." He took Wesley's face in his hands. "You're coming apart at . . . at . . ."

He looked into Wesley's eyes. Wesley's determined, unyielding eyes . . .

151

And he knew. He realized what had happened.

The Knack. His Knack.

He was making Wesley do this.

It had been unintentional. His own anxiety had caused his power of suggestion to completely envelop Wesley. He hadn't intended it to do so.

Or had he? Now he wasn't sure. After all, he was in control. Was Wesley, in fact, doing exactly what Jaan wanted him to do?

He paused a moment, uncertain of what to do. He had influenced Troi deliberately, that was certain. Troi had been making accusations, veiled innuendo. She might have given Picard a report on Jaan that would have prompted the captain to throw Jaan off the ship. Besides, she was a damned attractive woman. Attractive, and uncertain in recent days about the value of her ability. Put it all together and he'd had several reasons why he was perfectly comfortable with having given Deanna Troi a little push. Indeed, he'd have happily given her a little more if Riker hadn't shown up.

But this business with Wesley, this was unintentional. Except . . .

Except the Knack was not some sort of mind-controlling power. All he did was give certain priorities to thoughts and feelings that were already there. Deanna found him attractive. Deanna didn't really want to have to recommend he be sent home. So it was simple to convince her of that with finality. And Wesley . . . he wasn't *forcing* Wesley to do anything. Wesley wanted to help him. Wesley wanted to save him.

And maybe he could? Hell, he'd saved the ship several times. A thousand lives. This was just one life. It should be easy.

So the Knack was making Wesley compulsive about it. So what? What was the harm, really?

That stuff that Troi had said, about Jaan being willing to do anything to live, well, that was just wrong-headed. He wouldn't kill to live, right? He wouldn't sacrifice someone else, right? But this wasn't evil. This was just giving Wesley an additional push to achieve the greatness that he certainly already had within him.

That was all. Nothing wrong with it.

He realized that Wesley was staring at him blankly. He put a hand to either side of Wesley's face and said gently, "It's okay, Wes."

"Is it?" said Wesley.

"Sure, Orange. Look . . . I understand what you're doing. I understand why. I've never had a friend like you, and I know I never will again."

"Oh, you'll have lots of friends, Jaan. I'm going to save you. And you'll live for years and years."

"Okay, Orange. You keep at it. I'll be back in touch with you to check on you from time to time."

"Sure, Jaan."

Jaan stood and walked quickly out of Wesley Crusher's quarters. When the door closed, Jaan leaned back against the wall of the corridor and let out a trembling sigh, wondering how much of his soul he'd just sold off in the hopes of living.

Chapter Twelve

THROUGHOUT THE GALAXY, like bits of intergalactic flotsam and jetsam, mysterious objects had long been turning up. Here a bit of machinery, there an artifact that defied description and hinted of civilizations far advanced and farther gone. For years, various archeologists and starships had been stumbling over the findings, debating over them, categorizing them. Wondering about the technology that was cast off like so much dross.

By far the largest such find was DQN 1196. It was the farthest out in space. It had offensive capability beyond imagining. And at the moment it had several Kreel crawling over it, continuing the work that had been done by the earlier exploring party.

No Klingons had dared come near the planet, and the Kreel cheerfully took the weapons that they found and set forth to harass the Klingons. Except the Klingons had been fighting back, and unfortunately those weapons the Kreel found, while marvelous and plentiful, couldn't be everywhere. As much as the Kreel had hurt the Klingon Empire, by the same token the Klingons were laying waste to those Kreel outposts and ships that were as yet unequipped.

What the Kreel needed was time. Time to overcome the one great handicap of the weapons.

Power source.

While on the planet, the weapons worked fine. But they appeared to have only minimal energy reserves, for when they were removed from the planet, their energy drained off within a very short time. DQN 1196 apparently acted as some sort of giant battery. Removing the weapons meant having to find alternative sources, and the amount of power the weapons required was massive. When mounted on Kreel ships, it tapped virtually everything they had when fired. Indeed, eight ships had actually blown themselves up in the process of attacking Klingons, without the Klingons having fired a single shot.

Hence the bid . . . the bid for peace, and for time. Time to get the hang of the weapons' full potential.

A Kreel science team (a phrase any Klingon would have immediately designated an oxymoron) were busy continuing the work that the earlier landing party had started. They explored the underground outpost on DQN 1196 room-by-room, carefully testing each weapon and finding out what they could do.

The planet had been Kreel-held since the very first, and several Klingon attempts, in escalating numbers of ships, had been repelled by ground fire with absolutely devastating range. A Klingon warship could lay waste to the entire planet, but only if it got close enough. The planetary defenses (which, if the Klingons had known amounted to precisely one gun, would have probably resulted in mass suicide) were simply too devastating.

They tried circling the area to prevent Kreel ships from getting in and departing with weapons, but they had to be so far out in space to avoid being picked off from the planet that it was pointless. Kreel ships simply slipped into warp space like sneaking through the back door.

The upshot was that the Klingons conceded DQN 1196 and concentrated on fighting back at other more vulnerable points.

Just before the *Enterprise* rendezvoused with the Kreel diplomatic delegation (to the Klingon's, another oxymoron), however, there was a small mishap. It happened as follows:

There had been a six-member science team experimenting with the weapons. That number had been reduced to five when one of the Kreel scientists made another endeavor to get through the large, jagged-toothed door that had melted the late, unlamented Budian. He was certain that he had worked out the code on his computer and endeavored to punch it up on the multicolored keypad. His confidence evaporated along with the rest of him.

So it had been five scientists who discovered a particularly fierce-looking weapon in one of the lower rooms. It had been the only weapon in the room, and the room had had glyphs on it that were utterly unreadable to them. This did not deter them from bringing the weapon topside, mounting it on a tripod and testing it. If they had been able to read the sign which, roughly translated, meant "Remarkably stupid weapon. Do not use," they very well might have tested it anyway.

The test was quite simple. They picked a small mountain several hundred kilometers away, aimed the weapon, found the trigger, and fired it.

At first, it seemed to work extremely well. A deadly blue bolt ripped out of the bowels of the weapon and, inside of a second, had drilled a hole right through the mountain.

The ray then, in total defiance of logic, adhered to the curvature of the planet and kept going.

The immediate result was that as the Kreel scientists were congratulating each other on finding the deadliest weapon of all, the beam, in little more than an instant, completed its circuit of the planet and struck them from behind. The beam blew holes through two of the scientists who were in its path, struck the weapon and blew it up. The resulting explosion wiped the remaining Kreel scientists from the planet, not to mention from the annals of Kreel science. The subsequent fire burned itself out in a day.

The end result was that the planet, for the first time in a month, was utterly unoccupied by Kreel. Since the ground fire gun had never been set on automatic, DQN 1196 was now completely unprotected. If so much as a Klingon scoutship had arrived, they could have taken the planet and everything would have ended. But the Klingons were giving DQN 1196 a wide berth, since coming within parsecs of the place had been nothing less than suicide.

The foregoing provided three lessons: Never fire a weapon if the instructions are incomprehensible; if you must fire such a weapon, do so from a distance; never concede a planet, since anything can happen.

So after a month of activity, the planet was now peaceful once again. But now, having yielded up some of its secrets, the planet seemed to be waiting for something else to happen. As if it anticipated a long-delayed meeting were at last about to occur.

Chapter Thirteen

THE OTHER SHOE DROPPED.

The Kreel arrived.

Picard was extremely cautious in the *Enterprise's* first contact with the Kreel diplomatic ship. But Worf's careful sensor scan of the Kreel vessel revealed no hint of the extraordinary technology that the previous ship had carried. So it was with a bit more relaxed, but nevertheless cautious attitude, that the *Enterprise* had lowered her shields and made ready to transport the Kreel diplomatic party aboard.

Picard made damned sure to greet the Kreel in exactly the same manner in which he'd greeted the Klingons.

A security team would have been advisable, but the Kreel would have viewed it as a sign of weakness by Picard—that here, on his own ship, he felt the need to protect himself with armed guards. Still, Picard had such a team hovering within a hundred feet, out of sight . . . just in case.

Riker and Deanna were at his side as the transporter chief locked on to the coordinates of the Kreel ship.

The only one missing from the welcoming party that had been there earlier was Worf, for obvious reasons.

"Do not," said Picard, "under any circumstances, break eye contact with them when standing face-to-face."

Riker nodded. "Yes, I've heard about that. They'll consider it a sign of weakness."

"You're talking as if you're mapping out a battle strategy," Troi said.

"That is a fairly accurate assessment, Counselor. All right, Transporter Chief . . . beam them aboard."

Riker suddenly decided that he was standing a couple of feet too close to the transporter and moved back. He never cared to forget that what was happening within the parameters of the transporter field involved the molecular unscrambling of anything (on the platform) and its subsequent reintegration at a specified point. It was a formidable process.

Riker remembered a time in Starfleet Academy when a much-detested instructor was about to beam down to headquarters to accept an award no one felt he deserved. So Riker and one of the computer whizzes had performed some hot-wiring to the transporter console. It was staggeringly simple, really. Minutes before the instructor was sent down, the transporter was programmed to extract from the molecular mix any molecule that was not biologically based. Synthetics, for example.

The result was that when the instructor materialized on the other end, to be greeted by a welcoming committee of twenty distinguished sorts, his clothes didn't make it down with him.

It was quite a scandal and mass punishments were threatened, but the students closed ranks and the head of the academy (who privately thought that the prank was absolutely brilliant, not to mention deserved on the part of the instructor) eventually let the matter drop.

But Riker always made sure to treat that particular technology with respect.

So he stood a safe distance back as the Kreel materialized.

They stood on the platform, muscles bulging, their minimally-clad bodies rippling with power. They looked around with the unabashed curiosity of those unaccustomed to the transporter. There were ten in all, just as many as had been in the Klingon party.

Slowly, cautiously, they stepped off the transporter platform, and one of them approached Picard. He was about half-a-head taller than the *Enterprise* captain and looked as if he could break him in two.

Picard wondered fleetingly if, racial considerations or not, it mightn't have been a good idea to have Worf on hand, anyway.

"I am Aneel," he said.

"You are the ambassador?"

His grin exposed jagged teeth, a couple of which, on the right side, were broken. "That is the rank to which I've risen, yes."

"I am Captain Jean-Luc Picard."

"You are in charge?"

"That is the rank to which I've risen, yes," said Picard dryly.

"Excellent. Where is the Klingon swine?"

Picard's jaw set for a moment. "The Klingon *ambassador* is in his cabin, and would like to meet with you at your convenience."

"Oh, would he?" There was the sound of snorting, derisive laughter from the others.

"Now, you listen here, *Captain*," said Aneel, and he roughly grasped Picard's shoulders in his three-fingered hands.

That was all he did, for the next second Riker's fist slammed in to the side of his head. Aneel released Picard, turning toward the first officer, and Riker shoved him back with a well-placed kick. He stumbled backward and was caught by the other Kreel in the group.

Picard tapped his communicator and snapped, "Picard to security."

And the Kreel laughed.

It was an unpleasant sound, like a pack of wild dogs. Picard, who was behind Riker, watched in astonishment as the Kreel envoys chortled among themselves.

"Excellent," said Aneel. "Excellent! This worthy gentleman, Captain . . . is he your head-of-security?"

Worf's voice came over the communicator, actually sounding concerned. "Security here."

"Stand by," said Picard cautiously. "Ambassador . . ."

"Aneel," he said, dusting himself off. "Merely Aneel. We Kreel are not as caught up in titles as the Federation and the Klingons"—and they all spat—"seem to be."

Picard walked around Riker, ignoring the first officer's restraining arm. He went straight up to Aneel.

In no uncertain terms, and looking the Kreel right in the eyes, he said, "There will be no spitting on my ship. There will be no fighting on my ship. And diplomatic mission or no, if you can't be trusted, there will be no freedom for you on my ship. Is that understood?"

Aneel once again smiled that toothy smile. "Perfectly, Captain."

As if his manhandling of the captain moments ago had been forgotten, he casually introduced the other members of his group. It seemed to Picard that whereas the Klingons accompanying Kobry had been

161

an honor guard, the Kreel who had materialized with Aneel seemed to be his drinking buddies. Aneel may have been the ambassador, but the rest of them appeared to be little more than rabble-rousing troublemakers.

Picard decided to take no chances. Whereas with the Klingons he'd waited until he could discuss the matter with Kobry in private, with the Kreel it would be best if he acted immediately.

"I need to take your hand weapons in to protective custody."

That stopped the chuckling and good-time attitude immediately. Aneel frowned. "Why?" he asked dangerously.

"Because I want to make sure no one blows someone else's fool head off while you're on my ship" was the terse reply.

"And if we refuse?"

"Then we send you back to your ship."

At that moment the transporter chief said, "Captain, the Kreel ship has already moved beyond transporter range."

Aneel grinned fiercely. "And *now* if we won't give you our weapons?"

Picard stepped closer until he was practically nose-to-nose with the Kreel, although Picard had to crane his neck.

"Then you walk home."

There was a strained silence for the moment.

Aneel pulled out his large disruptor, and Riker immediately started toward him, ready to yank the captain out of the way. But Aneel quite calmly reversed the weapon, proferring the butt-end to Picard. "Be my guest," he said.

Riker breathed an inward sigh of relief as Picard, taking the gun, said calmly, "Actually, you are invited

162

to be *our* guests. As long as you behave in a manner befitting guests."

Aneel gestured that the others should likewise hand their weapons over to Picard. It was Riker and the transporter chief, though, who actually went through and collected the weapons. Aneel half-bowed, with a graciousness that seemed completely inappropriate to him.

As Picard watched all this, Worf's voice came over the communicator. "Captain . . . security still standing by."

"It's all right, we have a handle on it here. Picard out." He cut off the communication before the Kreel could notice it and identify the voice coming over the communicator as that of a Klingon.

"All we wish is to make successful, peaceable inroads," said Aneel. He smiled again, that same unpleasant smile.

"My attitude precisely," replied Picard.

"Good. Now . . . where is the Klingon swine?"

Picard sighed inwardly. *What's the use?* he thought.

"Follow me," said Picard, and led them out of the transporter room.

They made a bizarre procession. Picard and Aneel in the front, a troop of lightly-clad Kreel behind them, and Riker and Troi bringing up the rear, Riker laden down with an assortment of Kreel hand weapons. They attracted stares from everyone they happened to pass, and Riker was so self-conscious he was starting to get an idea of how that academy instructor had felt.

"Truly a magnificent ship, Captain," said Aneel.

"Thank you."

"Despite our recent advances, we Kreel have nothing compared to this. Or, for that matter, to that marvelous transporter. What a pity that technology is not shared equally by all, wouldn't you say?"

"Technology," replied Picard, arms folded behind him, "is usually developed by a people when they are ready to handle it. Not before that."

"That is the convenient excuse given by all advanced cultures to make certain that those less fortunate remain so."

"That is simply not true, Aneel. There have been too many instances in our history of a people advancing before they were ready, because of outside interference."

"Such as ourselves?"

Picard glanced out of the corner of his eye as they continued to walk. "You said that, not I. What I was leading to, Aneel, is that we are governed by a prime directive which compels us not to interfere with the development of a culture. It would be doing you a massive disservice."

"Pretty words. The Kreel are not much on words. We prefer results."

"Aneel . . . let me explain something. There was a time, only a few centuries ago, when the people of Earth had very much the same attitude as you do. Any advancement was thought of in terms of how it would best be used to aid the military. Even the beginnings of the space program—the technology that eventually resulted in that which you see around you—that was thought of in terms of how the needs of war could best be served. Instead of putting all money and investigation in to creating space stations on which people could work and experiment and learn, governments were interested only in creating orbiting weaponry."

"So?"

"So?" Picard said incredulously. He turned and stopped walking, facing the Kreel. "So those beloved orbiting weapons provided the tools for mankind to launch World War Three. We almost didn't make it out here because of short-sightedness, wrong-headedness and stupidity."

"But what's wrong with military applications?" demanded Aneel.

"What's wrong is this: If someone had come from the future, or from another more-advanced culture, to Earth in those days and offered, say, transporter technology to our ancestors . . . it would have been misused. Hideously. The chances are the first thing our ancestors would have done was use transporters to materialize bombs in selected places, and we wouldn't have made it out of the twentieth century."

And Picard privately congratulated himself that he had thought, before the Kreel came onto the ship, of tapping the computer banks and putting a temporary seal of confidentiality on all information pertaining to technology the Kreel did not already possess. They would not, for example, be able to call up research articles and specs on the workings of the transporter.

At that moment, they rounded a corner and ran into four Klingons.

The reaction was automatic. They all reached for their weapons.

Fortunately, the weapons weren't present. More Picard foresight.

"I take it you all know each other," said Picard laconically.

"All too well," said Aneel slowly.

The Klingon who had introduced himself as Tron earlier looked at Aneel, and his eyes narrowed. "I remember you. I only heard that damned voice of yours, but I wouldn't forget it. You were on DQN 1196."

"As were you?"

"I was part of the Klingon landing party you attacked."

"Really?" Aneel grinned maliciously. "And you're still here to tell of it? My aim needs improving."

Tron lunged toward Aneel, and the others started to converge on each other.

Riker, thrusting the disruptors into Troi's arms, grabbed Picard to pull him out of harm's way, so that he himself could intercede. But Picard pulled away and, to Riker's shock, thrust himself between Tron and Aneel, who were just getting their hands on each other. With more strength than Riker would have credited Picard with, he shoved the two of them apart.

"That's enough!" he thundered with such fury that it brought everyone up short. "This is a *diplomatic mission,* damn it, and if there is so much as one more disturbance, no matter how minor, *I'll have the lot of you clapped in irons! Is that understood!"*

The seething anger between the two groups was practically something you could touch, but Picard's presence had created a barrier between the two that neither was willing to breach. At least not yet.

"All the Kreel have ever wanted," said Aneel calmly, "is respect. All Klingons have ever wanted is dead Kreel."

"All the Klingons have ever wanted," replied Tron, "is for the Kreel to cease acting like the parasites that they are."

"Parasites?" said Aneel hotly. "Parasites!"

"Gentlemen," Picard's tone was dangerous, "I have the leg irons being prepared."

"Captain," Aneel was saying, turning toward Picard, "we are supposedly your guests here. Yet these . . . persons . . . insult us with impunity."

"No one can insult a Kreel," said Tron smoothly.

Riker reached for his communicator, prepared to call security. He hadn't wanted strong-arm tactics this early in the game, but Picard's safety was the most important concern right now. He also noticed, to his annoyance, that other crew members were rubbernecking, as if oblivious to the danger of the situation.

And at that moment, a low, slightly bemused voice said, "Is there a problem here?"

The onlookers parted as the Honorable Kobry and Gava stepped through.

Aneel took one look at Kobry and started to laugh. A loud, raucous, disgusting laugh, and the others joined in. The Klingons bristled, furious at this cavalier treatment of one of their most honored individuals.

Now, the Kreel were laughing so hard that Aneel and several others were clutching at their stomachs, spasms shaking them. Picard and Riker looked from one group to the other and felt mortification for the small Klingon diplomat. Picard even took a step forward, but Deanna Troi placed a hand on his forearm and said in a low voice, "No, Captain . . . it's all right. The Honorable Kobry is . . . at peace with himself."

And indeed, Kobry did not flinch from the hysterics his appearance elicited. He merely smiled that same, enigmatic smile that Taka Nagai had found so intriguing, and walked slowly forward toward the laughing Kreel, right up to the doubled-over Aneel.

And he waited. Arms folded, face serene, he simply waited.

The Klingons looked at each other, uncertain of what to do. If the Kreel had attacked Kobry they would have been entitled to defend him—which is what they wanted. But as long as the Kreel made no move, and as long as Kobry was on the scene and refused to order them to do so, the Klingons were stymied.

And, as Kobry knew they would, the Kreel eventually laughed themselves out.

When the dust settled, and the Kreel had laughed for as long as they could sustain it without any further provocation, they stood there wondering what they should do next.

Kobry didn't give them time to think. He simply said, "If you wish to laugh some more at my deformity, I can wait."

Aneel shook his head, staring in wonder at him. "Who *are* you?"

"I am called the Honorable Kobry." He thudded a fist against his chest and held it out, knuckles down. "You are Aneel?"

"Yes."

"And the one who was with you in the original party that explored DQN 1196 . . . Deni. He is here, too?"

Nearby, Deni half-raised a hand.

"I see." Kobry paused a moment. "You have my sympathy for the Kreel loss of life in this meaningless conflict."

This caught Aneel flatfooted. From anyone else, it would have seemed some sort of admission of weakness. But Kobry seemed so self-confident, so self-assured, that weakness seemed out of the question.

"My . . . sympathy for the loss of Klingon life as well," said Aneel slowly, not quite believing what he was saying. Neither could any of the other Kreel. He stared at Kobry. "What . . . *are* you?" he asked.

Kobry bowed slightly. "A humble servant of the Emperor, as are we all. This is my aide, Gava."

Aneel looked at her appreciatively. Up, and then down. Then he laughed roughly.

"You remind me of a Klingon woman I raped once."

Oh shit, thought Riker.

Tron lunged forward, even as Riker threw himself against the Klingon to hold him back. *"You lie!"*

"Tron, stay back!" snapped Kobry.

"You're right, I'm lying!" Aneel shouted. "Actually, it was more than once! And by the end, she was begging for more! She loved it! She—"

That did it.

Tron hurled Riker aside as if he were a poker chip, slamming the first officer against the wall, and lunged at Aneel. Picard summoned security. Kobry shouted, trying to make himself heard. And the Kreel and Klingons slammed in to each other, forming one giant mass of flying fists.

From nowhere, it seemed, the other Klingons in the honor guard showed up and set to against the Kreel. The only thing that prevented the struggle from becoming a bloodbath was that they were all crammed together in the corridor, with no room to maneuver. Whatever weapons the Klingons might have been packing remained unpulled because there wasn't space to do so much as pull a knife from a boot.

"Stop it! That's an order!" shouted Picard, and then he was shoved aside and almost trampled by frantic civilians who didn't really see him but were intent only on getting out of there. Gava fell back, and Deanna Troi helped pull her away.

One of the Kreel broke from the crowd, and saw the Betazoid counselor still holding the disruptors Riker had given her. He lunged for her, snarling. Gava stepped between them, and without hesitation brought her foot up in to the Kreel's crotch. He went down, gagging.

Then Gava shrieked, *"Kobry!"*—the diminutive Klingon had just gone down in the middle of the crowd.

Riker pulled himself up and hauled Picard away from the scene. Then he said tersely, "Captain, permission to—"

"Yes," agreed Picard.

Riker pulled out his phaser and fired blind, waist high, into the middle of the crowd.

Klingons and Kreel went down in a heap, collapsing on one another. Within moments, the entire struggling mob had lapsed into unconsciousness.

There was silence, and then a low moan from the midst of the pile.

"Kobry," said Picard, and immediately he and Riker went over to the pile, shoving insensate bodies aside to get to the Klingon ambassador.

Slowly, Kobry emerged, hauled out by the captain and first officer. Having been below the level of the beam, Kobry hadn't been hit. But all the bodies had fallen on top of him.

At that moment a security squad, Worf in the lead, came running up. He put up a hand, and the squad skidded to a halt.

Gava, from nearby, said, "You missed it."

Kobry was shaking his head. "I suppose it's possible that things could have gotten off to a worse start, but I'm not really sure how."

Gava knelt down next to her father. "This isn't going to work."

And Picard said, "It is our duty to make it work, as much as we may dislike the position into which we've been put."

"The captain is absolutely right, Gava," said

Kobry. "Our respective governments are counting on us to stave off a full-scale war. There is a cease fire in effect for as long as this mission seems to have a possibility of succeeding. But if the twenty of us cannot live with each other for the time it takes to get to DQN 1196, how can we possibly hope that our two peoples can coexist?"

"Good question," said Worf.

Kobry stood and brushed himself off. "Captain, I need to sit and talk with the Kreel ambassador alone."

Picard nodded. "Lieutenant Worf," he said briskly, "have the Klingons brought to holding facilities on Deck 2, block A. Have the Kreel brought to Deck 18, block Z detention facilities."

"That's on opposite sides of the saucer section," said Worf.

"Precisely. They're going to be as far away from each other as is possible until we get things worked out."

"When will that be?" Gava murmured to Worf.

"When hell freezes over," he replied, much too quietly for Picard to hear.

Or so he assumed. But Picard turned and said, "Hopefully, Lieutenant, it will be a bit sooner than that."

Chapter Fourteen

JAAN WAS WALKING down the hallway, on his way to Dr. Pulaski for further treatment, and he slowed down as he noticed the change that seemed to have occurred in the corridors.

Usually, people had always been quick to greet him with a wave or a smile—the women, in particular—and he hadn't even needed to use the Knack for that. People were just attracted to him. He liked that, thrived on it.

But now it appeared to him that everyone was giving him a wide berth. Or those that were near him gave him sympathetic looks, or asked solicitously, "How are you?" And all of them had sorrowful faces pasted on them like cheap jewelry.

They felt sorry for him. Him! It was humiliating. He didn't want pity or sorrow. He wanted to continue his work. He wanted to continue to live. *(That wasn't so blasted much, was it?)* And slowly he started to resent the other people on the *Enterprise*—resent them for their attitude, for their damnable pity, and for their

172

lives. The lives they would continue to have, and he would not.

At that moment Bobbi Chase approached him, looking concerned.

It irritated him. He knew what she was going to say. She was going to utter meaningless words about how she hoped he was feeling okay, and if there was anything she could do he should let her know, and so on.

If he hadn't been ill before, certainly this type of treatment would have put him over the edge.

Although Bobbi was hardly the major offender, he decided to let her have it. She would start in with all the sympathy nonsense, and he'd rip into her sanctimonious prattling. And then, when he'd reduced her to tears, well . . . maybe he might suggest other things to her.

Yes. Yes, that would certainly be amusing . . .

After all, an elf should never pass up an opportunity.

She walked up to him and said, "Jaan, I need to talk to you about something."

He leaned against a wall and forced a smile. "What's the problem?"

"It's Wesley."

He stared at her blankly for a moment. "Wesley?"

"Yeah. You know, I really thought he liked me, and I know I liked him, but he's become so obsessive lately. It's a little scary, you know?"

"Wesley is who you're concerned about?" He was stung. "What about me?"

She looked down for a moment and said, "I'm . . . concerned about you, Jaan. You know that. But . . . ." She looked up into his eyes. "You seemed to me to be the kind who doesn't want a lot of pity. So I wasn't going to do it."

She was right, of course. But to hear it stated like that, so matter-of-factly . . . it angered him more than he would have thought possible.

He was starting to sweat as he snapped, "Oh, is that what you think? Well you don't know anything. Not a single thing!"

"But—"

"Shut up! Just shut up! Just . . . leave me alone! Go be with your precious Wesley!"

Now others were staring at him and he couldn't stand it, so he shoved past Bobbi and rushed blindly forward . . .

And slammed into Aneel.

The security guard escorting Aneel had been standing just behind the Kreel, so he was out of position to see Jaan. Aneel paid little heed to the sudden obstacle in his path. With a swing of his powerful arm he brushed Jaan aside, sending him skidding across the floor in the opposite direction.

Jaan pulled himself up and felt his legs beginning to give out. *I will not pass out,* he thought furiously and staggered toward the turbolift that would bring him to sickbay.

Aneel watched him go. "Wasn't that an elf?"

"Yes," said the security guard. "Come on."

"What's the matter with him?"

And Bobbi, hearing this, and still confused and embarrassed over what had happened, snapped, "What's the matter with him? He's dying, okay? He's dying of the Rot and it's unfair!"

"So where is it stated that life is fair?" replied Aneel, but he wasn't really thinking about his reply. He was dwelling on what had been said.

He knew elves. He knew them quite well. He'd captured a few sometime back and had great fun playing with them, until he had released them—

slobbering, burbling wrecks. They were attractive and had a certain degree of grace, but as a whole they were not the sturdiest of races, physically or mentally. Which was curious, considering what they were capable of doing with their minds.

All of which set Aneel on an intriguing path of thought.

"When do we get to the conference room?" he asked.

"In a while," said the security guard. "I've been given an order, though, to make another stop with you first."

Since it was supposed to be a diplomatic meeting, personnel were kept to a minimum. Picard was there, of course, as was Troi. He would have liked to have had Riker there as well, but he wanted his second-in-command on the bridge during this rather tense time.

Also present were Kobry and Gava. The rest of the Klingons and the Kreel, except for the shortly-to-arrive Aneel, were securely in holding facilities.

"Do you think you'll be able to accomplish anything, Kobry—Honorable Kobry?" corrected Picard.

Kobry made a dismissive wave. "Please feel free to ignore the 'Honorable' aspect. It takes too long to say. In answer to your question . . . I know I'll be able to."

"How?"

"I have to know." The Klingon smiled wanly. "If I only thought so, then I wouldn't be able to. I have to *know* it." He glanced at the chronometer. "I think that Aneel should be just about finished with his detour."

"Yes, I was curious about that little tactic," said Picard. "Is that a common maneuver in diplomacy?"

"More common than you would imagine."

As if on cue the doors hissed open and Aneel entered, still escorted by the guard.

The Kreel was in a very good mood.

"Sit down, Ambassador," said Picard, and Aneel did so, seating himself across the table from Kobry. He thudded into the chair and looked cheerily across the table. "Tell me, sir," continued Picard, "how did you like the Ten-Forward Room?"

Aneel smiled that toothy smile and nodded his head. "That," he said in a deep voice, "is hospitality almost on par with what we Kreel are capable of providing."

"I take that as high praise," said Picard. "Now . . . Ambassador . . . the Honorable Kobry has requested this meeting. I myself would just as soon have the lot of you off my ship, but we all have to live with the requests of our respective governments. The Honorable Kobry feels that he has a solution to all of this."

Aneel turned and stared slightly bleary-eyed at Kobry. Aneel was not drunk by any means, but he was certainly relaxed. Still, more than enough of the famed Kreel bluntness remained in him. "You seriously expect me to deal with you?"

"Yes," said Kobry evenly.

Picard glanced over at Troi, clearly trying to get a silent assessment from her as to how matters were likely to go. She shrugged her shoulders. It was a toss-up.

"It's ridiculous," said the Kreel soldier-turned-ambassador. "I could step on you. How is it that you are supposed to be the Klingon mediator?"

Kobry smiled. "You know, most of my people used to be very much like you. They did not take me seriously, either."

"Oh really?" said Aneel, feigning surprise.

"Really," affirmed Kobry. "But you see . . . that is how I managed to survive in the Klingon Empire. A hierarchy noted for promotion through back-stabbing, assassination and double-dealing. I left the Empire for a while, was educated within the Federation. Came back at a time when my people were wracked by internecine warfare.

"I began to gather followers, people who were influenced by my words rather than my appearance. Those above me—they paid me no mind. They never took any of my activities seriously. They merely continued as they had been, plotting against each other and planning, always planning. They were so good at plotting and planning that they managed to kill each other off. No one noticed that those above me were dropping, one after the other, and that I was still there. And when the Emperor looked around, he suddenly discovered that all his advisors were gone. Undone by each other.

"And here was Kobry"—and he shook his head in amusement at the memory—"whose followers had now swollen vastly in numbers. Kobry, who preached moderation, who preached alliances with the Federation rather than the Romulans. We had to grow, you see. We had to grow up, and go forward as a people. We could not remain savages forever. Aggressive, hard, yes. That is bred into us. It makes us strong. But strength has to be tempered with intelligence, with knowing when to fight, and when to talk."

Aneel made a dismissive wave. "The Kreel always know when to fight. It's when anyone else challenges us."

"But it has to stop," said Kobry. "You have to move forward. And we have to help."

"You're only interested in *helping* because we now possess weapons that pose a threat."

"There is that," admitted Kobry. "But it merely alerted us to a situation that should have been rectified ages ago."

"Rectified through extermination is what you're saying."

Kobry leaned back, tapping his fingers on the arm of the chair. "Once, that would have been the case. Once—before we realized the self-destructive nature of that course. No longer, though. But that is why this journey to DQN 1196 is so important. That is why . . . Captain, how long until arrival there?"

"At Warp 6, about five days," said Picard. "I only wish, for your sakes, that it could be sooner."

"No," said Kobry. "No, this is probably better. Ambassador Aneel, the journey to DQN 1196 is important for two reasons." He ticked them off on his fingers. "First, it was necessary to bring two groups of our people together for a sustained period of time to open a dialogue. To prove that we can coexist. Granted we have not gotten off to a good start, but that is no reason to assume that it's hopeless. The second reason is that the heart of our dispute is that planet. The weapons on it are powerful beyond comprehension. Your scientists, no slight intended, are out of their depth when it comes to examining them. If the Kreel are given free access to them, you know that, at best, it will mean all-out war. At worst, it will mean the extermination of both our races."

"Or the extermination of the Klingons," said Aneel slowly.

"Or," replied Kobry, "the extermination of the Kreel. Are you willing to take that chance? To lose everything? My understanding is that the Kreel were battling for respect. So tell me, here and now, as a representative of your race . . . which is of more importance—respect or genocide?"

Kobry had violated, at this point, one of his main rules for diplomacy, indeed for life; namely, never ask a question to which you do not already know the answer. The Kreel was still a wild card, his answer capable of going either way.

Still, he waited patiently for the response.

Aneel studied him a long time, then looked at the others in the room. He liked the way they were looking at him: with concern for what he was going to say, with a certain degree of fear as to what he was going to say. He was aware that he, Aneel, held in his hand the key to what direction matters would take.

And best of all, what he said right now didn't matter all that much, for he had other plans already developing in his mind. Definitely, that was best of all.

"What did you have in mind?" he asked slowly.

"A treaty?" said Tron incredulously.

The Klingons in the holding cell stood grouped around Kobry in a loose semicircle. As a precaution by Picard, Worf was standing just outside the cell. The holding force shield was off at Kobry's request, so that he could address his people and have them feel less like they were prisoners.

Gava was hanging back, standing next to Worf. He felt her fingers brush in an "accidental" manner across his leg, and he took a half-step away. Now was certainly not the time for distractions.

"Yes," said Kobry. "I have signed a treaty with the Kreel ambassador . . ."

Several Klingons spat.

"Stop that!" said Kobry with the first real flash of anger any of them could recall seeing. "By the Emperor, it's like dealing with children! There will be no spitting at the mention of names. And that's final! Now, I have signed a treaty with the Kreel . . ." He paused a moment, to make sure that his anti-expectoration order was being attended to, and then he continued. ". . . ambassador. Copies will be made

available to each of you. It delineates the lines of cooperation between our two groups, and specifically designates the *Enterprise,* and the planet called DQN 1196, as neutral zones. *Not* strike zones. Do you understand? No matter what the provocation, there is to be no battle within these areas."

"And how," asked Tron disdainfully, "have the Kreel agreed to adhere to this treaty?"

"With their honor."

There were disbelieving snorts from the Klingons. "Honor?" said one of them. "The Kreel only know honor as something others have that they can use to their advantage."

"The Kreel," replied Kobry tightly, "whether we find them personally repellant or not, have grievances they feel must be answered, just as we do. These are grievances that must be worked out, just as the Federation and the Klingon Empire did with theirs. But before anything can be worked out, or discussed, we have to be able to look at each other without trying to kill one another. Now the Kreel have pledged not to hurl insults, nor to make any overt aggression against us."

"To act like perfect little gentlemen?" said Tron sarcastically.

"That's one way to put it. And, by the same token, we will behave in a like manner. Unless of course"—and he paused—"Klingons are incapable of behaving in as civilized a manner as Kreel."

Worf was filled with a large degree of admiration for the way the Honorable Kobry had phrased that. Naturally such a comment was designed to cut any Klingon to the quick.

It certainly worked in this instance. Almost as a unit, the Klingons squared their shoulders, their pride severely stung.

"Anything the greatest of Kreel can do can be matched by the lowliest of Klingons," said one of the guards sharply.

"I did not bring the lowliest of Klingons with me," Kobry said mildly, glancing at his fingernails. "I brought the best. Are you up to the challenge?"

They glanced at each other and Tron, taking a step forward, said, "A Klingon thrives on challenges. If the Kreel pretend to have a code of honor, then we can show them what a true code of honor is."

"Fine," replied Kobry. "I have the captain's permission that, should you agree to follow the terms of the treaty, your freedom to the ship is restored."

"That is fortunate," said one of the Klingons, a particularly burly fellow named Sklar. "We were concerned over the Honorable Kobry walking about unprotected."

Kobry sighed. "Don't be." He turned to Worf. "I'd like to return to my quarters, Lieutenant. I'm feeling somewhat fatigued."

Tron said briskly, "We will accompany you, sir."

"Oh, I think I'm safe enough with the lieutenant here. Make no mistake—if he were not Klingon, naturally I would need an escort. As it is, and considering we're in his environment, I'm certain I'm in safe hands. Correct, Worf?"

Worf nodded, surveying the Klingons in the holding cell. He tried to get a feel for what they were thinking, but they were masking it rather well. He got the distinct impression that Tron, for one, was not happy over what had been decided here this day.

The Honorable Kobry turned and started back for his quarters, with Worf to his left and Gava to his right. All three Klingons walked with even strides, Gava and Kobry looking resolutely ahead, while Worf cautiously scanned all sides of the corridor. He was

181

expecting trouble. He was always expecting trouble, even when there seemed little likelihood. One could never be surprised by something that one was always expecting.

"Tron made a legitimate point," said Worf. "You should not be unescorted at any time."

Kobry made a dismissive wave. "Lieutenant, I was surviving long before I had any honor guard of any sort. I've gotten quite good at it. Do you know what the key to my survival is?"

"No, sir."

"Twofold. First, I'm a small target, as I said earlier. Second, I always know what's going on around me."

"I see."

They walked a few more steps.

"So I understand you and my daughter are lovers," said the Honorable Kobry.

The simple declaration threw both Gava and Worf out of step. Worf stared at Gava who gestured helplessly, making it clear she hadn't told her father.

"May I ask . . . how you knew that, sir?" said Worf.

"Weren't you paying attention to what I just said?" asked Kobry in mild amusement. "About knowing everything that's going on around you?"

Worf looked at Gava again, and this time she said, "I didn't say anything about it, Father. I pride myself on being discreet. How did you—"

"If I counted on always being told everything, I would have been long gone by now," said Kobry. "Assassins rarely say, 'I intend to kill you in a day or two.' One has to be able to perceive what is not being said. Body language, a gesture here, a look there. Detecting the unspoken. That is the key to survival, my child."

"Does the Honorable Kobry disapprove of my relations with his daughter?" said Worf stiffly.

At that, Kobry actually laughed. "The Honorable Kobry feels it's none of his damned business. I assume it's not against her will, and, you being a male Klingon, I'm certain it's not against yours."

They had arrived at Kobry's quarters, and the door slid open. Kobry turned and faced them. "My daughter is quite selective," said Kobry. "It speaks very highly of you that she has chosen you for a lover, Worf. It certainly confirms my initial opinion of you."

"Thank you, Honorable Kobry," replied Worf.

"For a woman like Gava"—and he looked at his daughter affectionately—"it's difficult to find someone she can respect."

"True," said Gava. She smiled in the same way that Kobry had. "I'm always comparing them to my father."

"Unfair competition, really," commiserated Kobry. "Compared to myself, anyone else is bound to come up short. Good day to the two of you." He vanished behind the door.

Gava and Worf looked at each other.

"I have duties to attend to on the bridge," he said.

"Of course. I certainly hope, however, you'll save your after-duty time for me."

"You can rest assured of that."

"I didn't intend to rest."

"What's the prognosis, Doctor?"

Jaan sat up, swinging his legs down from the diagnostic bed. Pulaski was looking at the test results.

"Jaan . . ."

"Uh-oh."

She held the test results against her chest. "'Uh-oh?' You can tell what I'm going to say, already?"

"It's the way you said my name—in the same tone as you would greet someone who's shown up unexpectedly at a party. By the way, I hear they may actually be making a party for the Klingons and the Kreel once we get to that planet we're heading for."

"A party?" She shook her head. "Klingons and Kreel, trying to be festive. I can't see it."

"I understand it was Guinan's idea."

"Oh. All right, then," said Pulaski. "Now . . . I think, Jaan, that you should be trying to rest a bit more."

"Why?"

"Because this is my first experience with this disease . . ."

"Mine too."

". . . and," she continued gamely, "it's progressing faster than I would have liked to see it."

"I should become an invalid, is that what you're saying?"

"No, that's not what I'm saying, Jaan," she said. "Just . . . take it easy."

"You said it's progressing faster. How much faster? Was six months overly optimistic?"

"I'm not sure," she said. "Perhaps. I don't want to alarm you."

"Alarm me?" he said, and for the first time, she was getting a sense of barely-restrained anger. "Alarm me?" And, suddenly furious, Jaan swept his arm around and knocked over a table of diagnostic tools. The noise brought assistants running from the med lab but Katherine gestured for them to stay back. *"How can I be more alarmed?"* he shouted. "Do you know how long my people live? Do you? Close to two centuries! We have time for everything!"

"Jaan . . ." she said.

But his fury, long pent-up, was bubbling over. "But not me! No, not Jaan Baat-Utuul-Bayn-Devin! I get a stinking fraction of that because my damned parents had a damned disease! I'll never have children, Doctor! I'll never leave anything behind me!"

"What about your writings?" She tried to get near enough to touch him, to console him. "You said your writings would—"

"To hell with them! Do you think lifeless words can make up for the years I'm losing? At least Orange cares! At least he's trying to do something to help me. Why aren't you trying to find a cure for this?"

"Because other people, with more talent for research than I have, have been trying for years and haven't made any headway," said Pulaski. "I can't cure everything! No one can. I know what you want, Jaan. You want me, or Wesley, to look over the work that's been done and hit ourselves on the forehead and say, 'Of course! How could anyone have missed that? It's so simple!' and synthesize a cure for you from penicillin and coconut oil. It doesn't work that way! I know that. Wesley doesn't yet, but he'll realize it soon enough."

She waited for his fury to continue mounting, to the point where he would have to be sedated, even lashed to a table. But it didn't happen. Instead, to her surprise, he pulled himself together, got a grip on himself. He forced himself to calm down, closed those marvelous eyes of his and, when he opened them, he was utterly composed.

"I'm sorry for the outburst, Doctor," he said. "I will try to slow down. Whatever you say."

Katherine felt relief sweep over her, but that was quickly erased by another, stronger feeling that maybe Jaan's reaction of fury and hurt was the better one. That was out in the open, that was something that could be seen and dealt with. What actually seemed to be happening, though, was that he was fighting to bottle everything up.

How long, she wondered, before he erupted?

Had Picard been right? Should he have been taken off the ship, immediately? But no, she couldn't go back to Picard now. After all the trouble she'd gone to, after their head-on collision that she'd survived and won, she couldn't go back at this point and say, "Captain, maybe you were right." Not if it wasn't absolutely necessary.

She prayed she wasn't making a mistake.

At that moment, the door to sickbay opened. Pulaski turned and stared in surprise at the newcomer. "Yes?" she said uncertainly. "Can I help you?"

"You are the Doctor here?"

"Yes. Dr. Katherine Pulaski. And you are—?"

He smiled. "The Honorable Kobry." The half-size Klingon extended a hand. "There is something of importance I need to discuss with you."

Chapter Fifteen

Two days had passed since the signing of the *Enterprise* Pact, as it had quickly been named. The Klingons and the Kreel had made a conscious effort during that time to give each other as wide a berth as possible. Although neither side was overly thrilled with the accord, they were endeavoring to live by it—the Klingons because honor demanded it, and the Kreel because they wanted to show they were as good as, or better than, the Klingons.

Nevertheless, Picard made certain that, at all times, *Enterprise* security men or higher-ranking officials had a visible presence to subtly reinforce the Pact.

Its first major test came, naturally enough, in the Ten-Forward Room. It was a preferred location for both the Kreel and the Klingons, but thus far they had managed to miss each other.

This particular day, Deanna Troi had just come from a frustrated talk with Wesley Crusher. She had never seen a young man more in need of help—help which she was finding herself unable to provide. The boy was wasting away before her eyes.

His physical deterioration was marked. His eyes still had that look of burning determination in them, but there were dark circles under them. He spoke now in sharp, clipped sentences, as if he really didn't want to waste time talking. When Deanna had come with food, she'd had to resort to threatening to have him confined to sickbay unless he started eating. He'd finished what she'd brought while she was sitting there, so at least she had the knowledge that she'd accomplished some good, no matter how insignificant.

Now, as she was walking down a corridor, half-a-dozen Kreel came up to her from a side hallway. In the front was the one called Aneel, and even if she hadn't been an empath she would have known what he was thinking as he openly appraised her.

They fell in to step with her, and Aneel said, "You're the Betazoid I've heard about, eh?"

His voice, his coarse emotions, grated on her, but she would not let those emotions show. "That's right. Are you enjoying the stay on our ship?" she asked, in an effort to be polite.

"I could be enjoying it more." He grinned his offensive grin. "But I'm making do. We all are, aren't we?"

The others grunted their agreement, and Deanna found herself wishing that Riker would show up. Even though she knew she wasn't in any real danger, she disliked the feelings she was getting from them. "I'm on my way up to the bridge," she lied.

"Well . . ."

Aneel stopped, suddenly noticing that Selelvian he'd spotted several days ago just ahead of them. The elf was waiting patiently in front of a large set of double doors, and then they opened and, to Aneel's shock, two people dressed in winter clothes stepped out. Flakes of snow seemed to blow past them and vanish as soon as they hit the hallway. The Selelvian nodded a greeting to them and stepped through the doors which closed behind him.

"What's that place?" said Aneel.

"That? That is the holodeck. Realistic computer creations allow you to live out virtually anything you can imagine."

"How interesting." He pointed ahead, down the hallway. "Will that turbolift take us to the Ten-Forward Room?"

"Oh yes," said Deanna, unsure of whether she'd been able to keep the relief out of her voice.

"Good. Come along, men."

Deni and the other Kreel reacted in mild surprise to their leader's sudden eagerness to get to the Ten-Four Room. But they said nothing, hurrying instead to keep up with Aneel as he sped down the hallway on his muscular legs.

"What's the hurry?" asked Deni.

"The hurry," replied Aneel, "is that something occurred to me that I didn't want the Betazoid to know about. How much have you learned about her, Deni?"

And Deni, who had been doing quiet investigations on all key personnel, said, "You needn't have been concerned. She can't read thoughts. Just sense emotions."

Another one of the Kreel snickered and said "I bet she was picking up a few great ones from me." There was raucous laughter from the others, which continued as they got to the Ten-Four Room and entered.

The usual assortment of off-duty personnel was there. There were also six Klingons seated around a table.

Chatter in the Ten-Four Room started to ease up as

the occupants slowly realized that there was potential for major trouble here. Six Klingons. Six Kreel. Twenty-four fists.

The odds were not promising.

The highest-ranking Klingon present was Sklar, and the others immediately looked to him for what lead to follow. Sklar, for his part, did not move. He knew what the Honorable Kobry had arranged, and what he expected. By the same token, he answered directly to Tron, and he knew how Tron felt about the Kreel—a feeling that he and the others at the table shared. There was, of course, honor to consider, but were the Kreel mature enough to comprehend honor?

Sklar and the others sat stiffly, as if bolted to their chairs. They were poised to stand quickly if need be, to attack lethally if it was required. Sklar allowed his right hand, which had been under the table, to drift toward the top of his boot where a knife rested comfortably. Next to him, Sub-Lieutenant Derl was prepared to yank his garrote from concealment in his belt buckle.

Swaggering, utterly confident, Aneel ambled toward them, arms dangling relaxedly. He had a lopsided sneer that Sklar was certain was indicative of total contempt. Sklar mentally chose a point two feet away where, if the Kreel crossed it, Sklar would consider that an act of aggression and pull his knife. Self-defense, of course. Pact or no pact, he wasn't going to let a Kreel scum get within choking distance.

Perversely, the Kreel stopped just short of that mentally drawn line-of-no-retreat.

Aneel folded his arms across his barrel chest. He was staring directly at Sklar with those damnable pig eyes of his, and Sklar waited for him to *do* something.

From the bar, Guinan called out to the new arrivals, "Can I help you gentlemen?"

Aneel paused and then said slowly, not to Guinan but to Sklar, "I'll buy you and your people drinks . . . if you'll buy me and my people drinks."

Sklar blinked in surprise. It was not at all what he'd been expecting. Hardly any sort of violation of the shipboard treaty. He glanced at the other Klingons but they were just as surprised.

"Well?" said Aneel. "Are you going to show that you're less hospitable than we?"

Sklar's lips thinned, his heavy brow bristled, and then in a low voice he called to Guinan, "Bartender . . . drinks for the Kreel."

And Aneel promptly responded, "Bartender . . . drinks for the esteemed Klingons."

"On the house," Guinan said.

Normally, the Klingons preferred something a bit more in the rotgut category, such as the swill they'd brought on board, but in this instance Guinan used discretion and reached for the synthenol.

The liquid began to flow.

"Estimated time of arrival at DQN 1196, Mr. Data?"

Data turned from his position at ops and looked curiously at Picard. "Precisely thirty-two minutes sooner than the last time you inquired, Captain."

Picard settled back in his command chair and sighed. "The sooner this business is over with, the happier I'll be. I feel as if there's a clenched fist in my stomach."

"So far, so good, Captain," commented Riker.

"No, Number One, you mean, so far, no one is dead." Picard shook his head. "I have an extremely bad feeling about this."

Suddenly a voice came over the intercom, snapping, "Security to bridge!"

Worf's head snapped around, beating Picard to the response as he said, "Bridge, Lieutenant Worf here."

"Disturbance, sir. Ten-Four. Knives being thrown. Mobbed down there, but we believe Kreel and Klingons are involved."

"Damn!" cursed Picard. "Worf, Number One, get down there!"

"Security team, meet me at Ten-Four!" barked Worf even as he darted for the aft turbolift, with Riker right on his heels.

It seemed ages ago that, in this very same arboreal setting, Jaan and Wesley had engaged in mindless hide-and-seek games.

Jaan now wended his way through the forest, phaser out, competing against a computer-created enemy. He had not wanted to disturb Wesley—Wesley who was his only hope. Wesley who was his only friend.

For the umpteenth time he considered somehow trying to undo the damage that the Knack had done to the young genius. But there was no point to it. Let Wesley go on trying. He might succeed. And even if he didn't . . .

His thoughts grew dark. Even if he didn't, who cared, really? So Wesley lost some sleep. So what? He, Jaan, was what counted. He was what mattered. He wanted to live. In most cultures, that wouldn't be considered a crime.

And the Federation—what had they done for him? —hadn't found a cure for the Rot. Oh, they'd been working on it, or so they said. But they undoubtedly had more important things to worry about, like building bigger and better spaceships. Who gave a damn about one life?

"The hell with them," he said, and at that moment a phaser bolt struck him square in the chest.

The computer-created seeker had found him, and Jaan was blasted back off his feet, caught totally unaware. A tree halted his backward flight, but he hit it with full impact and the world spun around him.

He slid to the ground and lay there helplessly, feeling humiliated. Once, he had been the best at this game. Even computer creations couldn't begin to cope with his speed, his stealth. Now his concentration was unfocused, his body movements stiff and clumsy. The disease was creeping through him, eating away at his nervous system.

The computer-generated human stood over him, unmoving, not making a sound. Why should it? It was just an unliving shell.

Which was what he was going to be.

"Damn you," he grunted and tried to stand. His legs had no strength, his stomach cramped up yet again. He felt a wave of nausea rolling over him.

He should have listened to Pulaski. He should have taken it easy . . . but for what? To prolong this non-life of his?

His face became wet with tears. It was unmanly. It was inappropriate. But he couldn't help it, and the computer human remained an impassive witness.

In a strangled voice Jaan said, "Go away!" Obediently, the computer opponent holstered its phaser and walked away from him.

He sank to the ground then, rubbing the dull pain in his chest from where the phaser bolt had taken him down.

Why was this happening to him? Why? What had he done? It was so *damned* unfair. He had tried to live a good, honest life, and this was his reward. Being cut down, not even in his prime. His prime was still years off.

He sighed, and even that stung. There was no point

to sitting here like an oaf in computer-generated woods. He stood, preparing to leave.

And that was when a figure, who'd been watching him, stepped out of the shadows of the trees.

Jaan heard the snapping of twigs and spun quickly, so fast that he almost lost his balance and fell. But he recovered immediately, throwing his arms out to either side to prevent it. He looked at the newcomer in surprise.

"What," he said, "are you doing here?"

And the newcomer smiled and said, "I thought I might have something I can offer you."

"Like what?"

"Life."

Worf and Riker pounded down the hallway, setting new speed records as they got to the Ten-Four Room. Even before they arrived, they heard shouting and yelling, challenges being tossed back and forth, all in the very distinct voices of Klingons and Kreel.

The security team of five was waiting, phasers at the ready, and the moment Worf and Riker arrived the Klingon security head said, "Phasers set on stun. At my mark and . . . go!"

The doors opened and they leaped in, phasers aimed, and they were hit by a now-overwhelming barrage of noise, except now it seemed that in addition to Klingon and Kreel voices there were others as well.

At first they couldn't see anything. *Enterprise* crew members had created a solid wall of backs, as if they were watching some sort of sporting event. They were bellowing out what now seemed to be shouts of encouragement, and Riker could have sworn he even heard betting being made.

What in the world—he thought.

"Out of our way," snarled Worf, and he didn't even wait for people to obey as he shoved his way through, followed by Riker and the now-completely-confused security team.

As people in the crowd realized who was trying to get by them, they made every effort to step aside. At last, the officers fought their way to the front of the crowd. There, they stopped and gaped in disbelief.

Hanging on the wall, stuck there who-knew-how, was one of the leather tunics that the Kreel typically wore. Concentric circles had been drawn in the middle of it, and sticking out of the bull's-eye, just right-of-center, was a dagger.

Thirty paces away, a bare-chested Kreel, whose tunic it undoubtedly was, was taking aim with another dagger. He was surrounded by shouting Kreel who were urging him on, and equally raucous Klingons who were claiming that no way could he possibly match that throw.

Worf and Riker looked at each other, dumbfounded. They'd expected to find bodies on the floor. Not this.

The Kreel, who Riker now recognized as the one called Deni, let fly. The dagger soared straight and true and landed dead center of the bull's-eye.

A roar went up, and immediately everyone was shouting and arguing. The Klingons wanted a rematch. The Kreel were shouting that *this was the rematch, but sure, why not,* and it was all a madhouse, simply a madhouse.

And at the top of his lungs, Riker shouted, *"Everybody quiet!"*

Immediately a silence fell over the Ten-Four Room. Slowly, Riker walked across to the target, shaking his head in utter disbelief. He pulled the daggers out of the tunic and lifted it up. The wall was riddled with knife marks, where previously-thrown daggers had penetrated the tunic and gone through. He also noticed that the tunic was being held to the wall by the puttylike substance used to seal bottles of synthehol.

Derl of the Klingons, who had been the knife-thrower opposing Deni, said, with no trace of remorse, merely as explanation, "We tried to protect the wall."

Riker turned slowly and stared at them, stared at the crew. "You're out of your minds," he said incredulously. "You're throwing daggers around! Someone could have gotten hurt! Plus you're damaging Federation property. You're disturbing the tranquility of the entire ship with these dangerous stunts! Now"—and his angry tone made it clear that a reckoning was about to occur—"whose bright idea *was* this, anyway?!"

And every Klingon and Kreel, and every member of the crew, pointed and chorused the same thing:

"GUINAN'S!"

Riker turned and looked at the hostess for confirmation. From behind the bar, she smiled, giving him her most innocent expression.

"Oh," said Riker. He shrugged. "Okay, then."

A cheer went up and Riker said quickly, *"However."* And when the noise level had dropped back down to a safe decibel range, he said, more quietly, "However . . . these daggers are now property of the first officer. Namely me. If you all want to entertain yourselves, that's splendid. Try to do it with less-sharp objects. Is that understood by everyone?"

There were desultory nods all around, although the Kreel didn't nod so much as half-bow, because of their relative lack of necks. Taking this to be a sign of understanding by all, Riker and Worf left the Ten-Four Room, security squad in tow.

The Klingons and Kreel looked at each other. "They took the knives," said Deni.

"That's fine," replied Sklar. He lifted his arm, and the sleeve fell away to reveal a pair of daggers in tight holsters strapped to his forearm. "We have lots more."

Meanwhile, Worf and Riker reported back to the bridge, where Captain Picard looked less than pleased as they explained the situation.

Deanna Troi couldn't help but observe, "It's better than their trying to kill each other, Captain."

"That is a matter in which I take small consolation," replied Picard. "Although you do have a point. Let's hope that business proceeds smoothly from here."

So the knife throwing continued in the Ten-Four Room, as Worf and Riker had secretly imagined it would. And the *Enterprise* drew closer toward DQN 1196.

And none of the participants had noticed that Aneel had vanished from the Ten-Forward Room in the heat of the knife-throwing contest.

Jaan stared up at the unexpected intruder, a burly member of the Kreel contingent, so recently arrived on the *Enterprise.* He pulled himself up to a sitting position, and brushed the dirt off himself.

"Life?" Jaan snorted.

"That's correct."

"Don't talk to me about life."

"Why not?" said the Kreel, swaggering toward him. "My name is Aneel, by the way."

He was a typical Kreel, Jaan thought. Obnoxious,

overbearing, and incredibly confident in himself, even when he had no reason to be. "Aneel the Kreel," said Jaan. "That's simple enough to remember. Well, Aneel the Kreel, the reasons I don't want to talk about it are none of your concern."

"Really?"

"Yes, really."

The Kreel sat down on the ground across from him, balancing himself with his massive arms. "Could it have something to do with the Rot?"

Jaan shot him a look that was pure poison. "How in the name of Kolker do you know about that? What is it, on damned subspace radio or something?"

"Oh, matters have a way of being found out," said Aneel, giving silent thanks to that chattering young girl in the corridors.

"Great. Well, if you know of my problem, then I'm sure you can imagine that I'm not in the greatest of moods." Jaan stood to leave and pain lanced through his chest, knocking the breath from him. He staggered, moaned, and fell back. The Kreel made no effort to catch him or aid him in any way.

"Feel your body shutting down?" said Aneel without a hint of sympathy. "Blood not pumping the way it used to? Arms and legs forgetting how to obey commands?"

"Shut up."

"Getting harder to see these days, isn't it?"

"Just shut up!" said Jaan with a fury that almost drained him. "Just leave me the hell alone."

Aneel, of course, did not move. "You know," he grunted, "I was one of the first to investigate Hellhole."

"What?" said Jaan, tired and disinterested.

"Hellhole. Oh, the official designation is DQN

1196. But we call it Hellhole. The place where all the advanced weaponry was found."

"So?"

"So . . . that's what the Federation and the Klingons think was found there, since that's all they've seen."

Jaan shook his head uncomprehendingly. "So?" he said again.

"So . . . what if I told you that wasn't all we found?"

"I don't think I could be less interested."

"What if I told you that we could cure the Rot?"

It took a moment or two for what he was saying to sink in. "Cure . . .?"

"The Rot, yes."

Jaan couldn't believe it. "That's—that's ridiculous."

"Why ridiculous?"

"You just"—he shook his head—"you just *happened* to find a bunch of weapons, and while there you also just *happened* to find a cure for the disease I just *happened* to have. You must think I'm some sort of idiot."

"I didn't say we found a cure just for what you have. There's cures there for virtually every known disease. One of them is for any disease that attacks the central nervous system and the respiratory system, such as the Rot. But"—he shrugged—"feel free not to believe me. It's of little consequence to me."

He stood and started to walk away, and was actually a dozen paces away before Jaan said, "Wait."

Got him, thought Aneel, before he turned and said, "Yes?"

"What do you want?"

199

"Want?" said Aneel.

"Yes, want," said Jaan impatiently, "and don't try that innocent routine with me. It doesn't work."

"Speaking of routines," replied Aneel, and, suddenly, he grabbed Jaan by the shirtfront and hauled the elf to his feet. For a brief moment, fear ribboned through him as the Kreel snarled in his face. "Don't bother trying that little mind-push trick with me. I helped dissect a Selelvian once, so I know everything you fools can do. You can't push me into giving you the cure if I don't want to, and if you try, I'll give you a second smile just under your chin. Is that understood?"

Numbly, Jaan nodded.

Aneel smiled, and let Jaan go. "Good. Now, in answer to your question—we want just one thing. Something I believe that you can help us with."

"And . . . and if I help you with that, then . . ."

"Then, when we arrive at Hellhole, I'll give you the cure for the Rot. Do we have an agreement?"

Jaan gulped deeply. He didn't trust the Kreel, not for a moment. But he was offering Jaan more than anyone else had—except for the beleagured Wesley—namely hope.

What if he was lying? But what if he was telling the truth?

Jaan had everything to gain and nothing to lose. When you're dying, certain priorities rearrange themselves.

"All right," said Jaan. "What do I have to do?"

"We call it quits for now." Geordi sighed.

Data stared down at the alien weapon, commiserating with his friend. The rest of the tech crews were already dispersing back to their usual assignments.

"Perhaps," said Data slowly, "we were not meant to figure out the workings of this weapon."

"Sorry, Data, I don't buy that. I don't believe in that 'there's some things men aren't meant to know' stuff." Geordi shook his head. "Whatever we want to know, whatever we want to do, we should be able to know it and do it. The rest is just making excuses, that's all."

"No, you don't understand, Geordi. I mean perhaps someone—"

"Or something," said Geordi. "That's always got to go together."

"Very well," said Data agreeably. "Someone or something does not want us to discover how this weapon works. It wants to make sure that we return to the planet of its origin in order to find the answers. Perhaps . . . in order to make contact."

Geordi shook his head. "Why? Why go to all that trouble?"

"I do not know," said Data. "I do know this: There have been a lot of 'loose ends', if you will, in our exploration of the galaxy." He paced the confines of the engineering deck in a comfortingly human manner. "Artifacts, discoveries, and even some of our own recent encounters with entities that were beyond our comprehension. All of which would seem to indicate a sort of master race, perhaps dropping clues for us to discover."

"Or just going on about their business and not really caring about us one way or the other," offered Geordi. "Don't read too much into things, Data. Whoever this *omniscient* race of yours is, maybe they're just lousy about picking up after themselves."

"Or maybe," said Data, "this has all been some sort of test."

"Oh God, don't say that," moaned Geordi. "After

Q, and everything else we've been through, a test is definitely the last thing we need."

Ensign Tom Chafin, who had been very vocal in his opinion that Wesley Crusher was an idiot, had been reassigned. Picard, deciding that the opinionated crew member needed a change of scenery, kicked him over to security under Worf's generous stewardship. Worf, for his part, had other things to do than train a new recruit, so he had assigned him a post that was nominally important and yet sufficiently safe that he couldn't get into too much of a mess.

He was guarding the weapons room. The door had been specifically encoded to respond to his voice alone—aside from the voices of Picard, Riker and Worf, and Chafin considered it a very responsible position. He would stand there, smiling at all the passing crew members, feeling very proud of himself.

Usually the weapons room didn't require a guard, but considering the warlike attitude of the two current ambassadorial parties, it was an extra precaution, one well worth taking.

So Chafin stood there, feeling significant, and when Jaan walked up to him and greeted him, he returned the greeting in a boisterous mood.

Jaan wasted no time. Coming close in on Chafin, he said, eyes glinting, "You know, Tom . . . remember that charming young lady you and I discussed a month or so back?"

"Amy?" Chafin's eyebrows went up a notch. "What about her?"

"I ran in to her." He lowered his voice. "She wants you, Tom."

"You're—you're kidding."

"I'm not kidding."

"Oh lord, I was praying she might notice me."

"She did," said Jaan. He drew in a step closer. "Here's what you're going to do, Tom. Are you listening?"

"I'm listening, Jaan."

"You're going to her quarters. You're telling her you know she's been craving you. I bet you'll get lucky."

"You—you really think so?"

"I guarantee it."

"But . . ." His devotion to duty was causing him to waver. "But I can't leave my post . . ."

In his Knack-induced confusion, however, he was easy pickings for Jaan. "It's no problem," said Jaan.

"It's not? I was trying to think of some way to get around it . . ."

"I'm going to do you a big favor, Tom. I'm going to stay here and watch your post for you."

"Really?"

"What are friends for?"

"Oh Jaan, this is . . ." Overcome with emotion, Chafin embraced him. "You're the greatest. You really are."

"I know. Oh, by the way . . . how do you get the door to open?"

"Well, that's easy," said Chafin, and in a loud voice, he said, "Computer voice code and match. Open weapons-room door."

The door obediently hissed open, as Chafin, eager to leave, said, "You see? Of course, it only responds to my voice, or a couple of the brass."

"Oh, of course," said Jaan, nonchalantly stepping in through the doorway. His presence broke the electric eye, and the door, designed to provide safety for crew members, did not close.

"Well, great! I'll see you later, then!" With great joy, Chafin ran off down the hallway.

From around the corner at the opposite end came

Aneel. He glanced at Chafin's departing form and said, "What did you do?"

"Gave him a blind date. Come on," said Jaan hurriedly. "Grab what you need."

Aneel was carrying a small sack that could easily be carried unnoticed over one's shoulder. He stepped into the weapons room and smiled.

Phasers. They were small. They were elegant. They were deadly. They were what he was looking for.

He stuffed a dozen in the sack while Jaan continued to stand in the door, preventing it from closing. "Hurry up!" Jaan hissed. "Move it!"

"Afraid, elf?" sneered Aneel, drawing the top of the bag tight. He stepped out of the room and Jaan moved out of the way of the door, which now shut securely.

They moved off quickly down the hallway, made it to a turbolift, and within moments were in Jaan's quarters. Jaan sank into a soft couch and said, "We did it."

"Of course. And by the time Chafin returns to his post—"

"He'll be confused as anything," said Jaan. "He won't even remember clearly that I was there. I made sure of that. The one who's going to have some explaining to do is the girl he's going after. She'll have no idea what led him on. Ultimately, neither will he." And now Jaan was shaking his head. "I don't understand. What did you need phasers for?"

"Because your beloved captain took our weapons away, and that puts us at a disadvantage. And, in arming ourselves, it's preferable for us to have something small and discreet. After all, we don't want them to know we're prepared for trouble."

"But . . . that's all it is?"

"Of course," said Aneel with false cheerfulness. "Just being cautious, that's all. We don't want trouble.

We even signed a treaty. We're just being prepared, that's all. Nothing wrong with being prepared, is there?"

"No," said Jaan slowly. "No, I suppose not. And when we reach DQN 1196—?"

"I haven't forgotten," said Aneel. "The cure will be waiting for you there. And you hardly had to do anything for it. Your luck is changing, elf." And he grinned his awful smile.

Chapter Sixteen

THE SUCCEEDING DAYS passed with surprising calmness.

Relations between the Kreel and the Klingons were still hardly idyllic. But at this point both parties remained cordial, each one waiting for the other to hurl the first insult. However, neither one *was* doing so, so they both had no choice but to act with a minimal degree of civility.

Still, as the proximity to DQN 1196 grew, so did the tension. Even the announcement of the proposed diplomatic reception—the party—upon arrival did little to alleviate matters. Both sides expressed reservations about such a reception, although naturally they both became more amenable to it upon being informed that it was Guinan's idea.

The latest hot rumor going around the ship was that Worf had himself a girlfriend. This news came after one alert crew member spotted Gava coming out of Worf's cabin with a very pleased smile on her face. "Out of such meager evidence do rumors come," grumbled Worf, and the fact that the rumor was entirely true did not alter his assessment one iota.

It was after Gava's departure one day, just before Worf was to go on shift, with arrival at DQN 1196 now just hours away, that Worf's door buzzed. Worf assumed that it was Gava, and he was finishing pulling on his left boot as he called, "Come in!"

He was first alerted to his error by the much heavier footfall. He glanced up, and there, standing just inside the doorway, was Tron.

"What are you doing here?" said Worf.

Tron cocked his head slightly. "You said I could come in."

"Yes," was the terse reply.

They paused a moment, sizing up one another.

"Gava is very attractive," said Tron.

"Yes."

"How loyal are you to her?"

"Mind your own business," Worf said, pulling on his other boot. Then he stood and faced Tron, topping him in height by several inches. "If you have something on your mind, be direct with it."

"I am merely interested."

"In matters outside your purview."

"No. In your opinion. And your views." Tron was speaking very slowly, very carefully, as if afraid to give away what was truly on his mind. "You were raised by humans, I understand."

"Is there some point to this?" asked Worf impatiently.

"A Klingon raised by humans. So—do you consider yourself loyal to the Klingons, or to humans?"

"I believe I have already addressed this question," said Worf. "I see no need to broach it again."

"Ah, yes. You are loyal to the Federation."

"As I have said. And demonstrated. Now I must be going . . ."

"And the Kreel?"

Worf paused. "What about them?"

"Are you loyal to them?"

He turned slowly toward Tron. "What are you talking about?"

Tron stepped closer to him; his voice was hard-edged, anger evident in his eyes. "I'm talking about the tolerance being displayed toward those animals on this ship," he said in a barely-controlled fury. "I'm talking of my own men fraternizing with them. I'm talking of Klingons becoming so weak of mind and spirit that they forget who their enemies are. Have you forgotten, Worf?"

Worf stood there, rooted to the spot, his mind spinning back to the most horrible hours of his life. Those hours trapped beneath the fallen shelter with only his mother's crushed body between him and certain death.

He had not told Gava everything. He had not told her of the stark terror that had filled his every moment, about being buried alive, trapped with only the least bit of stale air managing to work its way down to him. He had not told her that, at first, his efforts to dig his way out had stopped when he heard the gleeful and hideous chortling of the newest arrivals to the destroyed outpost of Khitomer.

Like laughing hyenas, the Kreel had swarmed over the planet. They had followed in the devastation by the Romulans, descending on the planet like flies swarming over a corpse. Perhaps the Romulans had even told them of the intended strike to add insult to injury.

Young Worf had lain there, buried under the rubble,

his ears assailed for endless hours by the brutal laughing, coarse jokes, and nauseating voices of the Kreel. At one point, as they were rummaging around above him, he wanted nothing more than to claw his way out, grab a knife or a gun or a rock, anything, or just crush the head of the nearest Kreel. The Romulans had remained in their ships, aloof and untouchable. They had laid waste and had gone, beyond his reach. But the Kreel, the Kreel were there, big and alive and something that he could hate and think about killing.

And yet, much to his subsequent shame, when discovery by the Kreel had actually seemed a possibility, he had burrowed farther down in fear, actually retreating to what seemed the safety of his mother's body. It was, he deemed later, pure cowardice. That he would most surely have been killed had he been discovered was of no consequence. That he was only a few years old and utterly helpless did not matter. All that he remembered was shaking with fear and impotent fury as the Kreel ravaged what was left of his home. It was a shame he had carried with him to this day, and not all the years he put between himself and that time, not all the great deeds he accomplished, not all the medals he acquired, could satisfactorily distance him from that moment.

"I have no great affection for the Kreel" was his carefully phrased answer.

Tron slowly nodded. "Nor do I, fellow Klingon. Now the Honorable Kobry has created his damnable treaty. Kobry is supported by the Federation."

"And by the Klingon Empire," Worf quickly reminded him.

"And by Gava," said Tron with ironic emphasis. "Let us not forget our priorities."

"Your point, Tron?"

"My point is, how much are you able to bury your instincts? How much will occur before the Klingon warrior within you screams, 'Enough! I have had enough!'"

"I dislike the drift of this conversation," said Worf dangerously.

"This is no conversation. This is a warning, from one Klingon to the other."

"Are you threatening me?" was the icy question.

"Not at all. It is not that sort of warning. If you will, take it as a caution to the head-of-security."

"That caution being—?"

Tron was thoughtfully fingering a double-bladed weapon that was mounted on Worf's wall. "That caution being that it is dangerous to ignore one's instincts. And your Klingon instincts, as do mine, scream that the Kreel are not to be trusted. Yet here we are, violating that instinct, trying to ignore the warnings our heritage provides us with. They're up to something. I can feel it."

"Do you have any proof?"

"Proof? Over a century of aggression, of back-biting and sniping, of parasitic feeding off of Klingon fortune and misfortune. That is my proof. I would hope that it would be good enough for you. It is certainly good enough for me."

And, having successfully prodded Worf's fundamental concern with the situation, he took his leave.

It was enough to prompt Worf to contact the bridge and inform them that he would be a few minutes late coming on to shift. There was a matter regarding internal security that he needed to check out. And then he headed straight to the Honorable Kobry.

* * *

"Approaching DQN 1196, sir," said Data crisply.

Picard breathed an inward sigh of relief. He had never thought they would make it this far without blood being spilled at some point. But damn, that Kobry had been absolutely astounding. He had arranged for the Klingons and the Kreel to actually get along with each other. They were hardly the best of pals, but at least the temperature in the room wasn't dropping twenty degrees every time the two of them got together.

Furthermore, it was his understanding that Kobry and the Kreel ambassador, Aneel, had actually been having lengthy discussions about mutual grievances, that the foundations for a long-term peace were actually being laid. Now, Picard had little doubt that Kobry was sincere—the diminutive Klingon seemed sincere in all matters. Whether the Kreel were trustworthy, well . . . that was another question altogether. But Kobry seemed to feel that the risk had to be taken, and who was he, Picard, to gainsay him.

"Standard orbit, Mr. Data," he said. "Open a hailing frequency, Mr. Marks."

Marks, substituting for the otherwise-occupied Worf, did so. They attempted to raise the planet and received no response. They continued to do so for several minutes. Finally, Picard looked at Riker with curiosity. "There are supposed to be Kreel down there. Yet they do not respond. What do you make of it, Number One? A prelude to hostilities?"

"I doubt that, sir. If they wanted to be hostile, they could have attacked us before we got anywhere remotely near them."

"Yes, I understand that's how they were *greeting* most Klingon ships. Very well, prepare an away team to make initial contact."

"All right. Data, Geordi, with me."

"Good," said Geordi. "I'm looking forward to seeing this place close up. Tiny," he referred to his pet name for the big, unfathomable gun, "had been giving me fits."

Data got up from ops and was briskly replaced by Marks.

"I'd advise at least one security guard," said Picard.

"Already decided that, sir."

"But not—"

"Worf—yes, sir, I know. If there's Kreel down there, why bring down the one crew member who might automatically set them off."

They stared at each other for a moment. Riker would never deliberately challenge Picard, at least not outside of the confines of the briefing room or the captain's ready room. Yet, he was clearly putting across a silent message. *I can pick my own away team just fine, Captain. Thank you for your contributions, but they are unnecessary. I have the matter well in hand.*

"Do as you think best, Number One."

"Thank you, sir."

"No need to thank me," said Picard dryly. "You would have done so anyway."

"True, sir." Riker smiled rakishly. "But I prefer having the support of my commander."

"You have, of course, my full support."

"That is much appreciated, Worf," said the Honorable Kobry.

They were in the observation lounge, Worf, Kobry, and two guards. Kobry was staring out the window with that curious smile of his. "I've always enjoyed just looking out at the stars," he said. "Comforting to be reminded how small all of us are in space, no matter how much pretensions we have to the contrary."

"That is true," said Worf neutrally. "However, I—"

"Guards," Kobry said abruptly, "I wish to talk with Worf in private. Kindly leave us."

The two Klingons looked at each other uncertainly.

Kobry sighed. "We're the only ones here, gentlemen," he noted. "Stand outside the door if you wish, so you can monitor who comes and goes. But I'm quite certain I'll be safe enough."

Reluctantly, the two Klingons retired to the corridor just outside the observation deck.

"What did you wish to discuss, Honorable One?" asked Worf once they were out of earshot.

"Nothing, actually," replied Kobry.

"Then what—?"

"I thought you might wish to discuss something aside from Kreel-oriented concerns."

"Nothing that readily comes to mind," said Worf.

"Ah yes. Klingons have never been much for discussing innermost concerns." He paused. "Gava tells me you and I have a great deal in common."

"Gava talks too much," said Worf sourly.

That actually prompted a laugh. "Spoken with true Klingon tact," said Kobry. Then, becoming serious, he said, "We are both orphans of the storm, you and I. Or so I understand. Both of us cast up in times of difficulty."

Worf said nothing. Nothing seemed needed to be said.

"Klingons do not forgive," said Kobry. "Nor do we forget. One of our prime motivations is revenge."

Still Worf made no reply.

"That is pointless," said Kobry. "Revenge never ends. At some point, it must give way to forgiveness."

"For some acts there can be no forgiveness."

"True. But lack of forgiveness does not necessarily go hand-in-hand with need for revenge."

Worf looked at him skeptically. "It does for Klingons."

"It does not have to. Certain acts get no forgiveness, that is fine. That should engender caution. But revenge needn't always follow."

"The night always follows the day."

"Ah, now you see, Worf. That's the difference between us. To you, the night always follows day. To me, the day always follows night."

Worf snorted. "Semantics."

"To you. To me, a philosophy. You, yourself, need to adopt a philosophy, Worf."

"Yours?" Worf asked skeptically.

Kobry shrugged. "You are not me. We may have things in common, but you are not me. Just as you have things in common with the other Klingons on this ship, but you are not them. Nor are you human, Worf, as much commendable loyalty as you might feel toward them. You are unique."

"On that we agree."

"I might, however, make one observation. Humans are more advanced in the art of living without taking revenge than are Klingons. That much you must certainly have absorbed in your time among them."

"Yes," said Worf slowly.

"That attitude toward moderation would certainly be in conflict with your Klingon instincts."

Worf hesitated. Kobry was, of course, absolutely correct, but no one had ever put it to him quite that way. "That is a possibility."

Speaking in a no-nonsense manner, Kobry said, "Do not feel that you have to deny the gentler side of your upbringing. Strength is marvelous. It is the way to survive. But sometimes the greatest strength can be compassion for your enemies."

"Compassion can get you a knife in the back."

Kobry smiled. "I said be compassionate. Not stupid. Anyone who turns his back on an enemy deserves what he gets."

As the *Enterprise* settled into orbit around DQN 1196, Picard informed the Kreel and the Klingons that their destination had been reached. This resulted in immediate petitions by both groups to head down to the planet surface, but Picard held firm to the idea that, since the Federation was mediating this dispute, a Federation team should head down first to see matters were clear. No one wanted to endanger the uneasy peace that had been established because of a potential head-long run toward the advanced weaponry that the planet had to offer.

Instead, Picard had suggested, now would be the perfect time to have that diplomatic gathering that had been suggested—by Guinan, he hastened to add—a notion that was unanimously, if somewhat cautiously, received by all sides. It was decided that the ideal place for the *soirée* was the Ten-Forward Room. It had a nice philosophical aspect to it—that place in the ship that was most forward, representing the future of the Klingon and the Kreel. It also had a very relaxing atmosphere to it. And best of all, Guinan, who had an incredible knack for putting everyone at ease, would be pouring out the drinks.

The *Enterprise*'s inability to raise anyone on the planet was dutifully reported to Aneel, but he expressed an utter lack of concern over it.

"You have to understand, Captain," he had explained, "we don't carry those marvelous, highly-transportable communications devices, as you do. We have one communications area set up on the planet, and if no one happens to be nearby it, you won't get a response."

"We've performed a sensor sweep as well," Picard had told him. "We can detect no life readings at all."

"There is your proof then. They're probably beneath the planet's surface, in the middle of their explorations. Remember that the entire planet was extremely resistant to sensor scans."

So, although he had misgivings about the situation, Picard had resolved to worry no further about it.

Deanna Troi slowed down as she approached the Ten-Forward Room. The party was already in full swing, and she could hear loud voices and chatting.

Parties always made the ship's counselor uncomfortable. At any large gathering, her empathic ability always made her feel as if she was under attack, as if a radio was turned up too loud and she was being assaulted by sound. For Deanna, her empathic ability was always on. She had to make a concentrated effort to screen out the feelings of others—a simple procedure for a full Betazoid, but somewhat more of a strain for one of mixed blood such as she. A party was a burst dam of feelings, and she had to put a mental finger in the dike so as not to be totally washed away.

She would have preferred to skip such events. But as ship's counselor, it was her responsibility to, at least, put in an appearance, and also to be available for her people at all times.

Nevertheless, it was actually with some degree of relief that she found herself being flagged down by one of the Klingons from Kobry's group. He was in the hallway alone, nursing a drink, and he actually seemed pleased to see her. *Now, which one was he again—?*

It was as if he could read the question going through her mind. "Sklar," he said.

"Honorable Sklar," she said.

He shook his head. "No. Mere 'Sklar' is correct. This is quite fortunate, Counselor Troi."

"Why is that?"

"I dislike parties. Too many opportunities for someone to slip a knife between your ribs."

Well, that certainly accounted for the feelings of free-floating anxiety she was picking up from him. What an attitude to have. "I also feel ill-at-ease at such gatherings," she admitted, "although hardly for the same reasons. I should really go in though—"

"Why hurry?" he asked. "It will be going on for some time. I do not have the opportunity to meet many other races. This is my first assignment off my ship in quite some time. Please do me the honor of talking out here for a bit, where at least we can hear each other."

She smiled. He was extremely well-spoken for a Klingon. "Very well," she said. "At least for a while."

"Thank you. I will admit something, in candor. You are very attractive and"—he looked down— "attractive women make me nervous."

She stared at him incredulously. It certainly explained that still-free-floating anxiety, but . . .

"Are you sure you're a Klingon?"

He looked up and said, in no uncertain terms, *"All* Klingon."

Inside, the party was progressing quite smoothly. Kreel and Klingons were still giving each other a healthy distance, but there didn't seem to be a lot of tension in the room. Guinan, behind the bar, was wearing a hat the size of Canis Major and cheerfully working on keeping everyone's glass filled. Clearly she was in her element.

Geordi who, with Data and Riker and a security man named Tuttle, would be heading down to the planet surface, was in a conversation with Aneel. "Anything I should be on the look-out for, while we're down there?"

Aneel ran through, in his mind, the things that they had discovered down there. Immediately, he thought of the door that had killed Budian.

He stared at Geordi and decided he didn't like anyone whose eyes he couldn't see.

"Nothing of any real concern," he said. "Don't point anything at anyone."

"Words to live by," said Geordi.

From across the room, Jaan watched Geordi in deep discussion with Aneel.

When Aneel had first brought up the cure, Jaan had toyed with the idea of simply telling the captain and making sure that it was the first thing that the away team looked for when they went down. Aneel had squelched that thought real fast.

"We found it purely by dumb luck," the Kreel had said. "One-in-a-million chance. There's no guarantee that, unaided, anyone else will find it. Ever. Certainly not before you're moldering in the grave. Now, if you mention it to anyone, I can assure you that the Kreel will offer no help. In fact, I'll even deny that it exists. If, of course, you'd like to take your chances, go right ahead. But just how many chances do you think you've got left?"

It had been an argument that Jaan was unable to counter. So he had kept his silence and had prayed that his actions thus far to save his life would not have serious consequences.

But how could they? Everyone seemed to be getting on well enough. Certainly the Kreel now had hidden phasers tucked away in their breeches, but no one needed to know that. Things were progressing smoothly. The odds seemed very much against any weapons having to be drawn. No one had missed the phasers yet, and the last time he had passed Chafin, the security man had been standing there still looking somewhat puzzled over what had gone on before. When he had looked at Jaan, it was with the same kind of semiblank stare one gives when one isn't sure whether something really happened or if it had just been dreamed.

Jaan looked to the other side of the room, and there was Data chatting with the Klingon ambassador . . . now, what was his name again?

"Honorable Kobry," Data was saying, "I'd like to ask you a question if that is all right."

"Certainly, young man."

Data brightened. "You are the first person ever to call me that. Everyone else seems to be able to tell by my coloration that I am an android."

"Are you?" said Kobry mildly. "I never assume anything, particularly when it concerns albinos. Excuse me a moment, though." He put his drink down on the table next to him, popped open his large ring, extracted a pill and swallowed it.

Picard, standing nearby, drifted over and said, "Still having health difficulties, Honorable Kobry?"

"Oh no, Captain. As I mentioned to you, it's simply a medicine I take at food or drink times. Makes it easier to digest. Advanced years. You understand."

"Of course," said Picard.

"Now then, young man . . . your question?"

Data said, "Why are you always addressed as 'Honorable'?"

"Data!" said Picard. "I think you could have phrased the question a bit more tactfully than that. You're implying that the Honorable Kobry is not worthy of that designation."

"Am I?" said Data. "It was not my intention. But you, sir, are not addressed as 'Honorable Captain', nor Commander Riker as 'Honorable Riker' nor Geordi as—"

"I perceive your meaning," said Kobry quickly. "You must understand that, to Klingons, names are very important. Those who are highly honored, like myself, always have such titles as 'Honorable' placed before their names in direct address. Others who have distinguished themselves in battle, or have reached extremely high rank, are given the ultimate honor of not having their names spoken in direct address at all. At least by other Klingons."

"Why is that an honor?" asked Data. Picard himself was curious over that one.

"To speak someone's name is to establish a degree of familiarity," replied Kobry. "It gives you a certain power over someone with whom you talk, either bringing you up to their level or them down to yours. It's done to some degree on this ship. Those you consider your peers you address by given names. But you would not dream of addressing the captain as Jean-Luc, nor would I."

"Why?" asked Data. "Because you would not want to bring the captain up to your level, or you would not want to bring yourself down to his?"

And Kobry the diplomat and great thinker stood there, open-mouthed, temporarily brought to a halt by the innocent question. Picard graciously stepped in and said, "Because it would imply a degree of familiarity that does not exist."

"Thank you, Captain," said Kobry in mild relief.

"I've dealt with him longer than you have."

"So you see, Data." Kobry tried to bring the conversation back on track. "Our emperor is simply called Emperor, although certainly his name is on record in our history. The Klingon commander who was in charge of the ship that brought me here—a highly-ranked, well-respected warrior, who is simply addressed as Commander. No crewman would dare speak his full name. By the same token, the greatest punishment that can be inflicted upon a Klingon is to take his name away completely. Do you have any idea, Data, what it is like to have no name?"

Data considered that for a moment and Picard dreaded the answer. Any answer.

"It would be terrible," said Data.

"Absolutely," said Kobry, and Picard breathed a sigh of relief. "You see—"

"For one thing, you could never get any mail," said Data.

Oh lord, here we go, thought Picard.

"No one would ever be able to send you party invitations," Data continued. "And if you were being attacked on a planet, you couldn't say 'So-and-so to *Enterprise,* beam me up,' which could be fatal."

Korbry was starting to look shell-shocked.

"And of course it impedes conversation. For example, if someone wanted to say—"

"Data, *shut up!*" ordered Picard.

Data smiled graciously. "Thank you, sir. An excellent example. Let's say that Captain Picard wanted to say, 'Data, shut up!' If I had no name, he wouldn't be able to direct the comment to me and I would not know that he wanted me to shut up."

"Data, you have a name and it still didn't help," said Picard.

Data stared at Picard, processing what he had just

221

said, and it started to penetrate. "Oh," he said in a small voice. "Have I been babbling again?"

"Like a brook," said Picard.

"It is quite all right, young man," said Kobry. "The Klingon race can be somewhat stolid at times. Your enthusiasm is a refreshing change."

There was a tap on Data's shoulder as Geordi said, "Come on, Data. Riker says it's time to move out."

"The Honorable Riker," corrected Data.

Geordi shook his head, not even pretending to know what Data was talking about. Bidding their goodbyes, they left the Ten-Forward Room, along with Riker, and headed for the transporter room.

"Well," said Kobry, "that was invigorating." He glanced up. "Tron, are you enjoying the party?"

Tron, who had been standing nearby, nodded curtly.

"You don't look it," said Kobry. "Klingons never do," he confided in Picard before turning back.

"Gentlemen!" Picard said in a loud voice, and as always his commanding tone immediately caught the attention of everyone in the room. He raised his glass. "I'd like to propose a toast."

Kobry glanced around and picked up his drink from where he'd left it. All around, others were raising their glasses as well.

"To a new era of peace between the Klingons and the Kreel"—and he swung his glass in a slight arc— "the Kreel and the Klingons," he continued, ever mindful of the ego involved in both races. "We are pleased beyond measure that two races renowned for their prowess in battle were willing to come to the Federation and ask for aid in avoiding war that would have served no purpose. We have all come so far in our development, and we have brought ourselves this far by our own diligence, and intelligence, and dedication to a greater good."

"Hear-hear," was murmured throughout the Ten-Four Room.

"To the crew of the *Enterprise* and to her guests, I say . . . this is yet another signal that the best is yet to come."

He tilted back his glass and drank, as did the others.

There was a burst of applause and Picard smiled, bobbing his head slightly. From behind him, Kobry said, "Well spoken, Captain. You would make an excellent diplomat."

"So much of my job is diplomacy, Honorable Kobry, that it would not be much of a stretch, I assure you."

"I remember my early days," said Kobry. "I . . ."

Kobry staggered, suddenly grabbing for the edge of the table. He dropped his glass. The crashing noise was barely audible in the hustle and chatter of the party.

"Honorable Kobry?" said Picard. "What's wrong?"

Gava was standing a few yards away, talking with Worf, but with some sixth sense, she suddenly turned and saw her father. "Kobry!" she shrieked.

That brought attention immediately. All talk stopped as the dwarfish Klingon lost all control of his muscles and toppled over, gagging and clutching at his throat. His body was trembling and he was trying to talk, but he couldn't get a word out.

"Kobry!" shrieked Gava again, as she made it to him and dropped to the floor. "Father!"

"Picard to sickbay!" Picard shouted into his communicator, "Dr. Pulaski, emergency! Ten-Four Room!"

Kobry's pale eyes glazed over, and it was as if he

223

was looking straight through his daughter. His mouth moved but no words came out.

Worf picked up the fallen glass and studied it. He saw a faint residue along one edge.

"Poison," he said.

Picard's head snapped around. His voice a hoarse whisper, he spat out, "Are you sure?"

Worf nodded wordlessly.

Pulaski barrelled in, with a medivac cart and two med techs behind her.

"Out of my way!" she snapped, dropping next to Kobry and practically shoving Gava to one side. The Klingon woman staggered back, fighting off tears because Klingons did *not* cry, no matter what happened. She moved against a solid, comforting chest and knew without looking that it was Worf, but he said nothing to her, made no comforting gesture. His mind was racing forward, grasping the implications of this sudden, shocking scene.

Kobry had stopped moving, stopped breathing. Pulaski was running her medical tricorder over him and whatever it said, it couldn't have been good, because she quickly pulled a hypo from her bag. She injected him; the hiss of the hypo was the only sound in a room that had previously been deafening.

From the far end, Deanna Troi entered, having been in the hallway with Sklar when Kobry went down. Immediately, the ship's counselor was assaulted by wave-after-wave of concern, panic, anger, fury, all indistinguishable from one another.

Pulaski passed the tricorder over him one more time and all the blood drained from her face. Slowly, ashen, she turned to Picard.

"He's dead, Jean-Luc."

Chapter Seventeen

WILLIAM RIKER, Geordi La Forge, Data, and Security Man Tuttle materialized on the planet that the Kreel had termed "Hellhole." It was quickly evident to them why it was called that.

"Well, this is certainly pleasant," said Riker sarcastically. He glanced around and saw no signs of habitation. "We're sure these are the coordinates of where the Kreel found the weapons caché?"

"Absolutely," replied Geordi. Then he pointed. "Over there."

"Where? I don't see anything."

Geordi grinned. "Shame you don't have my eyes. Over there. I see signs of a fire. Carbon traces."

They headed in that direction and soon came upon a desolate sight. There had indeed been a fire there, a particularly nasty one: the entire area was scorched and charred. Riker glanced behind them, and saw that they had left a trail of footprints in the ash.

"This is definitely weird," said Geordi.

Data was crouching next to a small pile of metal

and was picking up a fragment, looking at it curiously. "Geordi, take a look at this," he said, extending the fragment to the chief engineer.

Geordi held it up to his face and ran a full spectroanalysis on it. Then he nodded. "Has the same bizarre trace compounds that the big one up in engineering had. This is the place, all right."

"So where are the scientists?" said Riker. Then he raised his voice, shouting, "Hello! Is anyone here? We're from the *Enterprise!*" He paused. "You should be expecting us!"

His voice echoed and eventually dwindled into silence. "No go," said Riker.

Data was studying his tricorder and now he pointed. "I'm picking up readings from that direction. Approximately five hundred meters, just over that ridge."

"Then that's where we go," said Riker with a shrug.

They started off. "Don't see why we had to do this now," Geordi grumbled. "We could have waited until the party was over."

"You Kreel bastards! You *poisoned* him!" howled Tron. His hand barely seemed to move, and suddenly there was a small, ugly looking blaster in it. *"Death to the Kreel!"*

"NO!" shouted Picard.

And the Kreel, God only knew how, produced phasers.

Immediately, the room was alive with screams, and Guinan ducked underneath the bar, wondering if perhaps this hadn't been such a hot idea after all.

With a blood curdling howl Aneel shouted, *"Death to the Klingon scum!"*

All hell broke loose.

The Kreel and the Klingons started firing at each

other, people started stampeding for the exits. It was complete chaos—Picard did not know which way to look first. It had been his greatest nightmare and here it was, on display for all to see. Not caring who was in the way or who got hurt, the Kreel and the Klingons tore into each other.

It took them mere seconds to realize that there were too many people for them to get clear shots, so the two groups charged toward each other, furiously hurling all others out of the way. The room was now filled with frantic people, falling over each other just to get out.

Worf tried to form a security squad to break up the riot but he was too late. They were outnumbered and outgunned, not to mention concerned about the safety of the crew members, something that worried the Klingons and Kreel not at all.

Gava crouched over the unmoving body of her father, and Katherine Pulaski threw one arm around Gava's shoulders, drawing her in tight. With the other hand she slapped her communicator and shouted "Transporter room! Three to beam directly to sickbay! Hurry!" Intraship beaming was hazardous, but Pulaski suspected the room was going to be even more so.

Within seconds, the transporter whine filled the room. Picard's head turned and he saw the doctor and the two Klingons vanish. *Quick thinking,* he thought, and then the flying body of a Klingon knocked him back off his feet.

He shoved the Klingon off himself and shouted, *"Worf! Stop them!"* Worf, however, was having his own troubles, for two of the Kreel had jumped him from behind, and smashed his face in to the floor. Pain shot through him and enraged him. He brought himself up to his knees, grabbed one of the struggling

Kreel in either hand, and hurled them against the far wall.

The Ten-Four Room was starting to empty out, and Picard realized, to his horror, that not only were the civilians vanishing, but so were the two warring races.

"My God! They're carrying this in to the corridors!"

And sure enough, he heard the sounds of phaser fire from outside, the sounds of screams and running feet.

A nightmare.

He had to take control immediately, had to do something. First things first.

"Worf!" he shouted. "Take your security people! Every able body you've got! Round up those lunatics and slap them in restraints. I don't care how many weapons the Klingons have on them. Strip them if you have to, but shut this down now!"

Worf turned, took five security men, and bolted from the room as well. Picard took two others, and went to the bridge.

What was left behind was a disaster area of overturned and broken furniture, as if a tornado had been through. Crushed and broken glass was scattered all over.

And slowly, Guinan's hat appeared, followed by Guinan. Her large eyes took in all the damage, the damage that would take forever to clean up.

"Last call," she said.

The away team stood before the large opening that served as the entrance to the underground. They looked at each other for a moment, and then Geordi made a sweeping "After you" gesture to Riker. Riker bowed slightly and walked in, followed by the others in single file.

They followed much the same route as the original

group of Kreel had, and eventually arrived at the same split in hallways.

"All right," said Riker. "Data with me, Geordi, you take Tuttle."

"Where do you think the scientists are?" said Geordi, utterly unaware that several charred lumps they had passed without even noticing on the way in, would have supplied the answer to that question.

"That's what we're trying to find out," said Riker. "Everyone stay in communication. No surprises. There's supposed to be a cease-fire, but you never know. Anything could happen."

"Attention all hands!" The captain's voice boomed over the entire ship. "We are in a state of emergency! All families are to remain in their quarters until the all-clear has been given. There will be no exceptions! If you leave your quarters, your lives may be in danger. Report to your quarters immediately and stay inside! There are Kreel and Klingon warriors fighting throughout the *Enterprise!*"

From all over the ship, wherever they were, there was a mad rush to get inside and out of harm's way. Lounges, and the like, were not safe, but private quarters at least could be locked.

Down in engineering, First Assistant LaVelle heard the announcement and wondered *what the hell* the problem was. She turned back to her work just in time to be blasted by a stray phaser blast.

Panic swept throughout the engineering deck as a Kreel warrior came charging through, with two Klingons hot on his heels. Lieutenant Palmeiro, on duty high up near the dilithium-recrystalization shielding, saw what was happening and shouted into his communicator, "Engineering to bridge! They're here! They're—"

The Kreel soldier heard this and took a brief moment to turn and fire off a perfect shot that picked off Palmeiro and sent him hurtling down three stories to land with a hideous crunch on the deck floor below. Then the Kreel dove headlong over a circuitry table as the Klingons opened fire with their blasters.

Then it was the Kreel's turn. The Klingons sought shelter behind the dilithium-chamber windows, but the phaser cracked through them, sending a shower of plasticene all over the infuriated warriors.

Trying to find shelter, one of the Klingons, who happened to be Derl, said, "I am an engineer."

The other Klingon, not quite seeing the point, said, "So?"

"So, if I have the layout of this place figured correctly, the Kreel bastard's hiding behind the console that channels the transporter circuitry to the power source. We manage to blow that, we not only take him, but we make sure that none of his friends manage to get away."

The other Klingon nodded. "I'm with you."

Of one mind, the two Klingons leaped into the open and charged the sheltered Kreel, howling at the top of their lungs and firing furiously.

The miniblasters the Klingons were packing weren't anywhere as deadly as phasers, but they could be devastating nevertheless. Several shots hit the console dead-center, blowing it apart. The Kreel warrior who had been hiding behind it was flung backward, and when he landed he screamed because a piece of metal had embedded itself in his leg.

Sparks flew and open circuitry lay exposed as the Klingons closed in on the now-helpless Kreel, and at that moment a security team led by Worf charged in.

The Klingons spun around, and Derl shouted,

"Worf! We have one of the bastards who poisoned the Honorable Kobry! Help us kill him!"

Worf aimed his phaser and fired. The blast took out the two Klingons, knocking them backward and into unconsciousness.

Worf crossed quickly and shoved his phaser into the face of the helpless Kreel. He thought about Kobry's unmoving form, and the grief-stricken Gava, and said tersely, "If you weren't defenseless right now, you'd be dead." Then he turned and stalked away from the Kreel as he slapped his communicator. "Worf to bridge." Without waiting for acknowledgment, he continued, "One Kreel, two Klingons out of commission. We're working on more."

Up on the bridge, Picard said, "Excellent, Worf. Keep at it. In the meantime, I want the bridge secured. No one to get up or down. I'm shutting down the turbolifts from here. That only leaves the emergency-access ladder that opens onto the deck below. Station two men there with a portable forcefield generator. The last thing we need is any of the combatants managing to get control of the bridge."

Even as he spoke, he was moving to the engineering station, where Marks was aiding him in carrying out his intentions. "Blast. I need Geordi back up here. This is taking too long. Picard to away team! Come in!"

On the planet surface, Riker stopped dead in his tracks. Data had had his interest piqued by a sign on the door of an empty room they had passed in one of the lower floors.

Riker touched his communicator. "Away team. Riker here."

"Mr. Riker, I'm bringing the four of you back up. In fact, I'll have you beamed directly here to the bridge."

"What's wrong, sir?"

"A bit much to explain at the moment, Number One. Transporter room . . . lock on to away team and energize."

Riker waited for the familiar mild feeling of disorientation, followed by his appearance on the bridge. But there was nothing. "Riker to bridge. What's happening up there?"

He heard a rather unexpected profanity from his captain, and then Picard said, "We're having trouble with the transporters, Number One. I'm afraid you'll be down there for a while."

"Captain, if there's something I can do to help . . ."

"I'm afraid the answer is no. Don't worry, Number One. We'll have the matter in hand. Picard out."

Riker had never felt quite as helpless as he did now. His place was aboard his ship, not here rummaging about some dusty ruins.

Data turned to Riker and said, "You may wish to take a look at this. These glyphs on the wall are identical to those found in a similar archeological dig decades ago. At first they corresponded to musical notes, but eventually a simple alpha-beta applica—"

"Can we skip all that, Data?"

"If you wish, sir."

"Can you read the sign? What does it say?"

"It says something to the effect of, 'Remarkably stupid weapon. Do not use.'"

Riker stared at him. "You're joking."

"I was? How splendid," said Data.

In the meantime, down another corridor, Geordi and Tuttle had made somewhat faster progress, but had resulted in arriving at a dead end.

"Now that's impressive," said Tuttle. He was pointing at two massive doors that came together in a vertical zigzag formation—doors that looked as if they had massive teeth clenched together. Next to the door was a multicolored keypad. On the floor was absolutely no trace of two small piles of goo which had been there at various times.

Geordi approached it. It gave no reaction. Unlike all of the other doors they had approached, this one did not seem the least bit interested in opening.

"I wonder why it won't open?" said Geordi. He ran a hand over the smooth metal, marveling at its perfection. "There must be something really important behind this."

"Only one way to find out," said Tuttle. He pulled out his phaser. "Stand back, sir. I'm going to blast it open."

Unfortunately, the individuals who could have told Tuttle what an exceptionally bad idea that would be were currently running around on the *Enterprise* endeavoring to kill Klingons. And one other individual—the one who had lost a hand in his abortive attempt to open the door—had been reduced to one of the aforementioned piles of goo. So he wasn't going to be of much help.

Tuttle took aim.

"Blast," grumbled Picard to Deanna. "I had the perfect idea, too. We could have done a sensor sweep of the inside of the ship, picked out the life readings of the Kreel and the Klingons, and beamed the lot of them into a transporter room with a security team waiting for them. Dangerous, but effective. Still . . ." He turned to Dykstra who was manning the ops station while Data was planetside. "Ops. Locate and track all Klingons and Kreel. Screen out Lieutenant Worf's personal biological profile. The least that we can do is give him some help by telling him where to look."

Jaan was hiding in his quarters, quaking with fear.

What had he done? In the name of Kolker, what had he done? It had seemed so harmless. No big deal. But it had all horribly, horribly backfired.

Suddenly a loud thudding sounded at the door. Jaan hesitated, and the sound was repeated. A gruff voice said, "Security!"

Quickly, Jaan went to the door and released the lock. The door slid open . . .

And Aneel, Deni, and two other Kreel shoved their way inside.

"Get out!" yelled Jaan.

Aneel shoved the elf against the wall. "Shut up," he snarled. "You're going to help us take the bridge."

"Like hell!"

Aneel drew him back and slammed him into the wall again, so hard his head rang. "Now you listen to me, you little slug! You're in as deep as we are. The Federation's going to want to know where we got the phasers, and if you don't help now, we'll tell them!"

"You—you wouldn't!"

"What would stop me, hmmm? Conscience? Sympathy?" he said derisively. "What do you think I am?"

"I'll . . ." Jaan tried to summon his bravado. "I'll tell you what you are"—and he tried to infiltrate Aneel's mind.

And their thoughts touched, and Jaan recoiled with a shriek, so overwhelmingly fierce was the Kreel.

"No, I'll tell you," said Aneel, ignoring Jaan's mental pain. "I am the one chance you have—the one chance of not being tried and convicted by the Federation and spending what little time you have remaining left rotting in prison. The one chance of living more

234

than the paltry few months your disease has given you. You need me, and if you don't realize that, I might as well put you out of your misery right now!"

There it was. One final test of Jaan's character. One chance to make up for what he had done by fearlessly facing down his captors.

"All right!" howled Jaan. "Just—just don't shoot!"

"Why shouldn't I shoot?" asked Tuttle.

"Because," Geordi said patiently, "I don't want you to damage this metal. Besides, there's no point. If it's anything as tough as the gun we have back up in the *Enterprise,* there's no way that your phaser's going to be able to cut through."

"So what do we do?"

"Well, I could always try the combination lock."

"The what?"

"This thing," said Geordi, indicating the keypad. "Probably touching it in a certain order will open the door."

"How do you know what the order is?"

"I don't," said Geordi cheerfully. "It'll take some experimentation, but I've got time." He turned, his hand hovering over the keypad. "After all, what's the worst that could happen?"

Chapter Eighteen

FIVE MINUTES BEFORE Geordi's hand hovered over death, Wesley Crusher floated in and out of consciousness. All he wanted to do was sleep, but he couldn't. He had to keep going, had to accomplish what he set out to do.

And he was so close. So close. It was there, just beyond him, just out of reach. Formulas he didn't quite understand, theories that danced just past his ability to assimilate. If he could just gather in the threads, he would be fine.

Just rest. But there was no time.

Something roused him. He didn't know what it was. Sounded like rain? Thunder? A storm, inside the ship? Didn't seem likely. He half giggled to himself in his delirium. They'd been predicting sunny weather.

Then he remembered. He'd heard something. Captain's voice. Something about people staying in? Was it really raining? *Stay in so you won't get wet?*

Wesley picked up some notes that he had written to himself. When he'd scribbled them, at the time, they had made perfect sense. Now, though, someone had replaced them with garbage. He stared at the notes in confusion. Gibberish. Gibberish in his handwriting.

Who had done this? Who was trying to sabotage his work? And why was it so damned hard to think clearly?

He scratched his face and was astounded to find beard stubble. But that was ridiculous. He was only sixteen, and his facial hair came in very slowly. It took him the better part of a week to acquire five-o'clock shadow. He couldn't have gone without shaving that long. He'd only been working on the cure, what, two days? Three at the outside? How long?

"How long?" Wesley heard his own voice croak.

There was more running, more shouting.

An emergency. There was an emergency on the ship.

He stood, swaying in his cabin. What was he doing in there, hiding, if there was an emergency? He was needed, dammit. He was an acting ensign. And it was high time he started acting like one.

He staggered into the bathroom, leaned over the sink, and allowed the jet spray of water to hit him in the face. He turned away, water dripping from him, his hair and the front of his shirt now soaking wet.

"Got to help them," he said. "Got to get to the bridge. They need me."

He lurched out into his room and fell, slamming into a computer console. He yelled and made a grab for it as it fell to the floor with a crash, and he heard something inside it shatter. Oh, man, Pulaski was going to kill him. But that didn't matter.

He turned away. None of it mattered—just saving the ship. That was his job. That's why they paid him "the big money." He laughed merrily at an expression that had lasted even though it no longer had any meaning.

He stepped out of the door of his cabin, still chuckling to himself, and got run over.

The portable force-shield generator had been created by none other than Wesley Crusher. At one time, it had been rather effectively used to keep the embattled *Enterprise* crew out of the engineering section during the occasion that the whole crew had run amok. Since then, it had been slightly modified and was now a favored tool of the security team in situations just like this one.

The security team of Meyers and Boyajian, a team with ancestors going all the way back to the *Enterprise* Model NCC 1701-A, had been chosen to man the access ladder that was the only available means of getting up to the bridge. The turbolifts had been shut down, as Picard had ordered. The access ladder was to be used only in emergencies, but was always open. No one had ever considered the possibility that anyone would *want* to cut off the bridge.

So Meyers and Boyajian had positioned themselves at the bottom of the ladder, crouched on the floor, the shield created by the generator providing them with more than adequate cover. From where they were, they had a clear field of vision in either direction down the hallway. Any shots at them would bounce harmlessly off the force shield. They, by the same token, could return fire with impunity; their field of vision was completely unobstructed behind the translucent shield.

At first, the halls had been filled with running, frantic people. Now, however, the action had died down and it seemed long minutes since they had last seen anyone.

And then a figure came around a corner.

Boyajian saw it first, swinging his phaser up and shouting, "Halt! Stay back!"

"Hold it," said Meyers. "It's the elf."

Sure enough, hands draped behind his back as if he were taking a leisurely Sunday stroll, Jaan walked down the corridor, whistling lightly.

"Didn't you hear the captain?!" shouted out Meyers. "Stay in your quarters!"

"We're at *red alert,*" seconded Boyajian.

Jaan stopped a few feet away and stared directly into their eyes. "Haven't you heard?"

"Heard what?" said Meyers slowly.

"Oh for the love of—I can't believe they didn't tell you! It's over! They rounded up everybody."

"They did?" said Boyajian. "I . . ." (and why was it getting hard to concentrate) "I was hoping they would, but—"

"Well, of course," said Jaan, coming closer, smiling in his friendliest manner. "I'm surprised you hadn't been informed. Everything's back to normal."

Meyers sat back on his heels. "Wheeww"—he let out a *whooosh* of air—"That's certainly a relief."

"Glad we got that settled," said Jaan.

"You bet! Thanks. We'd have looked like idiots crouched behind here."

Meyers stood, stretching his legs as Boyajian reached down and snapped off the force-shield generator.

The moment he did, Jaan hit the floor.

"Are you okay?" Meyers started to ask, and then both he and Boyajian were cut down as the high-pitched whine of phasers surrounded them. They fell, clawing at air as they were knocked cold.

Aneel came toward them, along with the other Kreel, and he was shaking the phaser in irritation. "I

239

thought I had it set to kill finally," he said. "I thought this knob was all you had to turn. You must have to do something with the power lever too. Oh well"—and he waved his phaser in the direction of the access ladder. "Let's go."

"I've done all you asked me to," said Jaan.

"So far. You can still continue to be valuable, elf, so you're coming along."

"No more!" said Jaan furiously. "I went with you this far, but—"

"It's always easy to say you'll go just this far and no further, isn't it?" Aneel sneered. "One more easy step on the road to hell, and before you realize it you're knocking at the door. Now if you want that cure, get up there!"

Jaan stood there, bristling for a moment, but in short order his resolve failed, and he turned and started to climb up the ladder.

Tron made his way cautiously down the hallway, darting inside Jeffries tubes, looking for whatever cover he could find.

A phaser bolt shot past him just off his shoulder. He dropped, pulled a throwing star from inside his sash and hurled it without even looking. He heard a satisfyingly truncated scream and turned just in time to see a Kreel staggering back, the throwing star embedded in his forehead. Blood was pouring down and it was nothing short of miraculous that the Kreel was even alive, much less on his feet.

Tron slowly advanced on him, grinning, and he grabbed the dying Kreel, whose pig-like eyes had already lost their focus, and he snarled in his face, "You sleep in hell tonight, you bastard."

The Kreel slammed his head forward, the throwing star still jutting out.

Tron screeched as the throwing star ripped into his eye, and he hurled the Kreel back, grabbing at his ruined face, clutching at the now-destroyed right eye socket. Pain such as he had not imagined possible threatened to overwhelm him. The throwing star clattered to the floor, Klingon and Kreel blood comingled, and Tron clapped a hand over his lacerated eye socket and staggered forward.

He tripped over the corpse of the Kreel, who had predeceased him by mere seconds. But Klingons, he swore, did not die so easily. He plunged forward, scooping up the Kreel's phaser as he went, and stumbled into a turbolift.

"Sickbay," he groaned, for that was the only place he could think of to go. *The damned Kreel! The damned Kobry! Damn them all to hell!*

As the turbolift shot toward its destination he ripped off a piece of his tunic and, trying not to think about what he was doing, stuffed it into where his eye had been to stop the bleeding. He was gasping for breath and his mind was trying to shut down because of the pain, but he wouldn't let it. He . . . would . . . not . . . let it.

He was a Klingon, and while a single Kreel breathed, he would do whatever it took.

The turbolift halted and the doors slid open. Tron lurched to his feet and staggered out into the hallway.

No one around. And there, just ahead, was sickbay.

He ran up to the doors and slammed headlong into them.

They hadn't opened! The damned doors hadn't opened! Well they wouldn't keep him out! He swung the phaser up and fired point-blank, blasting a huge, smoking hole in the doors and eliciting a satisfying shout of alarm from within.

He stepped through, shouting, "Doctor! Where's the damned Doc—"

And then he froze in midword.

There, standing next to a med table, was Gava. Lying on the table was the Honorable Kobry.

Sitting up. Staring at him. Alive.

Alive.

"You . . . it . . . you can't be," stammered Tron. "I—"

"Poisoned me?" said Kobry, and he still sounded weak. But alive, impossibly alive. "Is that what you were going to say?"

"No," Tron said. "No, I . . . I didn't . . ."

"I realized afterward that you were standing nearby when I was foolish enough to put my drink down," said Kobry, clearly annoyed with himself. "And here I had been talking about turning one's back on an enemy."

"It's a trick!" yelled Tron.

"Someone should take care of that eye," said Kobry mildly.

"What I'll do is take care of *you!*" shouted Tron, and he brought his phaser up point-blank, aiming at the Klingon ambassador who lay helpless a mere ten feet away.

Gava leaped over the bed, prepared to intercept the phaser blast with her own body.

And at that moment a twenty-pound Wasserman Chamber came hurling through the air from med lab II, crashing into Tron and knocking him back. He smacked into the wall and the world, which was already less than solid, began to spin around him.

Standing in the doorway, adrenaline pumping, Dr. Katherine Pulaski summoned all the fury and indignation she could muster. *"Get the hell out of my sickbay!"* she bellowed, at the same time hitting her

242

comm link. "Security! There's a lunatic in my sickbay! Get him!"

Grabbing at his bleeding eye, Tron lunged out into the corridor. He heard the sounds of running feet coming from one end of the corridor, so he headed down the other.

Blood was now starting to work its way into his other eye. He reached up, tried to wipe the blood away, and, for a moment, was completely blinded.

That happened to be the moment that Wesley Crusher stepped out of his quarters.

The Klingon crashed into Wesley, and, if the Klingon had been at full strength and concentration, Wesley would have gone flying as if he were weightless. As it was the two of them went down in a tangle of arms and legs.

"Get off me!" howled Tron as he shoved Wesley away.

And Wesley was now completely snapped out of his confusion and lethargy, except that he now found himself staring down the business-end of a phaser.

Tron had scrambled to his knees and he snarled, "I'm ready to kill something and you're it."

A booted foot kicked Tron in the chest.

He fell back on the floor, grunting as his head hit once again. Now he was completely blind and someone of great strength was hauling him to his feet.

"Still wish to know where my allegiance is?"

Tron recognized the voice immediately. "Worf! You've got to help me."

"Shut up," snapped Worf, and he drew back and slugged the Klingon once across the face. Mercifully, Tron fell into unconsciousness.

Tossing Tron over his shoulder, Worf headed for the nearest holding cell.

"Worf, what's going on around here?"

"The Kreel and Klingon ambassadorial parties are endeavoring to kill each other." That was all Worf had any interest in saying. When he got to the holding cell he heaved the Klingon in and activated the force screen.

"But—but Worf!" said Wesley. "He's bleeding in there!"

"So what?" replied Worf as he tapped his communicator. "Worf to bridge."

"Picard here."

And Wesley suddenly said, "I know what to do!" Worf's angry scowl did not even begin to quiet him. "We do an internal sensor scan, find all the Klingons and Kreel, beam them all into one transporter room and you have them all rounded up!"

Picard overheard this and said tightly, "Thank you for your insight, Mr. Crusher. How nice of you to rejoin the living, at least temporarily. However, the transporters are down. The power coupling circuitry has been destroyed in engineering."

Immediately, Wesley called to mind the schematics for the transporter. "All right," he said, and it was as if his thoughts were a million miles away. "All right . . . give me five minutes and I can rewire a transporter console. A cargo transporter would be best. It's got the largest circuit board. It's the easiest to work with. And it's the largest capacity, which is what we'll want."

"Captain, did you hear all that?" asked Worf.

There was a momentary pause and then, with great reluctance, as if bowing to the inevitable, Picard said, "Yes, I heard. Worf, can you get him there?"

"Of course," replied the Klingon. He turned to Wesley and said tersely, "You have a bodyguard. Let's go."

* * *

On the bridge, Picard was shaking his head and he turned toward Deanna Troi, who had arrived scant minutes before. "That's all we need," he said. "Mr. Crusher saves the ship . . . again."

"It would certainly be grist for Dr. Pulaski's mill," agreed Deanna. "But better to—"

Suddenly, her head snapped to the side, and her back arched in the chair. Immediately, Picard was on his feet. "Counselor!"

"They're coming!" shrieked Deanna. "I feel them! Loathsome! Hideous!"

"Who's coming, Deanna?" Picard shouted. "Who!"

At that moment on ops, Dykstra said, "Captain! I've tracked down three more Kreel! They're . . ."

"On the bridge."

Aneel had completed the sentence. He and the other Kreel had their phasers out and aimed directly at Picard and his crew.

"Back away," said Aneel. He waved his phaser at the seated officers at conn and ops. To their credit, they looked to Picard for guidance. He made a subtle gesture that they should rise from their seats and back up, which they did.

"What do you want?" Picard said slowly.

"We want your ship," replied Aneel. "All for us."

"It's what you wanted all along, isn't it?"

"Yes, Captain. Exactly what we wanted. With the kind of technology that can make us great."

"The kind of technology you're not ready for."

"Oh, how kind of you to be concerned for us." Aneel's voice was dripping with sarcasm. "Place your hands behind your head. That's right. That's better." He eyed Troi in particular, as she did so, and grinned that broken-toothed grin.

"I want you off my bridge," said Picard with barely-contained fury.

Aneel was impressed not at all. "I'll just bet you do," he replied. "I'll just bet."

But now Picard wasn't even looking at the Kreel. His attention was drawn to the tall, ethereal-looking youth who stood at the back of the bridge, quivering in misery. "Jaan?" he said. "What the devil are you doing here?"

"Oh him?" said Aneel indifferently. "He sold us himself, a little piece at a time. Don't worry. It didn't hurt." He studied the small cluster of humans carefully. "We promised him a cure for his disease in exchange for his help."

Jaan closed his eyes in pain. There went any hope of his ever recapturing his past life. Then again, what was there to recapture?

"Poor, pathetic bastard," said Aneel. "You know, he's worked so hard for it. I think I should give him his cure right now."

He swung the phaser around at Jaan and aimed.

It took Jaan a full second to realize what was happening. In that instant, Picard lunged for the Kreel leader, only to be knocked back by Deni. Troi tried to shout out a warning, for all the good it would have done.

The phaser beam lashed out and surrounded Jaan. Even as it did, in a last ditch effort he reached out for Aneel. He hadn't made it half a step when Jaan, with an agonized shriek, saw the world split apart.

Then there was nothing, no sound at all except the noise of air rushing in to fill the vacuum that the Selelvian had left.

Aneel made a satisfied grunt. "So that's how 'kill' works on this thing. Any other takers?"

"You . . . monster!" shouted Picard in outrage.

"You still say that? You insult me, Captain. All you had was a stinking traitor in your midst. I helped isolate and eliminate him for you. And I didn't even lie to him, really. He wanted a cure for the Rot. Well, death cures everything, doesn't it?" And he laughed that coarse laugh.

And at that moment, a familiar voice came over the intercom.

Unaware of the crisis that had occurred on the bridge, Worf's voice came over the speaker saying, "Worf to bridge. Come in, Captain."

Picard hesitated, realizing that silence would bring the security squad on the run. He saw Aneel aim the phaser at him in a no-nonsense manner, and then Aneel suddenly swung the phaser around and aimed it directly at Deanna Troi. His intention was unmistakable, as was his expression.

"Picard here," he said carefully. "Yes, Lieutenant?"

"We made it to cargo Transporter Room C, sir. Wesley is working on the transporter circuitry now. In a few minutes, if all goes well, we'll be prepared to transport all the Klingons and Kreel here. That should effectively end the crisis."

"Good work, Lieutenant," he said. "Picard out"— and he broke the connection before Worf could inadvertently give anything else away.

It was too late, however. Aneel spun around and snarled at the others, "You stay here! I'll get down to the transporter room and put a stop to this!" He grinned. "Worf. How marvelous. I've wanted a piece of that smug Klingon bastard from the moment I got on this ship."

The transporter chief was shaking his head in amazement as Wesley worked under the console, rerouting the relays so that the blown-out circuitry in engineering was being completely bypassed. "Amazing," he was saying.

"Quiet!" snapped Wesley, trying to keep everything straight in his head. He had been muttering almost constantly since he'd started, trying not to lose track of anything as he went. If he did the results would be seriously unpleasant.

At that moment a sudden alarmed cry came over the communicator. Wesley sat up so fast he slammed his head against the underside of the console.

"La Forge to transporter! Beam me up! Quick!"

Worf immediately tapped his communicator and said, "La Forge, the transporter is down. We're working on repairing it. What's wrong?"

No answer.

"Geordi! Come in!" This from Wesley, shouting urgently to the man who had become his mentor. "We're trying to fix it! Can you hang on a few minutes more?"

No answer.

"Oh God," moaned Wesley, and dropped beneath the console once more. And now his fingers seemed to fly across the circuitry with a life of their own. Inside of two minutes, he called out, "Okay! Try it now!"

The transporter chief manipulated the controls, and a familiar hum began to fill the chamber. But it was unsteady, its beams flickering in a most unhealthy manner. "I'm trying surface-to-ship," called the transporter chief. "But I'm not getting sufficient gain. There isn't a steady enough signal to calibrate around."

"One thing at a time," shot back Wesley. "Try ship to surface. Beaming down."

The transporter chief reversed the beam, and this time Worf, who was standing a couple of feet away, thought that the beam looked stronger, steadier.

"That's it," called out the Klingon. "That's better. That's . . ."

The Kreel's entrance was so swift, so savage, that it even caught Worf off-guard. The door was blasted open, and the transporter chief spun to shout a warning cut short as he was struck dead-center by the phaser and vanished into nothingness.

The Kreel darted across the room even as Worf whipped his own phaser around and fired. The blast sent sparks and debris flying from the wall behind as the Kreel darted behind the transporter console. The beams were still activated, shimmering blue lights rippling on the platform, projecting downward although there was nothing in them to go down.

Worf dodged to one side, and fired even as he went into motion. His phaser (unfortunately, he would later decide) was not set on kill. Only stun. He winged the Kreel, sending the hideous alien's phaser flying from his grasp in one direction while the Kreel himself fell behind the transporter console. Worf saw the phaser skid across the floor, safely out of the Kreel's reach, and congratulated himself on a excellent shot.

He couldn't see the Kreel from behind the console, but it didn't matter. He advanced on him, calling out in his deep voice, "Surrender."

"Death first!" came the Kreel response and then suddenly he sprang up into view. He had one arm around Wesley's neck. The other was against the boy's head, prepared to shove it very quickly and very efficiently.

"Now *you* surrender, Klingon. Before this boy's shoulders become lonesome for his head."

"Let go of the boy," said Worf warningly, his phaser never wavering, "and back away slowly, or you'll regret it."

"Not as much as he will," said Aneel. "Isn't that right, boy?"

He shook Wesley slightly, and Wesley groaned fearfully in his massive grasp.

"Worf," he gasped out, "get him."

But Worf couldn't bring himself to move. His phaser still didn't waver, but he made no approach.

"One step," said the Kreel. "Take one step and, snap, he's gone. Just like that." He moved so that Wesley remained between himself and Worf. "You think I'm helpless because I don't have a phaser?"

"I think you're helpless because you need a young boy to hide behind," said Worf with a sneer.

"Really? Well I should warn you, Klingon. I've killed one young boy today. A second will be even less of a challenge."

There was dead silence in the transporter room, broken only by the humming of the transporter beams.

"What . . . young boy?" said Worf very slowly, very dangerously.

"The elf," laughed Aneel.

Wesley froze as if his blood had turned to ice water. "You're . . . you're lying."

"The elf," repeated Aneel. "The one called Jaan. I blasted him out of existence myself, and enjoyed watching his face as he vanished. And you'll be next, boy, if you move. Now, Klingon . . . drop your weapon."

"You're—you're lying."

"Shut up, boy. I'm not talking to—"

"YOU'RE LYING!"

Furious, horrified beyond all imagining, Wesley suddenly planted his feet against the transporter console and shoved backward with all his strength—strength augmented by an overwhelming need to get his hands on the Kreel, to wring from him a confes-

250

sion that he had been lying, that Jaan was alive, was hale and hearty, that it hadn't all been useless. It had to be a lie. It had to!

It was as if Wesley had suddenly been jolted with a live wire. Given strength by hysterics, he started struggling wildly in the grip of the Kreel, totally oblivious to danger. He stomped, he kicked, he smashed his head against the Kreel's face, he did anything and everything and all the while screaming over and over—"You're lying! You are! You're lying!" —Over and over, like a chant.

Worf moved in quickly as Aneel found to his shock that he couldn't hold the boy anymore. And now there was no time, for Worf was upon him. There was no time to reposition his broken grip on the boy, so he did the only thing he could: He grabbed Wesley by the arm and flung him with all his strength against the far wall. Wesley slammed into it at high speed and slumped to the ground.

Aneel barely had the chance to bring his arms up to defend himself as Worf smashed into him, driving him back and slamming him against the wall. The Kreel brought his feet up, coiled like a spring and planted them against Worf's chest. Then he uncoiled, sending the Klingon staggering back with a grunt. He took two steps and leaped, covering the distance and grabbing Worf by the throat, pulling him down.

Worf's phaser flew out of his grasp, sailed across the room and into the transporter beams. It promptly vanished, projected down to the planet surface below.

Worf brought his fist around with high speed, bashing it into the Kreel's face repeatedly. His first blow broke the Kreel's nose, and the second and third caused a huge welt to swell up over the Kreel's right eye. It didn't slow down Aneel in the least, as he pounded at Worf with all the brute strength he had at his command.

They struggled, standing, throwing their full weight against each other, each trying to bear the other down. Suddenly Worf brought his leg around behind the Kreel's, jamming it backward and causing the Kreel's knee to bend forward. The Kreel slammed to the ground and then Worf was on top of him, and it was wonderful, just wonderful as his warrior blood sang to him and he dug his fingers into what passed for a neck on a Kreel. His corded muscles rippling, Worf started to squeeze in on the neck of the self-proclaimed murderer, on the enemy of the Klingons, on the stinking bastard Kreel.

The Kreel pig eyes bulged with alarm as he could no longer get enough air to breathe. Worf bore down on him and there was no pity in his eyes. His teeth were clenched and he felt his pulse pounding in his head, the pounding that demanded revenge, revenge for himself, for his parents, for Jaan and Wesley and who-knew-who-else, revenge all wrapped up in this beautiful complete package.

And the Kreel managed to grunt out one word.

"Mercy," he said.

Worf froze. Blood from ruptured capillaries in the Kreel's neck was already welling up through his mouth, covering Worf's hands. Aneel was choking, gagging under Worf's iron grip.

So easy. Just a quick twist. Just like in the holodeck. Remember how satisfying that had been? This would be even more so.

Just . . . so easy.

And, to Worf's astonishment as much as that of the Kreel, the pressure began to ease on the Kreel's throat.

"Mercy," said Worf, as if trying on a new shoe to see if it fit. "Mercy."

252

The instant he was able to take a deep breath, the Kreel brought a fist up straight into Worf's face.

Worf's head snapped back as if on strings, and blood gushed out of his nose. Another blow to the chest, and Worf fell over and landed on his back several feet from the transporter platform.

The Kreel scrambled about and leaped forward, bringing his knees down into Worf's gut and knocking the air out of him. Worf, the world spinning around him, tried to ward off the Kreel as he brought a series of furious punches raining down on Worf's unprotected head.

"This is for the years of oppression!" howled Aneel in a paroxysm of fury. "This is for my murdered fellows! This is for our slaughtered people! And this! *And this!*"

He tore at Worf's sash, and a dagger fell out of concealment. Hardly believing his good fortune, Aneel grabbed up the dagger and tried to bring it slamming down into Worf's neck. Worf barely saw it in time as he blocked it with his forearm. Aneel kept bearing down, bringing all his strength into play as the knife point hovered closer and closer to Worf's throat.

Through gritted teeth, the Kreel said, "You should have killed me when you had the chance, you bastard."

Worf, on his back, moved his leg slightly and then brought his knee slamming up in between the Kreel's legs. There was a hideous crunching sound and the Kreel screamed as Worf, with all his strength, shoved the Kreel forward and over his head in a last ditch effort to survive.

To his surprise, Aneel suddenly stopped struggling. Just like that. The scream of pain had also stopped just as quickly.

He rolled the Kreel's unmoving body off himself and stood. And then he saw, and he could scarcely believe it.

The Kreel's head was gone.

His head and his upper shoulders had vanished, just . . . *poof.* And then he realized what had happened. The Kreel had been thrust forward into the activated transporter beams. The rest of him had been held firm in Worf's grip, but the head and upper shoulders had been within the transporter field. And the transporter beams, being efficient, sent anything that got within their field to the point below.

Usually, of course, there was no problem, since people who were about to travel made sure that they were standing entirely on the platform. Aneel, however, was not.

Worf stood and dusted himself off. Then, so as not to be untidy, he picked up the rest of the body and hurled it into the beams. They followed the rest of the head to the surface.

Then he went to the transporter console to attend to other business.

The Kreel on the bridge were starting to feel a bit nervous. "How much longer do you think Aneel will be?" asked Deni.

At that moment everyone on the bridge vanished.

Virtually at the same time, they rematerialized in the transporter room. In the instants that it took the Kreel to realize what had happened, it was too late. Picard and Marks together hurled the Kreel from the transporter platform and Worf, having retrieved the phaser that the late Aneel had dropped, blasted them into unconsciousness.

Picard saw Wesley lying there unconscious and

immediately went to him. He knelt down, looked up at Worf and said, "Is he all right?"

"He took a bad spill, but I think he'll be all right."

"What about the other Kreel? He was coming down here."

"Oh him." Worf paused. "He got ahead of himself."

The rest of it took no more than fifteen minutes.

Worf, displaying laudable accuracy, sent the rest of the bridge crew back to where they'd been. Dykstra quickly located the rest of the Klingons and the Kreel who were stalking the *Enterprise* corridors, and fed the information down to Worf. To their shock, they found themselves one moment engaged in life-and-death struggles throughout the Galaxy-class ship, and the next they were suddenly in a transporter room, being held at phaser-point by an extremely irritated-looking security group.

Things were just starting to calm down.

"Now," said Picard from his command chair, "re-establish contact with the away team. Tell them that—"

And Deanna Troi gasped.

"Counselor?" said Picard.

Deanna actually seemed to shrink back in her chair and she pointed toward the viewscreen, stammering, unable to form so much as a syllable.

"Counselor Troi!" said Picard in alarm. "What's wrong? What's—"

And then he saw it, as did the rest of the bridge crew. He could have sworn he heard a collective scream from the entire ship.

The stars were moving.

"What the hell . . .?" said Dykstra.

Impossibly, insanely, all the stars on the screen

began to come together. Meteors, asteroids, all other astronomical phenomenon coalesced, spinning and swirling in an incomprehensible ballet beyond the grasp of physics. Beyond the grasp of sanity.

There, in the far distance, space fluctuated and rippled as the stars began to cluster in new configurations. They began to mold themselves as if being sculpted. But it was absurd! The stars they were seeing consisted of light from stars not as they were, but as they had been, since light needed time to travel. There could be no sort of phenomenon that could affect all stars at the same time!

"Away team!" shouted Picard. "Come in!"

And he heard Riker shout, "Captain!"

"Prepare to beam up! I'm bringing you straight to the bridge! Transporter room, activate!"

And Worf, down in the transporter room, acted upon the instructions.

And there, on the bridge, materialized Riker, Data and Tuttle . . . but not Geordi.

"Number One! Where's Mr. La Forge?"

"He's gone, Captain! He—" Then he saw what was happening.

The stars were taking shape. Forming the ridges of a face. A human face that spanned light-years in distance, that took up their whole screen. That was millions upon millions of miles away and was so close you could practically reach out and touch it.

The face hovered there in space, glowing with the light of a thousand-thousand stars. Meteors made up its eyes, comets formed its hair.

It stared at them.

And then it smiled.

"Oh my God," said Riker.

"Oh," said Data, now understanding. "Is that who it is."

Chapter Nineteen

"WHAT'S THE WORST that could happen?" Geordi had asked earlier, which certainly fell under the category of famous last words.

As he reached for the keypad, he heard Riker and Data, nearby, calling to them.

"Why don't you go check what they want," said Geordi. "Bring them over here. I'll be working on this in the meantime."

Tuttle walked off and Geordi proceeded to punch buttons experimentally, just to see if there was anything he could detect on any infrared or ultraviolet scale.

He heard a faint hum, which quickly became a high-pitched whine. Like something being activated.

What the heck? he thought.

Then he looked down.

Crisscrossed over his feet were horizontal beams of light outside the visible spectrum. They hadn't been there before. They had just started being projected out of the wall, about six inches off the ground. They were pencil-thin and overlapping in just such a way that, miraculously, Geordi was standing in between them. A half-step left, right, forward or back and he would have stepped right into them. And then—

Then what?

Suddenly, he got the distinct feeling that it would be better if he didn't know. He lifted one of his feet to try and step over them.

The beams began to widen.

Immediately, Geordi did the only thing he could. He leaped straight upward, and as the beams expanded, jammed himself into position above them, bracing himself with his legs on one side of the narrow corridor and his arms on the other. He was now suspending himself several feet off the ground, kept there by sheer muscle power and panic.

"Data!" he shouted. "Riker! Tuttle even!"

A distance away, the other three members of the away team reacted in surprise, particularly because they were heading in a different direction.

"Tuttle, I thought you said Geordi was this way," snapped Riker.

"I—I thought he was," said Tuttle in confusion.

"Data, where is he?"

Data had already consulted his tricorder. Each person's communicator contained individual biological information that made them easy to find. Easy, at least, when one wasn't being led astray by confused security men.

"Follow me," said Data.

Meanwhile, Geordi's hands were starting to sweat as he saw the entire floor was now one solid mass of beams about twelve-foot-square. There was nowhere for him to go.

He risked falling into them to slap his communicator and, indeed, almost did fall before slamming his hand back against the wall. *"La Forge to transporter! Beam me up! Quick!"*

The pause was brief and then he heard, of all people, Worf. "La Forge, the transporter is down. We're working on repairing it. What's wrong?"

Down? *Now* it was down?!

Realizing that the *Enterprise* was going to be of no help, he tried to tap his communicator again to open a new line to Riker. This time, however, he moved too quickly, jostling the communicator and sending it falling into the beams.

It dissolved.

Geordi felt his hands slipping, his boots unable to keep traction on the wall. He tried to readjust and it wasn't doing any good. And he shouted at the top of his lungs the one thing the Kreel had never said: *"HEELLLPPP!"*

And a polite female voice said, "Help requested?"

It seemed to come from everywhere and nowhere. Geordi looked around frantically as he said, "Yeah! Help requested!"

"Specify," she said calmly.

"Turn off the beams!"

"As you wish."

The beams promptly went off.

Geordi could scarcely believe it. It couldn't have been that simple. Tentatively he stepped down and, sure enough, he was still in one piece.

"Do you need further help?"

"Yeah," said Geordi slowly. "I wanted to get through this door. Please."

"As you wish."

He was through.

Geordi spun and looked behind him. The door had vanished. He was just simply on the other side.

"This is . . . this is crazy," said Geordi slowly. "All I had to do to get out of that death trap . . . and get through that door . . . is ask nicely?"

The disembodied voice said primly, "Good manners never hurt."

"Yeah, but . . ."

"It's indicative of intelligence. And maturity."

"Okay. Fine."

Geordi looked around to see the room that had been so securely guarded. The room that had almost cost him his life.

It was empty.

There was minimal light from a source that Geordi couldn't locate. Of course, he didn't need light. He looked around, trying to figure out the parameters of the room.

He couldn't find anything. He started to walk toward what he assumed to be a wall and, after several minutes that seemed like hours, it started to dawn on him that he wasn't going to get to there.

"You . . . still here?" he asked.

"Yes."

"Who are you?"

"Who are you?" it replied.

"Lieutenant Geordi La Forge. Chief Engineer. Starship *Enterprise.*"

"Greetings, Lieutenant. I am."

"You are?"

"Yes."

"Oh." That was of no help whatsoever. It was like trying to have a conversation with Data on a bad day . . .

Data! Of course! This thing was a machine.

"Are you a machine?"

"If it will help you to describe me that way."

260

Geordi sighed. "How would *you* describe you?"

"In terms you can understand?" She paused. "The welcoming committee."

"Did you welcome the Kreel?"

"No. They were merely a means to an end. They were not ready to meet us. We did not wish to meet them. But they brought you here, and so served our purpose."

"Served your purpose?" Geordi said incredulously. "They took your weapons and went crazy with them! They cost lives!"

"Lives cannot be cost," she replied. "They are merely different forms of energy, and energy cannot be destroyed. It's all the same."

"Look," said Geordi, trying to come at it from a different angle, "What's the big deal about this room? Why all those protective devices and everything for an empty room?"

"This room isn't empty."

"Well, what's in it then?"

She sounded so peaceful as she said, "Everything."

"What?"

"This room has no boundaries. It goes on forever, to all sides, to infinity. That is why it was important for you to enter here. You, Geordi La Forge, can see things as they really are."

"Uh-huh," said Geordi slowly, not understanding. "So?"

"Others would enter this room and see things as they think they are. It would drive them quite mad."

"Yeah. Well look, I have to admit I'm not feeling exactly too stable right now, myself. Would you at least tell me what purpose is being served by my being here."

"That's simple."

"I'm glad something is." Geordi sighed.

"When you entered this room, it served to summon them."

"Who?"

"The Cognoscente."

The star face floated before the *Enterprise,* massive beyond all measuring.

"This is . . ." Picard licked his lips, cleared his throat, and started again. "This is Captain Jean-Luc Picard of the Starship *Enterprise.* Identify yourself please."

There was a long pause. And when the face spoke it was without words, and yet they all understood.

We have a variety of names. We prefer simply the Cognoscente.

"Who . . . are you?"

We are those who have been waiting for you. We created this planet, with all its weapons, as a test to see how you would handle hostilities between two races. To see how well you could impart the lessons you've learned.

"Ah!" said Data brightly. "A test! I was right. Geordi won't be at all pleased."

"Oh no," moaned Picard. "Not a test."

"Oh yes, sir," said Data. "I was very certain that . . ."

"Shut up, Data."

"Yes, sir."

"Are you saying," Picard said, anger building slowly, "that all this—all the death, all the destruction and suffering—has been yet another test to keep beings like yourselves amused."

Not just this test. There have been other instances of death and destruction and suffering. They have always been for you to learn and grow.

"What?" said Picard, incredulous. "You've . . . done things like this before."

Always for a reason.

"Your reasons."

Yes. So that you could grow. And now the testing is over. Now we are here to take you by the hand. To—

It all came crashing down on Picard. All the tension, all the anger, all the fury, and now this—this damnable cavalier attitude by yet another race that fancied itself to be the judge and jury of mankind.

"NO!" shouted Picard. "I have had it! *We* have had it! All of us! We are sick to death of mysterious Alien races who think they know better than us! Who think that we're little white mice to run through mazes for their amusement!

"We are not test subjects! We are not guinea pigs! You, all you blasted 'superior' races, have the gall to arrange these massive, insane tests and act as if your ability to manhandle us makes you better. It does not! We have come this far, not because of beings like yourselves, but despite you all! Despite all those throughout history who have called us barbarians and sought to judge us. We have brought ourselves this far and we'll bring ourselves further still.

"And you can keep your hands to yourselves, and you can keep your tests to yourselves! Is that understood! We will not be threatened! We will not be pushed! We will not jump through hoops, and we will not, repeat, not, be subjects of tests anymore. Do you understand? *No . . . more . . . tests!"*

There was a long and ominous silence from the star face.

And then, it smiled.

Congratulations. We had hoped you would say that. That . . . was the final test.

Picard and Riker stared at each other incredulously.

"I don't think you got through, sir," said Riker.

Picard spun around and faced the screen again. "Now wait just one minute!"

"Captain!"

The shout of alarm came from Data, who had manned the tactical station. "Sensors detecting a—a rip!"

"What?"

And then they saw it too.

In front of them, beyond the planet designated DQN 1196, the fabric of space seemed to tear open, a thin horizontal rent that actually was light-years across.

And it started to drag the *Enterprise* toward it.

And far off in the distance, the star face of the Cognoscente was laughing.

Geordi felt the room begin to shake beneath his feet. He looked around frantically. "What's happening?!"

"We're going home." She sighed. "It's been so long."

"But my ship! The *Enterprise!* I've got to get back to her!"

"Well," said the voice, "it should be here somewhere. Everything else is. Maybe you'll find it. Maybe not. I have to leave now."

"Wait!" shouted Geordi. But there was no answer.

Geordi started to run.

"Full reverse thrust!" shouted Picard. "Engine room, give it everything you've got!"

The warp engines of the mighty starship blasted away from the spatial rip and the entire ship shook under the strain, as the warp nacelles pushed the ship one way, while forces they could not begin to understand fought to drag them the other.

Beneath them, the planet began to break up. Huge chunks of its terrain swirled off, spinning and spiraling away to be sucked into the huge maw of nothingness that had appeared. And beneath the places where the planet had been ripped away, there shone through huge metallic areas that glinted in the light produced by the face of a million stars.

And now that face, too, was breaking apart. The stars fell out of their alignment, returning to the positions in the galaxy that they must have always been maintaining, for certainly that had been a massive illusion.

"We're being pulled in!" shouted Marks.

"No. We'll make it," said Picard with incredible calm. Here, here was something he understood. The *Enterprise,* fighting a battle of wills, of strength—a battle that she would surely win.

Now the facade of the planet was completely gone, and its true nature was revealed. A solid metal sphere, gleaming, beautiful in space, and then it too was pulled toward the hole. It gave no resistance, happy to be going home.

Geordi La Forge ran, ran as if his life depended on it. Somehow he sensed something closing in behind him and he leaped frantically, desperately into the darkness ahead of him.

He cut through the darkness and was surrounded by light.

He crashed headlong into the protective shield around the matter/antimatter blender.

"Mister La Forge!"

He looked up and was astounded, but somehow not

too astounded, to find himself in the engine room. The engines were going full blast. "What's happening?" he demanded.

"We're at full reverse thrust," said the assistant engineer. "We're in trouble."

"What else is new?" said Geordi.

The gleaming planet disappeared from view, and the rift in space opened wider, as if to receive it?

No. As if to give a final view of what was through there.

They gaped in astonishment as they had a glimpse, just the briefest glimpse, of beauty beyond imagining. Cities floating and gleaming in space, circled by ships as large as planets and yet magnificent and graceful. The shape of the future, of the glory that was to be mankind, there for the asking, there for the touching . . .

And it was gone.

One moment it was there, the next—vanished. The rift had closed itself off, and whatever secrets, whatever wonders lay through there, would remain there. Untouchable and unknowable.

Picard sagged back in his chair, his face drained of all emotion.

"My God, Number One . . . what have I done?"

Riker considered it very carefully. "You've done one of two things, sir, or perhaps both . . . neither of which are quite so bad."

Picard looked up, and Riker had never seen him look so shaken or so vulnerable. "And they are . . ."

"Either you've prevented us from having something we were not ready for . . . and you yourself have stated the dangers of what can occur when that happens."

Picard nodded ruefully. "No matter how far we advance, every so often we run up against just how little we've learned. What's the other possibility, Number One?"

"Well . . . it may sound strange . . . but you might have just told off our parents."

Chapter Twenty

"MIRRORS, CAPTAIN. I did it all with mirrors."

They had gathered in the sickbay—Picard, Riker, Troi, Data, and Worf, all surrounding the remarkably resilient Klingon known as the Honorable Kobry. Gava stood nearby, smiling gently.

"Seriously, Kobry," said Picard. "How did you—"

"Survive? Honestly, Captain, one does not reach my age without picking up a few things." He held up his hand. "This ring, for example."

"With the pills," said Picard. "For your health."

"They're for my health, true enough. They're antitoxins. There are six poisons that are particularly popular in the Klingon Empire. Just one of these pills counters all of them."

"And Tron used one of those six?"

"No," sighed Kobry. "Unfortunately, he used one of the other one hundred thirty seven. One can't be prepared for every eventuality. But even in an instance like that, my little health pills—taken whenever I'm going to eat, remember—gave me enough protection so that the splendid Dr. Pulaski could revive me."

"The Honorable Kobry was kind enough to warn me ahead of time about the precautions he had taken," said Pulaski. "He also suggested that, should the situation arise, I pronounce him dead, just to prevent any further attacks on him while he lay relatively helpless."

"Yes, well next time I'd appreciate your telling me about such confidences and precautions. Is that understood, Doctor?" he said stiffly.

To his surprise she merely bobbed her head and said, "Yes, Captain."

"Actually, Captain, I blame myself," said Kobry ruefully. "I did not dream that my apparent death would escalate into warfare so rapidly. I did not allow for Tron's pushing my people forward and inciting them. Tron will of course be dealt with . . . and, I suspect, his commander will have something to answer for, as well. In fact, I would like to see Tron in a bit, if that is in order with the doctor?" Pulaski nodded, still looking a bit distracted.

"So what happens now?" asked Riker. "The planet's gone, so that removes the main point of contention between Klingon and Kreel. And I doubt the attacks with the advanced weapons will be continuing. Geordi"—Riker shook his head, still not believing that La Forge was back and wondering how he had returned—"Geordi showed me Tiny. His pet weapon? After DQN 1196 vanished, it cracked like an egg. There was nothing inside."

"Nothing?" Picard almost laughed. "Why am I not surprised?"

"I don't know, sir," said Data. "Why not?"

"One would think," said Kobry, "that with the

weapons and their source gone, there remains nothing to discuss. However, the Kreel do have grievances. They should be heard. They should not have to throw the equivalent of a tantrum to be attended to. There was a high cost, but nevertheless I will try to make things better for the Kreel. By the way, Counselor, I am curious about why, with your empathic ability, you did not detect Tron's murderous intentions at the party."

"I wasn't there," said Deanna. "I was kept occupied and distracted by the one called Sklar."

"Ah. Obviously, Tron was concerned you would realize and sought to keep you out until the deed was done. A good try, actually. Just . . . insufficient."

"Captain," Katherine Pulaski suddenly said, "can I speak with you and Data for a moment? In private?"

Moments later, in Pulaski's office, she said, "I just wish to admit some shortsightedness in some matters."

"Doctor, I hardly think that's necessary," said Picard.

"No. It is. I'm afraid that the entire matter with Jaan and Wesley grew somewhat out of hand and . . . it was my desire to see their needs fulfilled that prompted me to overcome your objections."

"Doctor." Picard smiled. "If you overcame any objections or uncertainties, it was not because it was against my will. I could have found ways to overrule you, you know. The redoubtable Katherine Pulaski can be overcome. If we erred in trying to accomplish something beneficial, that is hardly the worst way to do it."

Her mouth twitched in thought. "I suppose you're right. But there's one thing I should say. Data, you asked where the line between men and machines ends?"

"Yes."

"I still don't have the answer for that. But I'll tell you where it begins to blur for me. It's when a human feels the need to say to a machine . . . that she's sorry."

"That," said Data, "is an excellent place to start."

Tron, alone in his holding cell, looked up with his one good eye. The other was obscured by an eye patch.

The Honorable Kobry stood there, leaning on a cane.

"You are destroying the Klingon Empire and all that makes us strong," said Tron.

Kobry merely stared at him and then spoke four words.

"You have no name."

He turned and walked away, and the screaming that filled his ears was music to them. Perhaps there was something to the concept of revenge after all.

"You will be leaving with your father?" asked Worf.

"Of course."

"There is a place for you in the Federation."

"Not as long as my father needs me. Still . . . it's a small galaxy," smiled Gava. "Our paths may cross again."

"When?"

She paused. "How about now?"

"I cannot. I'm starting my second shift. So"—he stood and nodded his head once—"later then." He walked out of her quarters.

Gava sighed and leaned back.

Worf walked back in, and as the door slid shut behind him, he said, "I can always work three shifts tomorrow."

* * *

Wesley sat alone in his quarters, staring at the wall.

All the computer material had been removed, as had the journals, the experimental equipment, everything.

Wesley, rail-thin to begin with, had lost thirteen pounds. He needed to soak in a tub for at least two days. His face was the color of curdled milk and his eyes had lost their vigor. He needed, more than anything, a sound sleep.

Listlessly he said, "Come in," at the sound of the door buzzer.

Picard walked in and looked around. "Restored to normal, I see."

"Yes, sir."

"Mr. Crusher," and he sat down opposite him, "you've got to pull yourself together."

"I failed him."

"You didn't fail him. Jaan failed himself."

"No, sir, I failed him. I said that I would find a cure for his disease. I didn't even come close. I barely scratched the surface."

"You shouldn't have made promises that were beyond you."

"It wasn't beyond me," Wesley said with some degree of spark. "Or at least I didn't think it was beyond me."

"Mr. Crusher—Wesley—don't you see how far you've come? How many other young men have achieved the things you have? They don't have a fraction of your talent, of your intelligence . . ."

"It's not enough," he said sullenly.

"It's more than enough! Wesley, don't you understand? Jaan was pushing you in to trying to do what you had no business trying."

"No he wasn't."

"It was his ability that Dr. Pulaski called 'the Knack.' It—"

"It wasn't the Knack!" For the first time in his life, Wesley raised his voice to Picard. *"I did it! I wanted* to do it! I wanted to help him! I could have helped him! If I'd worked harder, longer . . ."

"You'd have killed yourself, son."

"Don't call me that! I'm not your son! I'm not anybody's son!"

Picard looked at him, shocked. "Wesley . . ."

"I had to do it, don't you see? I had to find the cure. I have to be able to do anything I set my mind to. Don't you see? Anything!"

"Wesley, no one can do *any*thing."

"I have to! I'm going to be able to! Not just engineering! That's easy for me. Too easy. That comes without my even trying. I've got to keep trying, working harder and harder, cover everything. Leave nothing to chance." The words were coming faster and faster, tumbling over each other. "No matter what happens, I'll be prepared. I'll know everything. I'll be able to handle everything. I'll come back. No matter what the mission is, no matter what happens, I'll always make it back."

"Of course, you'll make it back, Wes," said Picard in confusion, wishing like hell he'd forced Deanna to do this. "Of course you'll make it—"

"HE DIDN'T!"

"Who?"

"My father! He didn't make it back!"

Picard stared at him in shock. "Wesley, your father was a good man. The best. His death . . . it was an accident."

"I don't believe that! Any accident can be avoided if you know what to do! He didn't know what to do!

273

Something happened and he wasn't ready and he wasn't prepared and he didn't come back! That's not going to happen to me! I—"

His voice choked back in his throat, and tears of exhaustion and grief began to roll down his face. "I'm not going to—to go and have a wife, and a kid, and then go out there and get killed and—and not come—come back—"

And Wesley Crusher, the Brain Trust, the boy who saved the ship time and again, came apart. He started to sob piteously, tears and grief that had been bottled up for years, and he said over and over, *"Why* didn't he come back? *Why?"*

And Jean-Luc Picard, he who supposedly hated children, he who had brought back the body of Wesley's father, now held the shaking body of Wesley Crusher in his arms.

Picard didn't know what to say. He'd been on that ship when Wesley's father had died. He knew that there was nothing that could have been done. It was the idea of the Right Stuff, from the early days of aviation. If someone died in a plane crash, the other pilots would try and figure out what he did wrong so that they could take solace in the concept that it would never happen to them—that the dead man's "stuff" hadn't been "right" enough.

And Picard realized that he didn't have to say anything, that he just had to be there—be there as Wesley's father and mother couldn't. Be there . . . just for now. It wouldn't hurt anything. It wouldn't damage his reputation or destroy his ability to make decisions.

And he held him, just saying nothing, just being there, until Wesley succumbed to total exhaustion and fell asleep.

He picked the boy up and carried him to his bed,

shaking his head at the total lack of weight on him. As soon as Wesley woke up, which would probably be in a day or so, Picard would have Pulaski give him a full physical. And Deanna Troi, who, lately, looked like she could use a successful case, would spend time with him helping him deal with everything that had happened.

And, with luck, Wesley probably wouldn't even remember this little crying jag of his. He certainly hoped Wesley wouldn't remember that he, Picard, had been holding him as he was now doing.

In a soft voice he said, "I expect to see you on the bridge in seventy-two hours, Mr. Crusher."

And from somewhere in the depths of his sleep, Wesley said, "Aye, sir."

Picard nodded approvingly as he turned to leave. It was exactly the answer he'd hoped to get.

Decorum had to be maintained, after all.

STAR TREK®
THE NEXT GENERATION

GROUNDED

by David Bishoff

While answering a distress call from a scientific station in a remote part of the galaxy, the Starship *Enterprise* becomes infected with a mysterious alien life form which feeds on and transforms inorganic materials.

The U.S.S. *Enterprise* begins to gradually disintegrate, and Starfleet is forced to order its evacuation and destruction to prevent the dangerous infection from spreading throughout the galaxy. It's the end of an era for Captain Picard and his crew, who are scheduled for transfers that will split them up among different Starfleet vessels.

But even as the end draws near for the U.S.S. *Enterprise*, Captain Picard begins to formulate a desperate plan to save his ship and preserve his crew - a plan that will force him to defy Starfleet orders and lead him to a confrontation with a malevolent alien force which has the power to destroy the entire Federation.

STAR TREK®
THE NEXT GENERATION

A ROCK AND A HARD PLACE

Under the best circumstances, terraforming is a tough, dangerous task that pits the hardiest of pioneers against an unforgiving environment. When the terraformers on the planet Paradise fall behind the schedule, Commander Riker is given temporary leave from the *Enterprise* and sent to assist.

Riker's replacement on the *Enterprise* is a volatile officer named Stone whose behaviour soon raises questions about his ability and his judgement. Meanwhile, Commander Riker has become enmeshed in a life and death struggle with Paradise's brutal landscape. However, he soon learns that not all of the planet's dangers are natural in origin - as he comes face to face with Paradise's greatest danger and most hideous secret...

For a complete list of Star Trek publications, T-shirts
and badges please send a large SAE to Titan Books
Mail Order, 19 Valentine Place, London, SE1 8QH.
Please quote reference NG5.